THE
INDEPENDENT

THE INDEPENDENT

VICTOR P. LUXUS

ENLIBRE PRESS

To independent thinkers

. . . the public that once bestowed military commands,
consulships, legions and all else,
now meddles no more and longs eagerly for just two things:
Bread and Circuses.

– Juvenal, *Satire X*

MONROE TAYLOR AWOKE TO THE SOUND of his iPhone ringing. He had had a late night and turned off the alarm before hitting the sack. So the ringing was due to a call and after he fumbled for the phone, knocking it from the nightstand and finally retrieving it, he saw it was from his friend and associate editor Ted Polanski. Ted had no special ringtone because Monroe had never bothered with such technical intricacies. The phone was utilitarian; not a source of entertainment.

"Did I wake you?"

"No, I had to get up to answer the phone."

"Someone bought the winning Powerball ticket at the Sunoco on Ligonier Street last night!"

"Mmm. Wish it had been me. See you at the office. I'm running late."

"As usual. What time did you get home?"

"I dunno. It was after one. I still haven't finished the editorial, but I did finish the template for the web page. We gotta stop having working meetings over late dinners. I feel like hell."

"Me too, but at least I can get to work on time. Listen, I'm gonna put DeMario on the story about the ticket."

"What are you talking about? Why wouldn't you put Smith on the Commissioner election? He's the political reporter."

"Not the election ticket you moron. The Powerball ticket."

"Mmm. 'kay. Good night."

He fell back on the mattress and wondered why people in the movies are never startled from their sleep when a phone rings. The damn thing rings three or four times before they casually reach for it. Not him. Never. Every time a phone awakened him it was as if a guy in a mask kicked in his door. It was always all hands to general quarters. His heart rate decreased a little bit until he recalled that one night when he sprang for the phone.

"Fuck it. I might as well get up."

Vaughn Monroe Taylor was named for Vaughn Monroe, the famous singer from Jeannette, whom his mother adored. His father hated the name Vaughn, though, and compromised by correctly assuming that he could get away with calling the kid by his middle name. It was a grand, dignified name, and it had that hint of old New England money. The kind of first name that people with means name their kids. And also the kid's mother's maiden name was Monroe, so there was that.

Monroe was at his desk by 11 AM, about five hours later than usual. He gave silent thanks to his foresight in furnishing the bedroom with the room-darkening blinds that allowed him the luxury of a few more hours of blissful sleep, however fitful those hours had become. Maybe it was his advancing age (a concept he vehemently rejected), maybe it was his mattress or pillow, or maybe it was the pressure of trying to maintain a dying newspaper. Most likely it was a combination, but he blamed the latter. Franco DeMario poked his head around the door jamb, ostensibly to ask yet another dumb question. Monroe preempted him.

"Anyone claim that ticket? What was the final jackpot?"

"Two point six billion dollars. Largest in history. Of course, once you take cash and pay your taxes, then you're ONLY looking at 855 million. And there's probably like forty or fifty people who went in on it and bought five hundred tickets. Like we did here. Can you imagine what would happen if we hit?"

"Yeah, you would all retire and we would go out of business. Finally. So no one claimed it yet?"

"Nope. You'd be crazy to before you called your lawyer, your financial adviser, your accountant. And then you'd have to change your name and go off grid. Hire a security firm to protect you from all the relatives coming out of the woodwork."

"Mmm. Send Smitty in. I want him to get over to the courthouse."

"Smitty didn't come in today. Maybe he's the winner. Figures it would be a phallocephalus like him!"

And so it went. The day-to-day grind of running *The Latrobe Independent*, the area's local paper, which had a subscription of thirty thousand twenty years ago, and four thousand today. If it weren't for the website he would have closed years ago. His dad used to say that printer's ink flowed through his veins. But Monroe knew that the times were going to change, and if he had not invested in the apartments and the office complex, he would be in dire straits. He really had the ink in his veins too, though not quite like his dad. There was still a thrill to getting a story, meeting interesting people, following politics and current events on a local as well as national level. An information junkie, he had two flat screen TVs in his office. One tuned to Fox News, the other to MSNBC. An FM radio was tuned to the local NPR station, playing softly in the background. There were constant alerts on his second computer screen for Drudge, and always one of KDKA, WTAE, or WPXI; whichever one was irritating him the least at the moment. The bookcase along one wall was a built-in from floor to ceiling, and was filled neatly with biographies, histories, references, and local high school yearbooks dating to 1940. You never knew when you were going to need an old picture of someone who did something stupid or great. His dad had had a tradition of supporting the local school, and he was not going to break his father's tradition. A "Make America Cringe Again" sign was taped to the top shelf with a doodle that he made to represent Donald Trump.

Late in the day his desk phone rang. It was Nancy Maguire, his accountant. He owed her payroll data and taxes for his personal account. Being January 15, it was not too early to start pulling receipts together. As he cradled the phone he reached for a binder that he kept his business receipts in, each taped to an 8½-by-11 sheet of paper, and organized by date. He fished his wallet out to retrieve the receipt from last night's dinner with Ted, which he wanted to file. As she was yakking about her need for more office space, he glanced at the bill from last night, hoping like hell that she would not notice the tab from the bar. But he knew she would. She was a keen observer; just like a reporter. What distinguished her from any of his reporters was that she would have the good taste to not comment on the bar tab. He also pulled out some folded papers which he laid on his keyboard.

"Goddamnit! It drives me nuts when I can't find what I'm looking for!" he exclaimed to Nancy, who was accustomed to his rants.

"What did you lose this time?"

"My mind," he laughed. "Okay, so if I find the receipts for the charitable contributions, I'll walk them over to you." She was only up the street a few short blocks and assuming he could lay hands on them before either of them left for the day, it was nice enough weather for a walk, and he enjoyed getting some fresh air to clear his head.

Today was his lucky day. He found the receipts and made it to Nancy's office before she logged off her computer.

It was tax season, so catching up with her this late was not magic. He headed back to the office, which was by now vacant except for the janitor and a young journalist who was fresh out of college and looking to make a splash. In a dying industry. Monroe wanted to finish an editorial before he left for the day. He was writing about the County Commissioner's primary in April, and he was expected to endorse the Democrat, a female lawyer whom he despised. The Republican was no better, though, and if he had the time and wherewithal, he would have enjoyed running as an Independent just to mess with them.

He found the folded scraps of papers on the keyboard where he left them, and laid them on a bare spot on the desk. He hated clutter but his desk was mired in it, and that was also a stressor for him. Gas receipts, a ticket for a gun bash to support the Latrobe Fire Department, a lottery ticket from the Sunoco on Ligonier Street where he filled up the tank on the Prius last night.

* * *

2

HE HAD GIVEN EACH OF THEM a separate iPhone with a SatSleeve. It was only to be used to conduct business with him. They did not have to answer every time it rang, but when it did ring, they were expected to return the call within eight hours. It was not too much to ask: they were on retainer, and he was now their client with the highest priority. In Nancy Maguire's and Fred During's cases he would soon be their only client. Nancy was handing off her accounting clients to her partner, and Fred During, Monroe's lawyer for the past thirty years was doing the same. Albert Messing, CFP, was his money guy at a firm on Pittsburgh's North Shore. He was going to be handling the investments within his firm's portfolio, which would now be significantly larger.

The jackpot had not yet been claimed. They wanted to set up the internal mechanisms first, with provisions for gifting, trusts, guaranteed retirement, taxes, and so on. Monroe was doing his damnedest to not reveal the secret, but it was grating on his nerves. He was alternating between publicly acting like nothing had changed and privately succumbing to fits of giddiness. But this past week the conflicting displays were starting to overlap at work, and Ted confided in a few of the senior staff that he was afraid that the Editor was approaching a nervous breakdown, probably due to financial woes and their (the staff's) collective stupidity.

How the hell could they be committing the grammatical errors and ambiguous sentence structure?

"'Sutliff stated that the City Manger's report had not been completed in a timely fashion, and she did not have the resources to complete it.' Who did not have the resources? Sutliff or the 'Manger'? And where the fuck are we? Bethlehem? Don't you morons use spell-check?"

"Manger is a word, so . . ."

"Shut the fuck up! No wonder Monroe is losing his mind. I am too! You idiots are making me crazy! I never used to swear like this!"

"Who are you bullshitting? You came out of the womb swearing so much the nurses blushed!"

The staff meeting erupted with a cachinnation.

Monroe was spending so much time out of the office now that there was even money on whether he had checked in to an outpatient rehab clinic or was getting some action on the side. The guy was a lifelong bachelor who was not bad looking, but his personal life was a complete mystery to practically everyone in his professional sphere. They didn't know if he was straight, gay, or neuter. He had no personal artifacts in his office. The gag around the office was that Monroe did not even have a photo of a pet dog, cat, or gerbil.

During a time of urgent need they once hired a contract reporter who was given to making snide comments. Well, they all were, but this particular guy was over the top. When one of the staff mentioned the gag to the new guy during his orientation, he felt obligated to share his rapier wit, and made a homophobic comment about Monroe and the missing gerbil. Ted had a very brief but pointed talk with the guy.

Monroe was spending a lot of time with his financial team. Fred During was wringing his hands over his will and how the ticket would be claimed. Pennsylvania law required that the winner's name be made public, so there was some discussion about whether the ticket should be claimed under Monroe's name as an individual, or whether they ought to form a limited liability company to "be" the winner. Messing was adding two new financial analysts, and Nancy was busy shuffling between the tax implications and the off-loading of existing responsibilities onto her partner.

Messing had asked, "So what do you want to do with your life now, Monroe?"

"I don't know," he answered deliberately. "I've thought about joining the Peace Corps." They all laughed.

"No. I mean I'm kinda serious here. I'm not going to be satisfied to lay on a beach the rest of my life, or to collect rare cars or polo ponies. I actually thought about running for County Commissioner."

"Are you kidding me? What a pain in the ass that would be. If you were going to become a public servant, why wouldn't you take on US Senator at least?"

"You know, he's always been KIND of a public servant. Monroe is always involved in some kind of local project. USUALLY, but not exclusively charitable. . . . Fundraisers, Boy Scouts, Fire Departments. And being the editor, you really always have had a strong interest in politics."

"He is pretty smooth. I always thought he should have been a politician. Or a lawyer at least."

"Well, it only took me six years to finish law school . . ." His voice trailed away. Thirty-five years later and that late-night phone call still cracked his voice. There was a respectful pause. These people were really friends as much as they were advisers.

"You know, I thought maybe I should apply to Pitt's School of Public and International Affairs." He said it almost like it was a plea; asking for their permission.

"Might be fun, but don't you think at this stage in your life you could be a lecturer in that program? Who do you know that has more political and public affairs know-how than you?"

"What does it cost to mount a political campaign for senator?"

"Screw that. What's it cost to run for president? He's been exercised ever since Trump got elected!"

During whipped out his iPhone and Googled "What does it cost to run for president?"

"Trump spent 958 million dollars. Clinton spent 1.4 billion. You're going to be short!"

"Short yeah, but there is a whole fund-raising mechanism."

"Sure for Democrats and Republicans," smiled Monroe. "Independents have a rougher road."

"It could be done. Look at Ross Perot. He garnered a lot of popular support. People gave money to his campaign."

"Who's gonna write a check to a Powerball winner?"

"Who wrote checks to Donald Trump?"

"It's a lot of fun to think about," said During. "But Monroe doesn't know anything about running a campaign."

"Hello. I'm right here. I can hear you, you know. But you are right, I don't know much about running a campaign, but I sure as hell know about issues. And I can hire people who CAN run a campaign. AND I know a hell of a lot more about issues than Trump!"

They looked at him. It had struck a nerve and he was on the defensive.

"Settle down, Tiger," said Nancy. "Why not relax and enjoy life?"

"Look, I don't NEED the money. I've always done okay."

9

"You've done BETTER than 'okay,' okay? But if you don't NEED the money, I'll be happy to relieve you of the burden!" Messing chuckled. Albert was a little worried that a foolish lark might diminish the management fees he was entitled to. Besides, as a Certified Financial Planner, wasn't part of his job to protect the assets?

"No," Fred During drawled. "Our boy is serious here. We struck a nerve. Let's claim that dough, and why doncha take a vacation to a lower latitude and ruminate on the future for a few weeks?"

. . .

3

IT WASN'T THAT IT WAS A BAD IDEA. And now that he was about to be in some major money, he was not about to fly commercial. He chartered a corporate jet out of Arnold Palmer Airport to St. Lucia, downing a couple of vodka and tonics while he answered emails on the fly. He settled into his room at the resort, and immediately regretted being away. It seemed like there was a lot to do, and laying on a beach was an indulgence that could not be afforded. Well, of course he could afford it, but he could not condone it. He called the travel agency and changed his return flight to the day after tomorrow. Fred and Nancy and Albert had nearly finished with the planning. The winning ticket was in a safe deposit box, and they said he would be ready to claim it when he returned in two weeks.

"Might as well hit the beach while I'm here," he said aloud to no one. He could have invited any number of friends, female or male, but he felt like he needed to be alone to contemplate the future. The arrangements were made by Fred, strictly on the QT.

After ditching some beach gear under an umbrella he took a jog by the surf and then tried to relax. Futile. He felt like one of those fish that live their lives at the bottom of the ocean, and when they are brought to the surface they explode because the pressure decreases.

"This is ridiculous," again to no one. At least there was plenty of scenery. He went for a dip in the gentle surf and decided to head back to the room, shower, and get ready for a nice dinner. It never bothered him to dine alone, though he always felt uncomfortable watching others do it.

Two days later he was back in Latrobe with a tan and traces of white sand in his Docksiders. Ted demanded to know what was going on.

"I can't tell you just yet. But trust me, your job is secure."

Ted came inside the office and closed the door. "Listen. Everyone is scared shitless here. They don't know if you are going to close the doors, or if you have finally gone 'round the bend."

"Hold on." He lifted the phone and called Fred. "Are we ready? Okay. Great. We do it Friday." Then to Ted, "Call a staff meeting for four this afternoon."

The entire *Independent* staff was crowded into the conference room on the second floor. Monroe had a reputation as a straight shooter, a no-nonsense kind of guy. When word circulated through the building that he was going to make a major announcement at 4 PM, no one knew what to expect. But they all knew that whatever it was, it was going to be important. The guy did not call staff meetings for the hell of it.

He strode purposefully into the room with his cuffs rolled up to his forearms, and with arms akimbo, announced, "I have decided that I am going to run for public office."

There was a silent pause followed by an ejaculation of chortles. He was a little disappointed, but he had actually anticipated such a response.

"Dead serious. Friday we will go public with this. Some of you are going to continue with your duties at *The Independent*, and some of you will be working full-time on the campaign."

"Boss, really. We all know you hold some strong views but c'mon. You're a newspaper guy." It was DeMario. He punctuated his declarative with his hand raised, like a plea for sanity.

"Not exclusively. And I agree: I hold some strong views. But the time has come to pronounce those views to more than a few thousand subscribers."

"Well what office? Mayor of Latrobe? Dog-catcher?" This was Barlow, one of the county reporters-at-large. He had a good sense for politics.

"National office," answered Monroe evasively.

Barlow continued. "There's a whole process. There's exploratory committees formed, there's money to be raised. There's a whole infrastructure that has to be assembled! People don't just announce! Wait. This is a joke, a gag. Ah, I get it. You're jacking us, right?" He looked around the table, sure that this was a set-up for a prank. The boss was clever! He was pranking the shit out of someone! "Yeah," he wagged his finger. "You're jacking us!"

Monroe placed both palms flat on the table and leaned in. He looked Barlow in the eyes and said, "I jack no one." He followed his gaze around the room, connecting with thirty-five pairs of eyes. "Effective immediately, Frank DeMario is the new editor. Sheila Burns is the new Associate Editor. Ted Polanski is my new campaign advisor and editor-at-large."

The meeting was quickly adjourned and Monroe was the first out the door. Barlow turned to Smitty as they filtered out of the room and whispered, "Wow! If that was real, I hope his first press conference goes better than that."

"Yeah," said Smitty derisively. "If that was real." Smitty recalled that a local farmer once announced he was going to run for president. It just confirmed his earlier suspicion that Monroe Taylor now officially had a substance abuse problem.

On Thursday morning they leaked that the winning ticket was going to be verified at the Sunoco station. There was only one winner, and the ticket had already been examined many times by Nancy, During, and Messer. During knew it would have no standing in court if the ticket went missing, but he prepared an affidavit to cover the contingency of someone stealing the ticket and presenting it later. They had a year to cash it in. The leak was transmitted to the three TV stations in Pittsburgh, who would share with their affiliates in Philadelphia, Altoona, Harrisburg, Erie, and Scranton. The regional newspapers were put on alert also. Everyone was told that the winner would be there between one and two in the afternoon; enough time to be edited to make the five o'clock news. The coverage would be national. Monroe worked on a brief statement, which was going to exhibit by turns, thankfulness, humility, and hubris, which would be couched in the blanket of wanting to perform public service.

Nancy and Albert had thought that the final number would come in around 850 million after taxes. They could have gone for the 30 annual payouts of only 34 million. Only. "Heh. ONLY 34 million!" he thought. He wanted the large payout now to fund a war chest, donate to charity, establish some legacy funds, and to actually provide for retirement, because, let's face it, nothing was going to come from a political campaign except him stirring the pot. He understood that and accepted it. But he had spent a lifetime covering politics, he was a student of history, and he did, in fact, hold some strong views that he honestly felt could matter to the public welfare.

At heart he really was a public servant, as Fred had observed. If you thought about it, he had devoted his career to public life, though he was never on a ballot. Working with local politicians behind the scenes, offering advice and free analysis, keeping an eye on corruption. But no one was going to credit any of that. He had no political resume. All he had was the paper. And, very soon, $850 million. A guy could build a steel mill with that kind of money.

Monroe had asked the police chief if there was going to be a presence at the Sunoco on Friday. Traffic control, crowd control, security, that sort of thing. The chief had obviously thought about it and since he had informally been issued a notice of the event through the paper, he asked Monroe who the lucky winner was. Monroe claimed he couldn't violate the privacy of the individual, but now the chief knew that it wasn't a group of people. It was an individual. Some lucky bastard is going to be rich. Monroe briefly wondered if he should level with the chief so that he could provide a security detail from the bank safe deposit box to the gas station. He decided that no one had any reason to bother him during that short route, and he would be accompanied by Nancy, Albert, and Fred. They would show up on the pretense of being curious citizens, and if pressed they would say they were there in a capacity to offer professional services, which no one would believe. They were sworn to secrecy, and being on retainer for essentially the rest of their lives, they had every reason to maintain their secrecy and remain Monroe's devoted servants.

The news vans rolled into the parking lot Friday morning and set up around the parking lot perimeter, their satellite transmitter towers reaching nearly as high as any building in the little city. It was a cold, bright day, with a dusting of snow scattered across the roads. Maybe the cold would keep some of the curious onlookers away. No matter. He would announce today, and start the rollout on Monday. By this time next week, Monroe Taylor would be a household name.

Franco DeMario and Sheila Burns were transitioning into their new roles without any problems. They were veterans of the news business and Sheila had worked for some large papers across the East Coast before returning to Latrobe to take care of her elderly father, who had since passed away. Monroe made sure they were sending a photographer to the Sunoco before he left for an early lunch with Nancy and the gang at the train station. From there they went to the bank where he retrieved the ticket, and they drove in four cars up Lincoln Avenue to the Sunoco station on Ligonier. They had to park two blocks down the street, where they were directed by a patrolman. Aside from the news vans, there were two local police cars, a state police car, a fire utility truck from 5th Ward, and a local ambulance on standby. The chief was definitely prepared.

There were about sixty people ringing the counter area, and every time a regular customer approached the onlookers held their collective breath. Everyone would study the face of the person buying gas or a five-hour-old breakfast sandwich. "This guy looks stupid enough to have won that kind of money," they'd whisper, or "She doesn't look excited enough." Monroe, Fred, Nancy, and Albert took their places in the ring and studied the crowd. No one really knew what Monroe's plan was. He waved at the chief, at *The Independent's* photographer, at Ted Polanski who had tagged along, and each of the three reporters from Pittsburgh, whom he had come to know in a professional capacity over the years. After about five minutes, he turned to hug Nancy and then broke ranks and walked to the counter.

"I have the winner here," he smiled at the manager who was manning the lottery machine.

A buzz went up from the crowd at overhearing the word "winner." As the lottery scanner read the ticket and started to tap out a tattoo of ink on the winning receipt, cameras whirred and clicked and the manager shouted, "WE HAVE A WINNER! LADIES AND GENTLEMEN, WE HAVE A WINNER!"

Monroe turned to see Ted's eyes so wide he was a little afraid for his friend's health. Cries of "OH MY GOD!" and "How about that!" drowned out the "HOLY FUCK" that sprang from Ted's lips. Monroe was swarmed by local friends and well-wishers, and he knew that most were sincere in their appreciation of his amazing good fortune.

The crowd parted for the reporters to approach with their cameramen. He saw that this was not going to be a great venue to make the big announcement, the astonishing announcement, the announcement that would actually overshadow his winning of the largest jackpot in American history. One of the reporters predictably asked how he felt. "Blessed," came the humble reply. A barrage of incomprehensible questions overwhelmed his senses, so he held up his hands and tamped down the excitement. He had their attention now, and he spoke to all three reporters. To their credit, neither they nor their cameramen had jockeyed into a dominant position, but all had yielded space while maintaining good angles on Monroe.

"I want to start by saying that I am incredibly grateful. I have offered many prayers of thanksgiving for what is a totally random circumstance. I am far too humble to assign any divine intervention to this incredible good fortune, but I am also cognizant of the need to put this windfall to good use.

"So aside from first ensuring that I have a comfortable retirement," he paused and a good-natured chuckle arose from those assembled. "I have a general plan for this money. Second, I will be contributing to some of my favorite charities . . . my alma mater, Saint Vincent College, to establish a trust in honor of my parents, James and Angelica Taylor, a couple of local charities that assist the poor of underdeveloped countries . . . and the local volunteer fire departments. Third, we will be investing in *The Latrobe Independent*, to provide some additional capacity and promote a more sustainable future for publishing.

"Now that accounts for about 5 percent of the total. Today I announce my intention to run as an Independent for the office of President of the United States in 2020. The remaining 95 percent will be used to fund the campaign, which begins today!"

A collective gasp, and after what seemed like a full minute pause of crazy disbelief, some polite scattered applause that built into "WOO HOO"s and "YOU GO, MONROE!"

Monroe smiled broadly, wrapped his arm over the shoulder of Ted Polanski who had wormed his way through the crowd, and turning to him, shouted over the uproar, "'You go, Monroe!' Not a bad bumper sticker, huh?"

"You crazy motherfucker! You crazy motherfucker!" Ted was crying.

· · ·

4

"YOU SURE YOU WANT TO HAVE A PRESS CONFERENCE before you bring a consultant on board?" Monroe was putting the finishing touches on a half-Windsor in his bedroom. He was accustomed to these early morning visits by Ted.

"Listen. I agree it's not ideal. But we need to get out there and gain some traction." He always avoided the use of the personal pronoun. Monroe had always ensured that his professional team was more than competent. They worked well together and he was never bashful about sharing the successes with the team and deflecting praise to them. "What's the worst that could happen?"

"You could commit some *faux pas* of Trumpian proportions and exit the contest before it begins."

"Not gonna happen. You forget, I'm a trained professional. Besides, it will just be an intro. Nothing too wonky. We're going to lay out the personal details, state where we stand on politics in general, and then we see what happens. If I should happen to, I don't know . . . shit myself . . . I can take my 850 million dollars and retire to a Pacific island where they've never heard of me and that has no internet.

"Besides, we are going to need a million signatures to get on ballots. That means volunteers canvassing every state. And for all I know every territory too. We'll leave the detailed civics lesson part up to the consultants. Point is, we need to mobilize. Pronto."

They got into Ted's new company car, a black Toyota Highlander hybrid. Ted had taken to driving Monroe around at Fred's recommendation. What if he was in an accident? Every nitwit looking for a payoff is going to sue him. Monroe's reply was "That's why you are putting together these trusts! To protect the assets!" He did not want to be a slave to his fortune, and resisted the attempts to be restricted. "Jesus Christ, you're turning me into the last Emperor of China!" But until things settled down and the money was where it needed to be, he relented. He figured he could be pliant for a month or so.

"We need a modern venue. Something that seats at least five hundred people. There's plenty of spaces like that in Pittsburgh, but I want to keep it local. Bring some attention and cash into Westmoreland County. The Fred Rogers Center at Saint Vincent would be just the thing, but, you know, separation of church and state."

"Yeah, you'd be labeled a Papist first thing out of the blocks. How about the theater in Greensburg?"

"Yeah, I don't know. What we should do is build a theater-slash-conference-slash-mixed use space where the old ALCO plant used to be. LEED-certified, the whole nine yards."

"That would be great except it would take three years, and would blow half of your budget."

"We should really look at expanding the charities to include a renovation trust, Ted. I mean instead of just funding the fire department. Something more bricks and mortar for the community."

"Sweet, but if something like that were going to be sustainable, there would still be a movie theater and merchants in town. Remember where you're living."

"Yeah, you're right. Let's save it for the presidential library." He swept his hands back through his hair, a habit he had whenever he was frustrated. "I guess we need to reserve conference space at a hotel in Greensburg. At least that will encourage people to fly into Latrobe."

"You know, if you WERE gonna build an office complex, there's a lot of nice property along Route 30 by the airport."

"No, that would just encourage more strip malls outside of town. It's already looking like burger row out there. I'd want to bring the business downtown. That's where we need the help."

"Well I do like the idea of establishing a renovation trust. But it has to be sustainable."

"Agreed. Everything has to be sustainable. Including our campaign."

They had sent out a press release to invite the major networks to the official announcement of his campaign. The campaign staff now consisted of Ted and five staffers from the paper whom he co-opted from Franco, with no objections. Nancy and Fred were too busy managing the deposits from the jackpot to devote any time, regardless of how badly they wanted to pitch in. To replace the five staffers, Ted had sent out a call to his regional contacts in media, and the local colleges. He forwarded over one hundred emails to Franco, who hired ten new people in anticipation of a busy news season. By now, they were starting to get some attention from political consultants, who had smelled the blood in the water. Monroe figured he had a little bit of time to interview them after the official announcement.

The big reveal was scheduled for Tuesday at 9:30 AM at the Greensburg Sheraton's ballroom. Even without being micromanaged by a consultant, Monroe had a sense about how to proceed. He wanted to spend time in the room prior to the press conference, rubbing elbows with the reporters and establishing some rapport. No big intros, no fanfare, nothing too ostentatious. No gliding down an escalator or riding in on a horse. He would greet them, chat with them, and then ascend to the dais to deliver his prepared remarks, answer a few questions, politely thank them, and say goodbye. Ted would be close by in case anything untoward required a quick shutdown.

Press packets had been printed and a couple dozen volunteers had been carefully coached to assist in distributing the information. The local support ranged from college students to retirees who knew his dad. The staffers had established a nascent internet infrastructure through a social media consultant.

The press packets contained Monroe's bio, campaign contact details with dynamic QR codes and links to his campaign website, and a twelve-page glossy brochure that listed some of the issues that he felt were important without going into details. Still, there was enough there to establish why he was running as an independent. He had been writing editorials since 1982. It wasn't as though he had no material to draw from.

It was pretty early when Ted drove Monroe up the drive to the hotel. The access road was bordered by red, white, and blue "YOU GO, MONROE!" pennants that flapped in the stiff breeze.

"What? No band?" he asked Ted.

The Highlander pulled under the *porte cochère* as the Greensburg and Latrobe bands hit the first measure of *Stars and Stripes Forever*. The two high schools were rivals, but had coordinated this welcome for a Latrobe boy on Greensburg soil. Monroe laughed and exited the car, waiting respectfully for the band to finish before applauding, pumping his arm in the air, and thanking the two band directors for the thundering welcome.

Inside, all of the local network affiliates were once again there; this time joined by the national news organizations. As Monroe was chatting with the guy from CNN, Ted sidled up to him and whispered, "Are they here for politics, or is this a human-interest story?"

"My campaign manager wants to know if you're here in a political or human-interest capacity!"

Ted shot him a look. "Depends on how it ends I guess," laughed the CNN reporter. It went on like this for another hour, with people just wandering around like it was a cocktail party. At 9:25 AM, Ted gave him the high sign, and he worked his way to the dais through a mass of about three hundred reporters and cameramen, slowly joined by Ted and the dozen or so staffers. Twenty or thirty flags backdropped the scene.

"I want to thank each of you for coming out on this chilly morning to attend the official rollout of the Taylor for America campaign. By now you all know how I got here. By the time we close this event, it is my hope that you will understand also why I got here.

"My father James Madison Taylor was the owner and publisher of *The Latrobe Independent*. An infantryman in the Custer Division, he participated in the liberation of Rome during World War Two. He fought in three battles, and was awarded the Purple Heart and a Bronze Star. When he returned stateside, he used his GI Bill to attend college where he majored in English and Business Administration. Dad believed in the Bill of Rights, and in particular in the First Amendment. He decided to buy a newspaper.

"He instilled his appreciation of the Constitution in his only child. A child that grew up in the sixties and came of age in the seventies.

"I graduated down the road from Saint Vincent College in 1980 with a major in History and a minor in Economics. The plan was to go to law school and become a trial lawyer. But you know what they say, 'If you want to make God laugh, tell him your plans.' My father passed away in my third year at Georgetown Law School, so I returned home to take over the paper, with considerable help from Steven McMahon, my father's assistant editor. At Steven's suggestion, I went on to obtain my law degree, and pass the Bar Exam, though I completed my degree at night through the University of Pittsburgh.

"But by then, the publishing bug had already taken firm hold of me, and so thirty-six years later, I have yet to try a case. I have however managed to keep our sometimes snarky, always independent newspaper out of legal trouble.

"I don't have to tell a room full of media professionals about the trials of managing a newspaper in the internet era. I don't have to tell you that state-sponsored assaults on the credibility of news organizations is anathema. And I should NOT have to tell you that news should not be biased, because let's face it: the truth is bad enough.

"But I did not come here to tell you how we ought to act. I am here to tell you how I want to act. I want to act to preserve the Bill of Rights my father loved. I want to act to preserve an America which offers opportunities for all people who are willing to work for their prosperity. I want to act to end rule by oligarchs. I want to act to return the United States to a position of leadership in the world without cloaking ourselves in the cumbersome and dangerous mantle of imperialism.

"And so I come before you today to announce that I am announcing my candidacy for President of the United States of America. I will run as an Independent. I hold some strong views, and one of those views is that the two-party system has deteriorated to the point that it is now impossible to achieve any meaningful legislation or goals, since party and pride have co-opted common sense and decency.

"I have outlined some of these strong views that I hold. I will be addressing each of them in detail in the weeks that follow, because it is not sufficient to speak in generalities, or to deflect concerns with a vague 'We'll see.'

"Among the issues that have forced me out of a private and very comfortable life are: the economy, the homeless, climate change and the environment, gun control, national security, states' rights, and health care. And now, I'd be happy to answer any questions."

A reporter from an unknown entity lobbed a softball. "You're bio makes no mention of a spouse. Is there no significant other in your life?" This was such a high floater that some of the more seasoned professionals in the front rows turned with furrowed brows to see who asked the question.

"No, that is true. Just like the only president from Pennsylvania, James Buchanan, I am not married."

"Buchanan did not exactly have a stellar record," interjected ABC. "In fact he is often cited as the worst president ever."

"I would suggest that his record as president had more to do with his inability to avoid the Civil War, and not so much to do with his marital status. Be that as it may, the country was primed for civil war, and perhaps if he had possessed a stronger antislavery position, he could have addressed that issue more directly and not passed it on to Abraham Lincoln. And besides, there's a new front-runner for 'worst-president-ever'."

"Are you gay or straight? Or do you have something against marriage?"

"No, I have nothing against marriage." He was being baited, and this was NOT going the way he envisioned. *Who was this bastard?* "But you may not know that it is not a requirement to hold office."

"What is your position on gay rights?"

"I believe that all Americans should enjoy the rights guaranteed by the Constitution."

"How about pornography? Do you ever use pornography?"

Monroe caught a glimpse of Ted in his peripheral vision. Ted was rocking back and forth, ready to launch to the lectern and declare the press conference over. Monroe threw him a look that said no, everything is okay. In reality, Monroe knew that everything was not okay. In fact, he was processing information that told him that this was a giant mistake. Why was he not content to live the rest of his days in St. Lucia, impressing nubile young ingénues with his expansive knowledge of New World history?

His ears were hot. It always happened when he was becoming irate, and he feared that the cameras would catch the crimson tide erupting on each side of his head. And now his neck and face. He thought about how silly he had been to protest the makeup that the team wanted him to apply. They had even gone to the extent of hiring a professional makeup artist from one of the Pittsburgh studios. And then he thought about how thankful he was that he had heeded their advice, and had the lady mask him, ever so gently. They had reminded him that even though he wanted to get close to the reporters prior to the press conference, the reporters themselves would be wearing something for their own camera shots.

He thought about the consequences of deflecting the question, outright ignoring it, or addressing it head-on. "I mean," he thought, "the BALLS of someone to waltz in here and ask about pornography! If I say I have never seen the stuff, they are going to call me a liar, or worse, find some evidence of it. If I say I have seen it, what's the follow-up going to be? Well, what about CHILD pornography? What about GAY pornography? What about dwarf bestiality? Jesus, where is the bottom of this cesspool?"

He was light-headed. He was having a transcendent, almost out-of-body experience.

"Whoever these bastards are . . ." he thought . . . And then he forged ahead.

"I'm so sorry. Could you repeat the question?"

"Do you ever use pornography?"

"Use it 'how' exactly? I don't understand your question."

Cameras turned on a slender man with a thin moustache who was standing with an expression that was not quite a smirk, not quite a smile. He possessed an air of superiority, though it was unclear whether he deserved that level of arrogance.

The slender man persisted. "Do you, or have you, ever seen or viewed pornography as entertainment?" The question was designed to prevent Monroe from saying something lawyerly like "I know it when I see it."

"Listen." Monroe gripped the sides of the lectern and shifted ever so slightly from his normal speaking posture, erect with his feet shoulder-width apart, and into a fighting stance, with his right foot slightly back, as if he needed to be ready to kick the arrogant bastard. He paused, then proceeded slowly, enunciating clearly. "I am a healthy, fifty-nine-year-old, adult American male with moderate appetites. I have masturbated, fornicated, masticated, salivated, urinated, and defecated." Another pause. "I hope I have now illuminated."

The stunned crowd went silent, and as Ted walked to the lectern a roar of laughter and hoots erupted. Ted waved, announced the close of the press conference, and they left the dais while all hell was breaking loose in the ball room.

"JESUS CHRIST! What the fuck was THAT? You're going to be the jagoff candidate by this afternoon!"

"Relax!" Monroe snapped. "I put the unctuous little cock-sucker in his place!"

They were rushing him back to a suite that Ted had had the foresight to reserve. A state police trooper was leading the small contingent down a corridor, and Monroe felt like he was a ping pong ball in a drain pipe. He was just going along for the ride.

Ted turned around to see if they were being filmed, and to his grateful relief they were alone as he reached for his pass key. The door opened and there stood Fred. Nancy was glued to the TV set with a mien of incredulity.

Fred grabbed his hand and shook it vigorously while hugging his left shoulder. "That was INCREDIBLE! What a blast! What poise! What rhetoric! You shoulda been a lawyer Monroe, I'm tellin' ya!"

"Are you nuts?" asked Ted. "That was about as close to an unmitigated disaster as anything since the Hindenberg went down."

"Oh, the humanity!" mocked Monroe.

"The guy just shit the bed on national TV and he still cracks wise!"

"'Cause he has a sense of HUMOR, Numbnuts!" cried Nancy. "That was seriously so fucking awesome!"

There was a knock on the door. Ted peered through the peephole to see one of the staffers escorting a couple of suits. He chained the door then opened it.

"These are the gentlemen from American Advanced Strategies." They were at the top of the A-list for political consultants. Ted closed the door, unchained it and let them in. To the trooper he said, "Please don't let us be disturbed." The trooper gave a curt nod.

The gentlemen introduced themselves, their firm, and the first guy dove right in. "The first thing we are going to need is damage control. We can put out a story by tonight that because you are politically inexperienced, you provided a naïve response to a politically charged question."

"American Advanced Strategies has turned around many campaigns. Don't worry, we have resources for world-class speechwriters, pollsters. We've turned around literally hundreds of campaigns, as well as damage mitigation and control for many, MANY," here the second guy smiled broadly and chuckled, "famous celebrities."

Designed to alleviate anxiety and induce a state of confidence, his intro had the opposite effect on Monroe. "Thank you," he said shaking their hands. "With all due respect, I think it went pretty well. And since I am not planning to use speechwriters or pollsters, perhaps you can advise Ted here what other services you may offer before you leave today." He ushered them to the door.

"What a couple of smarmy boneheads!"

"I thought they assessed the situation pretty well!" protested Ted.

"They're just hacks like 95 percent of everyone in that business. I am not going to run a campaign the way everyone else does. Period. Get used to it. Who else is on the consulting list?"

Ted's cell phone rang. "It's a producer from your favorite Sunday evening news magazine. *About Time* wants to interview you next week."

· · ·

5

MONROE WAS ENJOYING THE ATTENTION, and he scolded himself for taking so much pleasure in what was supposed to be a serious endeavor. A production assistant was clipping a mike on his shirt, and though she maintained a professional air, she smiled and brushed her hair away from her face. A particularly feminine gesture that had always appealed to him, the draping of that straight wisp around an ear. The lady was attractive and under another circumstance, he might have told her so. In this climate, he wasn't even sure the species would survive. Was flirting against the rules now?

After the makeup was applied, the PA did a sound check and complimented him on his sonorous voice. "Great public speaking voice," she smiled. Was she coming on to him, or was this part of a ploy that *About Time* used to soften you up before they dropped the hammer on you? That's a strategy that he could never employ at the paper. Most of his female employees were thirty years past their kittenish phase. If they ever even had one. No one thought about them as sex objects. They were just competent people he enjoyed working with, like everyone else. No one was going to be accused of sexual harassment. He and Ted had joked privately about how lucky he was to have drawn one of the male journalists rather than Grace Halsey. They had admired her since she began national broadcasts in the early seventies. Samuel Rothman seemed like a safe bet.

They were in the offices of *The Independent*. The producer, his assistant and Samuel Rothman met with Ted, Monroe, Franco, and Sheila Burns to give them the lay of the land. They would do an interview first in Monroe's office. (Construction on the annex was suspended for the week.) Then some shots inside the newspaper, then some of Monroe and Samuel walking through Latrobe. Back tomorrow for some follow-up questions, and that was it. Easy. Some of the hard-cases at the paper had even put on pressed shirts and combed their hair. Rothman was amiable, and Monroe wondered if the guy ever stopped smiling. Maybe this really was a trap.

Monroe's office was not small, but the crew was accustomed to setting up lights and controls in any kind of space. It was interesting to watch the process, which required substantial effort. It was like a small-scale military assault. Rolling the gear out of the panel trucks, toting the lighting cases up the stairs, setting up the stands, light bars, diffusers. They buzzed around the office barely missing each other with the black stands, and occasionally bumped into each other with a good natured curse. "Get the hell out of the way, you oaf!" and "Excuse me, Lardo, but do you even know what the hell you're doing?" Monroe thought the "Lardo" comment was a bit rude considering the man's girth, but then the wispy PA stuck her head around the corner, smiled at Monroe, and then said, "Mr. Lardeaux, can you help Dave bring the other floods up?" Lardeaux shot her a sincere smile and hustled out the door. Apparently the PA had the crew bent to her will, which was no surprise.

Once the new floods were mounted and wired, a tech held a meter in front of Monroe's shirt, and gave the producer the thumbs-up.

They had three cameramen. Two were for the interview to catch different angles without having to set-up twice, and the third was a rover to do behind-the-scenes shots.

"We'll just ease into this," said Samuel, as he settled in the club chair opposite Monroe's desk and adjusted his mike and Brooks Brothers cashmere sport coat. The cameras had been running for a few minutes already. "It's been quite a few weeks for you!"

"Well yes," Monroe concurred, bowing his head and giving a sincere chuckle. "Of course there was the Powerball jackpot, and then my decision to run for office."

"Not just any office."

"No," his intonation raised and his voice trailed off. "Let's be honest. It's probably the most important office in the world."

"Has that sunk in?"

"It hasn't had to sink in. This is something I had fantasized about for many years. In our business, we have the opportunity to see policies and politics play out. Anyone with a modicum of intelligence can't witness that and not form opinions. I felt like the jackpot was the best chance of putting those opinions in front of the greatest number of people."

"So this is a fantasy for you?"

"It was until I hit the lottery. That does not diminish the sincerity of my campaign."

"A lot of people are going to ask if you're buying the office."

He laughed. "Of course I am trying to buy the office! But that is not without precedent. The difference this time is that the guy trying to buy the office has an appreciation for the Constitution and the United States' place in the world. One of the great problems we have as a nation is that it requires so much money to run for office. Term limits would help reduce that."

"But there are already term limits for president. And, as you know, President Trump is in favor of term limits for Congress."

"Well, no one is wrong all the time. Term limits are a great idea for all offices. Term limits for the president have been in place since Truman. But there is still too much money required to run for all offices, and it prevents a lot of qualified people from attaining office. But I take your point. Term limits do nothing to minimize the amount of money needed to mount a presidential campaign."

"So how much is in your war chest?"

"We have about 750 million dollars," he low-balled the number. "That's a lot of money, but it is still not enough to mount a serious campaign. And even though we will need to raise more money, as crazy as that sounds, that is not currently our biggest challenge. The biggest challenge is going to be to get the signatures we need to get on all the ballots in all the states, and that is why we need to gain exposure."

"You got some national exposure last week with your first press conference," Rothman smiled.

"Yeah, that was fun." Monroe deadpanned. He was not backing down.

"You really exhibited a flair for rhetoric."

"'When you work with words, words are your work', "he said, quoting Luther Heggs in *The Ghost and Mister Chicken*. He laughed and wondered if anyone would get the cinematic reference. Nothing worse than throwing out a reference and you're the only one who gets the joke.

There followed a long pause while Rothman studied him, and waited to see if he would continue. With the cameras rolling and the lights on, Monroe knew this was a different kind of rodeo than the interviews he and the gang at *The Independent* did. He looked around at the faces in the office, and realized this was probably a tactic to get him to expound. Obviously they were not going to let dead air on the program, and this was not live. So naturally there would be editing. But the silence was intended to produce anxiety in the interviewee.

Someone once said that Benny Goodman always gave a lousy interview; that while he was a great clarinetist, he probably couldn't ad lib a burp after a Hungarian dinner. It was amazing to Monroe how these thoughts just sort of popped into his head, but he was determined to not give *About Time* a Benny-style interview. He shifted in his chair, adopting a more natural, relaxed posture. He draped his right arm over the back of his chair and settled in.

"You know, I don't even know who that guy was . . . what organization he represented. He just comes out of nowhere asking about my sexuality and libido. I guess that's all acceptable now after the Trump/Rubio debates. I'd like to elevate the discussion to address issues that are maybe more appropriate to the demands of the office. Unless Americans really just want WWF-style politics. Which is exactly what they voted for."

Rothman was shifted askance in his chair now too, his thumb and index finger on his chin. His eyes were characteristically narrow and he waited for Monroe to finish. *Oh boy, here it comes,* thought Monroe. *Goddamnit. Why didn't we bring a consultant or a media coach on-board before we did this?*

"It was a pretty humorous response. Why the need to run as an Independent?"

What? That's it? He's not gonna dive deeper? Monroe's creased brow drew the cameraman's attention, and he slowly, silently zoomed into a full-screen shot of his face. Rothman, the cameraman, the producer, the PA, and the viewers would all think he was giving thought to a serious answer about having no political affiliation. Instead, he was concentrating on dodging the masturbation-candidacy.

Well, of course *About Time* was not going to bring that up. Ted was a moron for planting that seed. *Wait til we get some pros on the team. Wait til I get my hands on that idiot Ted.* "I'm sorry. What was the question?"

"Why the decision to run as an Independent?" asked Rothman.

"Well, I have no political affiliation. In fact, the only times I have registered in a political party was to cast a vote AGAINST someone in a primary. Pennsylvania is one of nine states with closed primaries. But my political philosophy probably derives from my dad's influence. I mean, the paper is *The Independent*!

"I've never understood why people have to straight-vote. Or even belong to a party. It must come from a need to belong. To belong to a tribe and identify with them. So you are going to sign up with thirty-two million other people? You have that much in common with them? I don't get that. It's like states' rights."

Rothman leapt at this opening. "States' rights? What's wrong with states' rights?"

"It's a canard! I'm a Federalist, plain and simple. Now let me explain why: If you subscribe to the concept of states' rights, it presumes that you are in agreement with everyone in your state. You are all of a like mind. Have you ever heard of anyone moving to any particular state because of that state's laws? 'Well, the age of consent in Alabama is sixteen, AND, it's an open-carry state. I'm moving there!' No, that never happens. You live where you do because of an accident of birth, or you moved there for a job, or possibly your health. No one moves to a state because of its laws!

"We all live in the UNITED States of America. Why should the laws in California be different from the laws in Maine? Did you ever have a disagreement with your neighbor? He lives in the same state as you! He might be a jerk, but he has the same ZIP code! Are you telling me that everyone in your state holds monolithic political views? Of course not!"

Rothman smiled. He was enjoying this, and his producer knew this was going to be a great preview for the episode. Monroe forged ahead, his body coming out of the chair. He was becoming so animated that the camera zoomed back.

"But let's say you don't buy that argument. Let's look at it another way. Let's say you think there ought to be rights assigned to each state that may vary, because there's just too much of a difference of opinion between people in, say, California and Pennsylvania. Well, Pennsylvania is a pretty big state too. Lotta people in Pennsylvania! Maybe Philadelphians don't agree with Pittsburghers. And there's three hundred miles of farmland and forests between those. Maybe there ought to be different rules that apply to those rural areas too. And then there is the South Side of Pittsburgh, and the East Suburbs, and the North Shore and the Strip District. Maybe they each want different rules. Maybe they want to open carry and to raise the legal limit for blood alcohol. Follow that logic and you can break it down to individual streets or households. It just makes no sense."

The producer had planned to break and have Monroe and Samuel walk through town after lunch, to get some color commentary and shots. But Monroe was so fired up, he did not want to lose the momentum. The producer gave a nearly invisible wag of his head to Rothman and they forged ahead.

"How do you think that's going to play in South Carolina?"

"I've spent very little time in the south. I know that the south is ground zero for states' rights. But I hope that an appeal based on logic, history, and common sense will sway enough people to vote for me."

"Let's run through a list of hot-button issues and just give me a few words on where you stand on them. Abortion."

"Can we all agree that abortion is not the preferred method to avoid childbirth? I mean, pro-life or pro-choice, that ought to at least be a common starting point.

"But how about Roe V Wade? Where do you stand?"

"Abortions should be legal."

"But you are a Roman Catholic."

"I know, and I might be refused communion the next time I attend church, which admittedly is not often. But let's leave my religious beliefs out of politics. Let's leave everyone's religious beliefs out of politics. There is no religious test. We are not electing a saint here. We are electing a leader; someone who may have to do some very un-Christian-like things in order to fulfill the duties of the office. We would all be speaking German if FDR had said 'Well, the Good Book says we should offer the other cheek.'

"Gun control."

"The Second Amendment was adopted in 1791. The basis for the amendment was to arm a citizen militia against a similarly armed invader. That worked in the Revolutionary War, but it would be a ridiculous notion today to think that any ragtag team of assault-weapons bearing citizens would stand a chance against a foreign invader. NRA members are fond of saying that the right to bear arms guarantees that the citizenry will not be forcibly oppressed by their own government. Again, they would stand little chance against a trained army or police force. The other argument they raise is that the best way to stop a bad guy with a gun is a good guy with a gun. That may happen occasionally.

"But stopping an attacker is harder than it looks. Most people would be as likely to shoot a bystander as the shooter. Not everyone is James Bond. When shots are being fired, who is going to have the coolness and the training to neutralize an attacker without inflicting casualties on innocent bystanders? That kind of training is rare, even within some police forces. And it has to be maintained. You don't get there by going down to the range once a month. The average citizen just is not going to be effective in an active shooter situation.

"And the whole notion of keeping guns out of the hands of the mentally ill is crazy. It completely misses the possibilities of: one, someone like the Sandy Hook shooter taking a legally owned gun that was inside the household, and two, a normally sane person just snapping, reaching their final breaking point, and going nuts.

"So, gun control? Let's have it! Let's enforce the laws that exist, and write new ones to prevent the supply and purchase of assault weapons and large capacity magazines. The NRA is paying off too many politicians. They won't pay me off."

"North Korea."

"Yes. Yes. That's a tough issue. Here I agree with what Rex Tillerson had to say about it: that a sensible approach is to invite North Korea to negotiate without preconditions. Isolation is never a good idea. Sanctions sometimes work, but the ones who really suffer are the innocent civilians. Look at Iran. North Korea illustrates why we need a sober leader in the White House, and a strong, well-trained, well-equipped military with a well-defined mission. The military needs to be a very strong deterrent force, and it needs the teeth to act when required. It is not a force to distribute aid during a natural disaster. It is a force to inflict casualties and mayhem. We need a new paradigm."

"A new paradigm?" asked Rothman. "What needs to change?"

"Maybe I misspoke. Maybe it's really reverting back to an OLD paradigm. Where the military is in the business of inflicting great violence. That's what militaries do: inflict violence. I'm not sure the military is effective when the rules of engagement are complex. The US won wars on two fronts against Germany and Japan. Two massive military powers. Now we're still fooling around in Afghanistan, and even with some kind of poorly-defined missions in Africa. Clear missions to inflict violence are what the military requires. Half-measures are only going to fail. Battles are won by generals, but wars are lost by politicians."

"The economy."

"The Dow Jones Industrial Average is up what? Six? Seven hundred points since Trump took office? That's good, and he is taking all kinds of credit for that, but will he be willing to take the responsibility when the market corrects? I doubt it.

"Listen, the market is cyclical. And furthermore, the companies on the Dow are NOT heavily industrial! Maybe a third of them are in heavy industry. The rest are retail, insurance, entertainment, finance. Come on. Thirty years ago two-thirds of the companies on the Dow were heavy industrial. Are you gonna tell me that as McDonald's goes, so goes the nation?"

"Illegal Immigration."

"Who is in favor of anything illegal? That's not the right question. The right question is, 'What should be done to prevent undocumented workers from taking jobs that would otherwise be done by taxpaying Americans?' And the answer is, make sure that employers are not gaming the system and paying undocumented workers under the table. Produce still needs to be picked, and Americans are not gonna do that hard labor for that low pay. If an immigrant worker wants to do it, then by all means, let's invite them into the country, process the necessary paperwork, get them to pay taxes, and make damn sure the employer is paying his fair share too."

"That ignores the issue of services provided to illegals."

"There are some services that are provided to illegal immigrants. Emergency Medicaid, WIC, SNAP. Those are federal programs. And the states and municipalities are required to provide K through 12 education to undocumented children. So yeah there are costs to provide those services, but as a percentage of national debt, it's probably insignificant, even though this is a hot-button issue that has REALLY been exploited by the right wing-nuts."

"Healthcare."

"Yeah. Okay. Enough already. I'm never going to be elected." Monroe gave a dejected laugh and ran his hands through his mane of hair. "Here is the problem with insurance. Once everyone has insurance, there is no incentive to reduce healthcare costs. The providers keep jacking up the rates, and then the insurance companies increase the premiums. It turns into an arithmetic progression."

"Not a geometric progression, or exponential?" Rothman smiled. He was obviously enjoying this.

"I'm not given to hyperbole," Monroe smiled. "What I think needs to happen is to provide for preventive care, you know, an ounce of prevention. Things like annual checkups and various screenings. And then also provide for major medical to cover major health issues. And for God's sake, can we finally get tort reform?"

The producer gave a quick twirl of his raised index finger. He wanted to wrap up this part, and there was the soft stuff they needed to do tomorrow. The PA came over, unclipped Monroe's mike, then tended to Mr. Rothman. Monroe looked out his office door to Ted, who gave him a surprised and approving nod. Maybe he wouldn't wring his neck.

. . .

THE *ABOUT TIME* SEGMENT WAS TO AIR the following Sunday, and in the week leading up to the episode Monroe and Ted interviewed four additional political consultants. Ted had done a masterful job of getting them on the schedule and the team had politely listened to their pitches during the meetings, which were not grueling so much as they were interesting, even though each one lasted four hours with limited breaks.

Officially the campaign staff was led by Ted, with the five permanent staffers from *The Independent* involved in all aspects of the campaign. That was going to change as soon as a consultant was brought on board, but for now, they all switch-hit, with primary responsibilities according to their tastes and abilities, which matched up pretty well.

So Ted was the Campaign Manager, Theresa Stamford was Field Department Head, Alice B. "ABC" Conway was Fundraising, Tom Loughery was Communications Department Chief, Pat Metiore was the Scheduling and Advance Guy, and Jenn Hensel, his long-time secretary, had been tapped for general duties, which really meant she was still in charge. The Technology Department, Legal Department, and Political Departments had been un-tended to, pending the consultant's input. The current thinking was that each of the current department heads would roll over into a "deputy" or "assistant" role once the pros were hired. That way they could be assured, or at least fooled into thinking, that Monroe's interests were still being served.

The first outfit to present was called American Political Consulting. They drove up from their headquarters in DC with three men in black suits and one woman in a black skirt and blazer. Monroe was impressed with their no-BS style but when they started talking about opposition research he interrupted.

"Why do we need opposition research? I'm not running in a primary, and we already know everything we need to know about Trump already."

Blake Mrzowski, one of the young suits spoke up. "You'll still be in the primary states campaigning alongside Trump and all of the Democrats who show up. You'll want to have some ammo to counter-attack."

It was a good point. Monroe shot Ted a look that he interpreted as "I like the way this kid thinks." Ted grudgingly acknowledged, but was thinking, *I love how these ethnic families give their kids WASPy first names. They'd have been better off calling him Stanislaus.*

The next group was Marvis Baker, also from DC. They had flown into Latrobe with five people, including a trendy Account Manager; a Senior Consultant who was afflicted with a plaid bow tie and elbow patches; another Senior Consultant with sad, moist eyes; a Social Media Consultant who surreptitiously scanned her iPhone for breaking events every single minute; and a middle-aged black woman who had a background in finance.

After introductions the conversation led to damage control. "Again with the damage control," protested Monroe impatiently. Ted raised both hands, effectively tamping down the flames of impending rage. Then turning to the new group he suggested,

"Wait until you see the *About Time* piece this Sunday. It went VERY well!"

"You let him go on *About Time* without being coached?" laughed the afflicted senior consultant. He was an arrogant prick.

"By a consultant?" asked the account manager, piling on.

"Excuse me," Monroe politely begged as soon as his cell phone rang. "I have to take this." It was Jenn calling him from across the table to give him an excuse to leave the room before he lost these five votes. He left the room and walked up the street to Nancy's office to hide out for a few hours and see how his personal investments were doing. They called Albert who spent three or four minutes talking about how Wall Street was preparing for a major correction.

"Doesn't matter," Monroe looked at Nancy while they were on the speakerphone with Albert. "We only have what? Less than 10 percent in stocks?"

"Yes, the other twenty-seven million or so of your personal account is in bonds, so even at 4 percent, you are grossing one million, eighty thousand a year."

"Well hell. I can't live on THAT!" he joked. He knew Nancy would appreciate the gag. Albert, not so much. "Let's pull another million out of the stocks and donate half to Puerto Rico and the other half to Appalachia. Can we do that?"

"We CAN . . . but you really ought to save something for contingency liquid assets for the campaign."

"Well, I'd like to do it. And anonymously."

"Are you crazy? Talk about losing political capital!"

"It's not really charity if you expect something in return, now is it?"

"As you wish," sighed Albert, with more than a hint of sarcasm.

Monroe marched back to the office, a late winter wind magnifying its chill through the hardscape funnel of buildings on Ligonier Street. He picked up his pace as his ears began to grow numb.

The other meeting had wound down fairly quickly after his exit. Tomorrow there would be two more firms to interview, with a full day of sitting there listening to idiots who thought they knew more than him. The first guys were pretty good. No way for the second crew. Bunch of hacks. *Well, I ought to have a more open mind*, he thought.

Three men from StratiPol Consultants in Atlanta flew in to Pittsburgh. They ran through the same spiel as the first outfit, but came prepared with a budget that included options for buying a used commercial jet or leasing one. A brand new Boeing business jet would go for about $70 million, but would have resale value after the campaign. Unless Monroe took a liking to traveling first class with fifty of his best friends after the election. At least these guys had a sense of humor. Monroe was now regretting the instructions he gave to Albert yesterday, and then felt a pang of guilt over his nascent philanthropist's remorse.

Ted and Theresa had vetted all of the consultants, and now they had only one left. Monroe felt that he could live with StratiPol, but he preferred APC right now. Predictably, APC's proposal was higher, but at this stage it was impossible to pin down the cost. It wasn't like anyone was giving him a lump-sum price on a fixed scope. It was going to be T&E, baby, with retainers, and options for research, policy coaching, and all the media attention that would be required to get the grassroots campaign energized. Spread the buzz, collect the required signatures in all fifty states to get on the ballots. That was going to be a huge challenge, and none of that was going to happen without the research, policy, and media.

Which is why he was gratified when the first thing the last guys did was unfurl a Critical Path Method schedule that showed the deadlines for filing in each state, and how much time they would have to collect the signatures and prepare the message.

Sam Balentine from Technical Political Consulting, Inc. led the charge. Sam was probably the same age as Monroe. They provided a roster of their firm, with bios and pictures of the core members, their specialties listed next to their photos. They had an org chart that had straight lines of responsibility. The crazy charts that showed an arrow to every box with every possible permutation drove Monroe nuts; as if everyone does everything, and has total accountability.

Sandra Pease, a forty-something Senior Field Operations Consultant, acknowledged Monroe's background, and even cited some of his editorials as evidence of a mature political philosophy. While he was not a seasoned politician, they were not going to be starting with a neophyte. Not that they would anyway. His political philosophies were developed. He couldn't wait for her to see the *About Time* segment.

Gary Davidson was TPC's media guru. He was an intense fiftyish mesomorph with wire-rimmed glasses, black hair graying at the temples, and a perfect black suit. He looked like the guy who ought to be running for office. Alice, the *Independent's* Advertising Director, reserved opinion, relying on her professional jealousy to erect that invisible wall of skepticism that so often accompanies a professional introduction.

Gary was all about a multipronged approach. "Look," he enunciated over a bar chart of dollars spent on the last presidential campaign, "everyone is excited about social media, and it cannot be ignored, but in order to mount a campaign, I believe the best approach still involves print and broadcast." That sealed the deal for Alice.

Fuller Thompson was TPC's Research Director. A reserved and attentive black man, when it was his turn to present TPC's case, he calmly laid out a concise yet thorough explanation of the many facets to be considered, including opposition research, counterintelligence research, and policy research. TPC had their office in Falls Church, a short drive from Langley, where Thompson had worked unassumingly as an analyst for the CIA for twenty years after graduating from Yale with a BA in political science.

The meetings finally over after two grueling days of interviews, Monroe's intimates met in the conference room for a debriefing over pizza and beer. Rolling Rock had eventually been sold to Anheuser Busch and was being brewed in Newark, so now they opted for Straub and Yuengling out of loyalty to the Commonwealth.

Ted passed out index cards and asked everyone to list their preferences in order. As expected, the group that Monroe had walked out on posted last on every ballot. APC garnered three votes for second, and the rest for third. StratiPol collected two votes for first, one for second, and the rest for third. TPC led the pack with five votes for first. Ted had actually rated them third, behind StratiPol and APC.

"I just liked StratiPol's thinking about the jet," explained Ted. "They had the best rates too. I know you're richer than God right now, but we need to spend money responsibly. We aren't the fucking federal government." He paused. "Yet."

"They all had their good points. Even Marvis Baker." It was Tom Loughery. Ted shot him a look. Monroe looked inquisitively at him with raised eyebrows. "Look, you can't just ignore that we are going to have to respond to that jerk in Greensburg. That's going to come up again."

"Come up again? Monroe's reply is gonna make the highlight reel for this campaign on *Showtime*."

Monroe stood, running both hands through his hair. "Tom is right, they all had their good points. I just have no patience for arrogance."

Ted looked up from an unadorned slice of pizza and addressed Monroe. "You're the one who has to make the final decision. If you are comfortable with a consultant, that's who we should go with. The rest of us will live with it. But you don't want to change halfway through a campaign. That sends a bad message."

"I get that," answered Monroe. "But I wanted your opinions. You're all trusted associates." He paused, recalling one particular employee he fired fifteen years ago. Terminated with extreme prejudice would be a more appropriate description. "Or else you never would have lasted fifteen or twenty years with the paper."

A familiar hush settled over the team, punctuated by several bottles being set down on the table. Jenn quietly folded her hands across her lap and pursed her lips as she reflected on the "Garrett Affair."

During coverage of a strike fifteen years ago at a local steel mill, James Plinther, one of the staff reporters, had been hit in the head by a brick. It wasn't intentional, but obviously it never should have happened in the first place. Wrong place, wrong time. Fractured skull, paralysis, it was a mess. And no one knew who threw it, so no charges were ever pressed. The paper had been hamstrung anyway. One of the female reporters had married and her husband moved to North Carolina for a job. So they definitely needed a hired hand to fill in the gap left by the injury. Ted had put the word out to his contacts to see if anyone knew of someone who could fill in and maybe even take the position permanently.

Monroe and Ted interviewed a guy who came highly recommended. Stan Garrett impressed them as a competent, reliable reporter, and he came with a pedigree. In fact, Monroe felt like an ass offering this guy the usual gunslinger rate (but it was a cutthroat business). He finally offered 20 percent more than Plinther was making.

It seemed like the smart play, but in a short while Garrett was providing running commentary on the state of *The Independent*. He commented freely on a perceived lack of professionalism and journalistic integrity.

The other reporters were getting pissed. There are no secrets in a news room, and word leaked that Garrett was making more than the rest of them. Not only that but the guy wasn't exactly setting records for meeting deadlines. There was a lot of "Maybe that's how they do it in the big city . . ." and "Now Franco, does this piece of yours meet the 'Garrett Standard'?" Ted had caught wind of the gossip and knew he needed to reel it in.

Polanski was preempted by a very agitated Franco DeMario, who pulled him aside.

"You gotta do something about this little cocksucker, Ted. He ain't safe!"

"Hold your voice down!" snapped Ted, grabbing Franco by the shoulder and dragging him into an empty conference room. "First, you don't tell me what to do! Last time I checked, you work for ME!" Ted had an independent streak himself and like most employees, it was more fulfilling to act on his own than to be instructed or lectured to. "Second, you ought to know better than to make threats in the workplace! Third, I am aware of the situation, and . . ."

There was a crash and a murmur of voices out in the fishbowl.

"Grab your SHIT and get the FUCK out of here!"

Franco and Ted looked stupidly at each other then darted around the corner to see Monroe standing over a tipped over wastebasket with Stan Garrett on the floor among scattered papers and a coffee mug. Ted quickly instructed Franco to get Monroe to a neutral corner, an office, or a broom closet while Ted rushed over to Garrett and offered a hand and any opportunity, however small, to save face.

There was a lawsuit (settled out of court), bad publicity, and a rumor going around the tri-state area that *The Independent* was going to shutter because the idiot editor had a bad temper and was being sued for breaking an employee's nose. And, oh by the way, the idiot editor was a LAWYER!

Well, the damage was not that bad. Monroe felt bad for pushing the guy, and the place did not close. Pressed by Ted for an explanation, Monroe explained that the little cocksucker had impugned his editorial style.

Water over the dam.

But every one of his staff had come by individually and without prompting to offer their support should they be asked to testify.

"Let's bring back TPC," sighed Monroe as he checked his iPhone. The rest of the group nodded and murmured approval as he read the fifteenth text this week from Albert Messing. *What is his problem now?* wondered Monroe.

Albert had never been a fan of Monroe's idea. His objections were transparent. Albert Messing was managing the total amount of the lottery winnings. There was a $30 million personal account for Monroe and another $810 million operating account for the campaign. The $810 million in the campaign would be drawn down throughout the campaign, leaving Albert with only the personal account. One percent of $840 million was a hell of a lot more than 1 percent of $30 million.

At first it was the questions related to quality of life: Why not enjoy life? Why do you want to put yourself through the scrutiny?

Do you have any idea how exhausting a national campaign is going to be?

He was now writing daily missives about how much more sense it would make to protect the assets with a variety of financial vehicles: Think of the good you could do by placing the money in trusts. It would be a full-time job to manage those! You could establish your legacy as a philanthropist on the order of a Carnegie, or Heinz, or Gates!

The pleading was grating on Monroe. He needed a clear mind to wade through these next few tricky months, and Albert's whining was a distraction. He called Nancy, who answered on the first ring.

"Albert is seriously killing me."

"I know."

"He's digging his own grave."

"I know!"

"You're going to have to settle him down."

"I KNOW!"

When he received five Albert-grams before noon the next day, Monroe called him. "Albert, this is not working out. I need you to calm down, or I'm going to find another financial planner."

"Monroe, it's my DUTY . . . ethically . . . to guide you to the best possible financial solutions to protect your assets . . ."

"Albert, Fred will be contacting you." He hung up. Fred was already aware of the issue and had scoped out a firm in Pittsburgh to handle the account. Fred and Monroe had actually talked about opening a second account right after the confirmation of the ticket to inspire competition and higher yields. Monroe had gone with his gut, which in this case was a combination of loyalty to Albert and complacency. Now they were going to have to find two firms so that this time there would be competition.

The first alternate was another firm just like Albert's, with a nice track record of protecting some of the region's wealthiest families. They could devote a Senior Vice President (everyone in these places was a Senior VP) to service Monroe exclusively. That VP's name was Khalil Menfadlak. Khalil was a first-generation American whose family had emigrated to the US during the First Lebanon War in 1982. He was ten years old then, and his father was a respected thoracic surgeon at Saint George Hospital University Medical Center in Beirut. The family landed in Pittsburgh where Khalil's father secured a position at the University of Pittsburgh Medical School. When the time came, Khalil went to Wharton to get an MBA in finance.

The other firm that Fred found was located in London. He had spoken with Mars-Enberg a few times and then visited them. Fred was impressed with their international clientele, as well as the prospect of sheltering some of the money off-shore. That VP's name was Blaise Conrad.

Satisfied that all was legal and completely above-board, Fred made the switch from Albert to Khalil and Blaise. Eight-hundred-and-forty million dollars was split in half and sent to the two new CFPs. Albert had really handled the money well, but he was out, and Khalil and Blaise were in.

. . .

THE *ABOUT TIME* SEGMENT WAS A SOFT PIECE and Monroe came across as sincere, intelligent, well-informed, and able to stand up for himself. The liberal media just might anoint this guy if he had no serious skeletons, and could keep his pecker in his pants for the next two years.

Sam and Sandra from TPC had driven up the previous Saturday, and watched the piece in *The Independent's* office with the rest of the campaign staff on Sunday night. After some moderate celebration they discussed where a permanent headquarters ought to be established. Would it be in Latrobe, Pittsburgh, or near the TPC offices in Falls Church?

"We cannot abandon Latrobe," Theresa said immediately. "This is the biggest thing to happen here since John Braillier."

"Besides," added Pat Metiore, "you're gonna want to appear to remain humble to capture that appeal to the heartland."

"We can tailor the appeal as needed," cooed Sandra. She had a voice like nectar, smooth and soothing. "The polling data will show us what to adjust."

"Look, I know you are experts at what you do, and I agree I will need coaching and advice on how best to present myself and my ideas, but I do not want to spend a lot of time and money on polls." Monroe had pulled on his caution face. The caution face was not for him; it was for others. "What I mean is, I am not going to be changing my views based on polls. If miners in West Virginia need to be told their mines are shutting down, I'm going to say that. If Iowans need to be told that the economics of ethanol are not there without subsidies, I'm going to say that. I'm not going to be lying because of the audience."

"Federal subsidies of ethanol expired in 2012," Sandra informed him, "Just saying."

"We take your point," said Sam. "And our advice right now is that you should probably start to spend some time in Falls Church. Closer to the action, get yourself seen around DC. . . . You're obviously going to be spending time in a lot of places, and it would make more sense to use Latrobe than Pittsburgh. You have the airport right here. But you don't have the available office spaces that you are going to need. Not even close."

"Told you!" said Ted and Monroe to each other in unison.

They agreed to have Metiore scout for office space on the east side of Pittsburgh, close to the Monroeville exit off the Turnpike. They would want maybe five thousand square feet to start, with the ability to double that in three to six months. In the meantime, Ted and Monroe were to drive the three-and-a-half hours to Falls Church on Tuesday to get the lay of the land there and find temporary housing. Unless Monroe fell in love with the area and decided to purchase a residence.

They all joked about that, and while there were definitely some pros to buying a property there, Monroe could not quite get his mind around spending money like a mega-millionaire. Fred, master of the obvious at times, had told him that he could do it as a business expense, and after the election he could sell it. So there was that angle too. But he had a lot of respect for the amount of money that was going to be required to survive this campaign, and he resisted the temptation to squander the funds. Temptation was not exactly the right word either. It simply was not in his DNA to waste money.

Monroe's parents were children of the Great Depression. He grew up hearing stories about how his mother was lucky to get an orange for Christmas, and those stories impacted his thrift throughout his adult life. Nor was he especially frugal. He paid fair wages to his employees and he ran the business, well, like a business. He thought of himself as a good steward and so he invested in the paper where appropriate, but when the internet started to steal subscriptions, he quickly invested in other streams of revenue generation.

For all of Sam's bitching about the lack of office space in Latrobe, TPC's offices were smaller than they had expected. What impressed Ted was the furnishings, which could be viewed from the atrium, outside of the private lobby.

"Apparently, image really IS everything," whispered Ted as they passed through silent, sliding glass doors and into the lobby. They were greeted by a very professional, very polite receptionist who knew their names and the way they took their coffee. She escorted them into a glass-walled conference room that was equipped with blinds for those occasions that demanded privacy. A Sony high-definition XD cam stood on a tripod in the corner.

"Every wall in the joint is glass," remarked Monroe.

"Where does a guy take a shit?" asked Ted rhetorically.

"You know, you have such a way with words!"

"Yeah. I should be a fuckin' writer," yawned Ted, picking up a crystal orb for closer examination.

Sam explained that they leased other space as required. There was plenty of office space in the area, and yes, it was ungodly expensive. Likewise the hired hands. Staff ebbed and flowed under the watchful eyes of the Account Manager. But there were always paid studies to perform and policy to research for industry lobbyists and the like. The receptionist entered the conference room with a smile and placed their coffee mugs on the table. Each was emblazoned with a different prototype "GO FOR MONROE" logo.

Gary Davidson, the media guru came in, along with Sandra, Fuller, and a man named Phil Ainsworth, who would be a Project Manager assisting Sam with scheduling and day-to-day operations. Phil was an affable fellow without being fawning; the kind of guy who was immediately likeable. As he explained the schedule arranged for the rest of the week, a natural excitement oozed out of him. Ted was thankful that some downtime was provided in the schedule. The week was going to be full of meetings to introduce the rest of the team and exchange ideas about Monroe's politics and how the campaign needed to progress.

After an hour of anodyne discussion, a tough-looking, bald son of a bitch with a goatee marched into the room and without preamble walked to the camera, positioned it, and turned it on. He turned to Monroe and interrupted Phil as he talked about where they would be dining tonight.

"What's your position on Obamacare?" he demanded.

Ted threw the guy a glance like he wanted to get up and punch him. But that was obviously an empty threat since the guy outweighed him by at least fifty pounds. Monroe was also taken aback. Flustered, he paused a moment, smiled, cocked his head slightly and after an inaudible throat clearing, answered in a clear voice.

"I believe that one of the main drivers in high medical costs is insurance. When a doctor or a hospital find out that a patient has insurance, what incentive do they have to reduce costs? And what incentive does an insurance company have to reduce premiums?

The answer is none, and the costs spiral out of control. In a perfect world, the costs would be set by the market. But in a medical emergency, you don't have the luxury of shopping around for a better price. And who wants bargain health care anyway? I am for limited insurance however, to cover two contingencies. The first," he said, raising his thumb, "is for catastrophic health care. Major medical. The second," the index finger went up, "would be for preventive care. Checkups, vaccinations, health screenings recommended by your PCP."

"Vaccinations cause autism!" If this guy was acting, it was a damn good act. His face was getting ever more crimson as he shouted.

Monroe shifted sideways in his chair and slung his right arm over the back of it. "Obviously I am not a physician, but I think that unless a definite link is proven between vaccinations and autism, or any other condition, it is wiser to err on the side of public health and not put larger populations at risk. Polio and smallpox have been eradicated through the use of vaccines. I can't support risking an outbreak of measles because of anecdotal claims." He was having a little trouble modulating his voice, and it was starting to creep into a higher register. *Damn! I know better! The lower registers always convey more authority.*

"You probably want my eleven-year-old daughter to get a goddamn HPV vaccine!"

"I want everyone to be protected by the protocols recommended by the CDC. They have the expertise to make those recommendations." This time his voice was down where it usually was when he was giving a serious ass-chewing to one of his reporters.

The guy paced over toward Monroe, leaning into him. Monroe observed tiny beads of sweat popping out on the guy's massive scalp. "That is such a liberal attitude!" he spat through absurdly pink lips. "Liberals always side with elitists! Why don't you just admit you are a closet Democrat!"

Monroe had to shift in his chair to gain a little space. "I have no political affiliation, because I adhere to no political platform by either party . . ."

Sam gave an approving nod to Gary, who stood and introduced the interloper. "Monroe, Ted. I'd like you to meet Kurt Bastille. Kurt is one of our media coaches." Kurt offered a beefy hand, a smile and a quick critique. "Nice job. Good composure. We need to work on your posture. If you're sitting down you want to avoid that arm over the back of the chair. It looks arrogant. And if you are challenged up close you need to hold your ground a little stronger. There are going to be a LOT of settings that are 'uncontrolled,' and we won't have an opportunity to clear space to get the best camera angle. You need to create that space yourself when possible, without looking like you are backing off. Move to the side. Never back up."

Monroe thanked him for the advice, but did not sound sincere. "We'll work on the sincerity thing too," called out Bastille over his shoulder as he exited the conference room, whipping a handkerchief from his back pocket and swabbing his gleaming head.

Next up was TPC's legal counsel, a youngish-looking Asian named Ronald Le Quang. His relatively wealthy parents had bribed their way onto an overloaded boat during the fall of Saigon in 1975, and made it to Los Angeles, where Ronald was born in 1982. His parents named him after Reagan. Ronald ran through some of the initial procedures that would be needed to begin filing for candidacy. He offered a binder full of tabbed dividers that outlined financial disclosure statements, the number of signatures that each state would require to get on their ballots, a Statement of Organization for the campaign, and dozens of other forms. He asked Monroe to arrange for his last ten years of tax returns and all his investments during that time to be copied and sent to TPC. He was also going to need to speak to Nancy, as well as his investment advisors.

"That might be a little bit of a problem," cautioned Monroe, while Sandra led Ted out of the room. "We're in a bit of a transition period with the financial guys, and one of them is in London. I can have you talk to my attorney, Fred During, about it."

The next day started at 7 AM, with a deep dive into Monroe's history scheduled for all day. They all gathered around the table in the conference room, and with the camera rolling to capture the details, Monroe laid out his bio, peppered with questions about details. Who were his friends in grade school? What did he want to be when he grew up? What did he and his family do on vacations? How did he get along with his parents? With other kids? Why didn't he have any siblings or cousins? Any sports? Little League? Youth football? By ten thirty they had finally plowed through junior high. He actually enjoyed recalling his early years. He was a happy kid with an ideal family life. Okay, it wasn't exactly Norman Rockwell every moment, but his parents were loving, and they got through most of life's challenges with only a moderate amount of tears and yelling at each other.

During the break at ten thirty, Gary Davidson mentioned, "You know, everyone who runs for president has to write a book. You're gonna be too busy to write one, so we're going to need to ghostwrite this. That's the other reason we are torturing you with these details."

"The other reason is we need this background to run counterintelligence," interjected Fuller Thompson.

"Yeah, I get all of that," said Monroe, "but I was thinking we might run a sampling of my editorials instead. That would be more transparent and probably easier to pull together."

"It's a possibility," offered Davidson reluctantly, "but even if we go that direction, the public is still going to want the human interest aspect. We can't just feed them editorials."

They got to the teen years, and right on cue the issue of his sexuality came up. He wanted to be careful to not be too assertive that he was a heterosexual. If only he had gotten married. But he never found the prospect particularly appealing. They didn't hit that too hard, which puzzled Monroe. They moved on to college and law school.

"I see you never finished at Georgetown. You got your JD from Pitt instead," observed Sandra.

"My father had a massive heart attack in my last year at Georgetown. He got up in the middle of the night to go to the bathroom, and my Mom heard a crash. He had fallen backwards into the bathtub. She called me from the hospital and she didn't even know he had already died. I just pulled on some jeans and drove home. The next week I dropped out of school. Mom needed me. The paper probably would have gone right along, but Mom was now the owner, and she was not prepared to sell. We limped along until things settled down. Which of course they never do after something like that. That was 1982. Dad was sixty. He was a rock. Was in great shape . . ."

Sam threw a look at Sandra across the table and she made a note to schedule Monroe's blood work and physical as soon as possible. He looked like he was in great shape too.

Monroe continued wistfully, his voice soft. "Mom was never the same after that. She became depressed, and lost the will to live. I came home late one afternoon six months later, and found her on the sofa. The coroner ruled her death natural, even though two bottles of her prescriptions were empty. She didn't leave a note, and so he didn't perform an autopsy. Natural death."

They wound that day down and reviewed the next day's schedule. Monroe was going to start talking current events and policy with Phil and Sandra. Ted would be there too. There would also be some media coaching by Kurt and Gary Davidson. TPC had a mock studio set up in a corner of the floor, and it was pretty convincing. Sam wanted to get some of the Latrobe team involved soon, so he was driving up to Pennsylvania tomorrow. It took no longer to drive than to fly.

Fuller Thompson quietly sent Tonya Jackson along with Sam to begin to ferret out dirt on Monroe. Also ex-CIA, she had operated as an Operations Officer in the Caribbean. A tall, slender, and very attractive black woman, she mixed seamlessly with the locals, discovering illegal drug trade routes from South America to Florida and the Gulf Coast. In Latrobe, she was going to stick out like a sore thumb, regardless of how demurely she dressed. But because she had also served in Yemen, she was also eager to have a discussion with Khalil Menfadlak. That would give her a chance to behave like a covert operative again, and exercise her Arabic.

The counterintelligence in Latrobe was a side matter. TPC had already embedded a mole at *The Independent*. A late-twenties graduate from Georgetown with a major in PoliSci, she had acquired a job there with the express purpose of collecting intel on Monroe in particular and the paper in general. If there was any whiff of corruption Sam wanted to know about it. Turned out she was a pretty good reporter too.

The paper had hired a few people to fill the gaps left by ABC, Tom Loughery, and Pat Metiore. So Franco was easily persuaded to hire the cute girl with the fake resume from Point Park University in Pittsburgh. She brought in donuts on her first day, and the fact that she could actually write seemed like a bonus. She fed encrypted status reports daily to TPC from her apartment in Lawson Heights. So far she turned up some gossip that Ted had gotten divorced due to some infidelity, though it was not clear yet who had cheated. The descriptions she got of Monroe were generally bathed in a reverent glow. She had given him the code name "The Saint."

. . .

SANDRA INVITED TED OUT TO DINNER the next night. When he heard about it, Monroe collared him and advised him to be on his best behavior. "What's wrong with you?" Ted asked with mock indignation. "Does everything have to be about sex with you? You should really seek professional help!"

"You know what I mean," whispered Monroe, a little too loudly. It came out like a threatening hiss. He looked around the office quickly to see if they were out of earshot. He grabbed Ted by the upper arm and ushered him around a corner. "I don't need you screwing another employee."

"Well, technically, she would be a contractor."

The exchange was caught by a TPC staffer who was too far away to hear the content, but nevertheless dutifully and discreetly reported it to Sandra.

"It looked a little gay," informed the staffer in a hushed tone, behind Sandra's closed door.

Sandra shifted her eyes and thanked the staffer, picked up the phone and called Phil. "It may be what we suspected."

"Well, ferret it out," answered Phil. "You know how to play it. He turned to Sam who was in his office. "Sandra is getting intel that our boy and his boy may be a 'thing'."

CHAPTER 8

"Well," replied Sam. "No one said running candidates was going to be easy." He exhausted an audible sigh. "Let's get the scoop before we invoke the 'Rainbow Option.' Even after eight hours of bio, we have no idea of this guy's preferences."

Sam had been back for a few days, having left Tonya in Pittsburgh. He arranged to bring down ABC, Tom, Pat, and Jenn from Latrobe. They would arrive in a week. Nancy and Monroe were trying to decide if they should buy an apartment building in Tysons Corner, and they were liking the numbers. It made a lot of sense, and Monroe did have good luck with real estate.

While in Pennsylvania Tonya debriefed the mole from *The Independent*, then arranged a meeting with Khalil Menfadlak. The mole reiterated that everyone at the newspaper liked Monroe and respected him. There was an incident awhile back with a journalist named Stan Garrett, who by all accounts was an ass. There was talk of a lawsuit for breach of contract, assault, slander, but it was all settled out of court. No one seemed to question Monroe's orientation, and there was even some anecdotal evidence of Monroe being a bit of a womanizer. He had the good sense to keep his relations private. On the occasions when he attended social events, he would sometimes be accompanied by an attractive woman from the Allegheny County Commissioner's office, but that relationship was seen by his colleagues as more professional than romantic. Her name was Amber.

Tonya had no reason yet to report the intel to the main office.

The next morning she drove into Pittsburgh to meet Khalil. She had invented a pretext in which she needed to hold some money from the sale of her Yemeni father's retail business, but she wanted to earn some kind of return on it even though it would be for a short term. She introduced herself in Arabic, then continued, explaining that she had found Khalil online and felt more comfortable conducting business with an Arab. Someone who would respect Sharia-compliant finance.

It was clear that Tonya had an excellent understanding of Muslim culture and religion, so her admonitions against *riba* were convincing. Khalil was sympathetic, and had a handful of Muslim clients in the tri-state area. But he explained that he was unable to take on a new client since his firm had limited his accounts to a single, ultra-high-net-worth individual. In fact, he said he had taken her appointment as a courtesy, but he was prepared to offer her the contact data of a Muslim acquaintance at another firm who could help her. She left the appointment with no information other than that Khalil was discreet and professional. Knowing about Monroe, she had already figured that this would be the case. She hopped back in her rental car and drove back to Falls Church.

Later that day Phil invited Monroe to dinner at a restaurant in DC.

Sandra met Ted at a contemporary restaurant in Falls Church. She had gone home to change, and was now wearing a clingy, scoop-back cocktail dress that highlighted her athletic figure. She ordered a Chardonnay as they were seated, and after some introductory small talk, she led into what Ted suspected was the real purpose for the get-together. "We learned all about Monroe the past few days, but no one really knows much about you . . ."

Having arrived early, Ted had already had a couple of Ketel One martinis at the bar. He was loose, but the red flags were up, and he knew not to give too much away. "What would you like to know?" he asked good-naturedly. "I'm an open book. What you see is what you get . . ."

Phil picked up Monroe at the Residence Inn where they were staying. Ted had the Toyota, and Monroe was not going to drive in any case. Phil drove to The Monocle, valet parked, and they headed inside. A few of the patrons recognized Phil and Monroe was gratified to see that TPC was on the radar. More importantly, several patrons also recognized Monroe. He was starting to generate recognition from not only the *About Time* piece, but also print media. The message wasn't out there yet, but the face and name were starting to be.

They enjoyed a convivial meal. Monroe had cultivated an approachable personality, and coupled with his natural openness, he made a great dinner companion. Phil took affability to another level. The conversation was uplifting, the meal was inspired, the service was discreet, and the atmosphere was warm and enveloping. Phil ordered an after-dinner drink while Monroe opted for a coffee.

"We didn't really get too far into your personal life during the deep dive. Is there anything we should know about?"

"Like what? I'm an open book. What do you wanna know?"

"How's your love life?" Phil asked matter-of-factly.

"Mmm. Private."

Phil chuckled. "C'mon Monroe. You are going to enter public life. Hell, you've already entered it. You just said you are an open book."

"I'm just reluctant to drag innocent people into it. It's not like they were in a position to provide informed consent."

The lack of gender specificity was frustrating Phil, but he was too much of a professional to let his frustration show to a valued client. "Listen," he said, rubbing his chin, "you are an unmarried fifty-nine-year-old. There is some speculation about your proclivities. It's 2018, and the world is a different place than it was even ten years ago. If we need to formulate an approach, we will. But we need to know what we're talking about here."

"Proclivities? Jesus Christ, Phil. Listen, move along. There's nothing to see here." Long pause while he debated about taking a humorous tack. "Mmm. Unless you are worried about 'The Incident'." He had waited too long and so the comedic effect was not as forceful. Phil smiled. Maybe Phil was more prudish than Monroe had deduced. "I get it. You guys need to understand what you are dealing with here. I just don't want a lot of innocent women to be dragged under the microscope."

"A lot? A lot of innocent women? How many innocent women are we talking about here, Monroe?"

"Look. It's like I told that asshole at the first news conference: I am a healthy male with healthy appetites."

"Okay. When is the last time you were laid?" So okay, Phil was not prudish. "We are going to need full names and dates."

Monroe dropped his head low and sighed. He looked up, glanced around to see who might overhear, and relented. "The last time was in St. Lucia. Mona Something. French."

"Wait a minute. Mona SOMETHING? You didn't get her last name? Or you don't remember it?"

"I don't remember it. But yes, Phil. It was pretty casual."

"That's gonna need some cover. And maybe a coat of paint," complained Phil with a touch of exasperation.

"Paint? I always prefer latex." Another long pause. "Before that, I mean . . . it's been awhile. There's a lady I've seen occasionally from Pittsburgh. Nothing too serious. Her name is Amber."

"Sounds like a stripper . . ."

"No no no! No strippers! Jesus Christ, Phil! She works in the Allegheny County Commissioner's office! We met when I was in town covering the G20 Summit in Pittsburgh."

"That would have been in what? 2009?"

"Right."

"At least that shows some stability . . . loyalty. You're not knocking off strange pieces on a regular basis." Wow, he was REALLY not a prude.

"No, of course not. Just the occasional piece." Monroe immediately regretted joking about it, but it was too late to take it back. What if Phil was a spy? What if he was wired? He just met the guy, but he inspired one's confidence. "Listen, I have had really good relationships with several women. Time spent at the paper, and my own inclinations, have not given me sufficient reason to get married. I do respect women. Yada, yada, yada. Fill in the blanks with the usual platitudes. I just also happen to love the way they look. And regarding names and dates, that's a list that is going to lack some specificity."

"Lack it how, exactly? Lacking dates? Or are we talking about lacking full names? Or names altogether?"

"Dates." Long pause. "And some names."

The night continued in much the same way. Phil briefly stated the obvious that the very fact that he was not married—that he NEVER had been married—was going to be a liability.

"Well, if I have to get married, I can find a candidate or two," he assured Phil.

"Or two million."

"This could be like the time Shemp had to get married to inherit his uncle's fortune! 'Hold hands you lovebirds . . .'"

Phil looked at him blankly. "Emil Sitka? Three Stooges?" Monroe asked in vain, in counterpoint to Phil's puzzled expression.

"Jesus, Phil! Didn't you have a childhood?"

They parted company around 11 PM outside the Residence Inn where Monroe and Ted were staying.

"Mmm," mumbled Monroe to no one. "No Highlander."

. . .

9

MONROE KNOCKED ON TED'S DOOR, and there was no answer. When he called his cell Ted picked up on the first ring. "Be right there, Buddy," he answered and hung up. Monroe looked out the window and saw the Highlander swinging into the parking lot. Ted scurried out wearing the same clothes he had on last night. He was met in the hall with a glare from Monroe. "Ten minutes, and I'll be ready!"

"Keys," demanded Monroe with an extended hand. "I'll load up." Monroe waited until Ted closed his door, then went to the Highlander and drove to TPC's office, leaving Ted to find his own transportation.

"He's not gay," announced Sandra as she breezed in late to the closed meeting the next morning. TPC principals always got an early start when clients were in the office. She was impeccably dressed and coiffed. She threw a twenty into the late jar, penalized a dollar for every minute she was late. The original thinking was that TPC would donate the penalties to charitable organizations, but that quickly degenerated into a beer-and-booze fund for late in-office decompression parties.

"Neither is Monroe," said Phil, rolling his eyes, irritated that Sandra had missed that part of the meeting. "And so now we have another problem. The USUAL problem! What has Tonya turned up about this?"

"Relax," said Sam. "It gives us an opportunity to showcase his masculinity. The guy just likes his privacy. And women apparently. Tonya is drilling into that. Now all we have to do is explain why he is a bachelor."

"All I know is it has to do with the Three Stooges . . ."

"Well, that certainly clears things up!" said Sandra sarcastically.

Fuller Thompson said, "Hold hands you lovebirds," and then started to crack up. Phil rolled his eyes.

"The guy does have a certain amount of sex appeal that can be exploited," noted one of the female consultants. "We should use that. It will get us ahead of any stories."

Sam explained they had a chance to put Monroe on any of the late night shows. The consensus was it was too early. They needed something of substance before he started doing more soft pieces. Gary Davidson was tasked with reaching out to *Sunday Morning with Jack Mauer, Face The Nation, This Week, Fox News Sunday,* and *State of the Union.*

"You don't wanna go for the 'Full Ginsburg,' do you? " asked Gary. The "Full Ginsburg" was a sweep of all five shows in a single day.

"No," said Sam. I don't want to dilute the impact. Let's try for two at most, then hit the rest in the following weeks."

Kurt related that Monroe would be ready. "In fairness to him, he was pretty good when we got him," he admitted. "All we're doing now is adding some shine . . . body language, facial expressions. Once in awhile his vocal register climbs but he is aware of that and works to control it . . . but he's never been a 'high-talker'."

The wonks at TPC hated high-talkers. People who end every sentence with a higher pitch. It always made them sound whiny and was the mark of an amateur. Kurt was already a believer in Monroe, but he was also a believer in preparation. He glanced out the glass wall to see Monroe conferring with Alice, Tom, and Jenn from Latrobe. No Ted though.

"How you doing?" asked Jenn, affectionately rubbing the back of Monroe's upper arm.

"Great, Jenn. The schedule is rigorous, and all these TPC guys keep warning me how tough it's going to get. But they act like no one ever works against a deadline. I complain a little here and there just to make them feel better." Alice and Tom laughed knowingly. Monroe was born with a strong work ethic.

Ted showed up a minute later. He greeted the Latrobe contingent and said hi to Sandra, making sure that nothing was "weird." He threw Monroe a look.

"Glad to see you could make it!" exclaimed Monroe.

"No thanks to you!" Ted retorted.

"Hey, Blake!" interrupted Monroe as a young man turned a corner, looking like he was on a mission. He shook his hand. "What are you doing here? You're with American Political Consulting!"

"I was with them, yes sir. But when I found out you went with TPC, I interviewed here and changed jobs. I want to be part of this campaign!"

Monroe turned and looked wide-eyed at the rest of the gang, while Blake continued around the corner on his mission. "That augurs well," said Ted. Monroe was speechless.

That afternoon Monroe was reviewing international policy with the team. It was a rapid-fire scenario designed to improve his mental reflexes and reduce the amount of time spent searching for a starting point. Monroe was an accomplished public speaker, but he did have certain verbal tics. The "mmm" he used while thinking before he answered was an annoyance to Kurt, but at least it was better than "ummm," "errrr," or the accursed "so," the prefix to every sentence uttered by a Millennial, and which had crept overnight into popular usage sometime in 2015. Or so.

About an hour into the session, Kurt threw out, "What about Aleppo?"

Monroe chuckled. "You know, they way they jumped on him was completely unfair. The guy was pilloried." He was referring to Gary Johnson's appearance on *Morning Joe*, when Mike Barnicle asked the Libertarian candidate for President what he would do about the situation in Aleppo.

"But when I think about refugees in Syria, I think about where they are heading. There are thousands of them making a very difficult journey to Northern Europe. And so you have to ask, 'Why do they want to go to Northern Europe?' And the answer is, 'those are wealthy countries . . . Germany, Netherlands, Belgium . . .' countries with wealth can afford to take care of them until they find their way on their own. But they are emigrating to cultures foreign to them. The question is: are there other wealthy countries that could accept them? And the obvious answer is Saudi Arabia, Qatar, the Emirates. And then it makes perfect sense. Why wouldn't they go there, where there is great wealth, and they already speak the language and practice the same religion? Most Syrian refugees are Sunni Muslims, just like Saudi Arabia. So why can't the UN, the EU, and the US apply pressure on those countries to accept more refugees than Northern Europe? That's what I think about Aleppo. Now having said that, I want to make two additional points . . ."

"Time's up!" announced Kurt. "You are talking too much. We need ten second bites."

"To match the little bitty attention spans of Americans," snickered Ted.

"Listen, we are going to have to educate the American public about politics," complained Monroe.

"You have a choice, Monroe. Either run for president, or get a talk show like Rush Limbaugh."

"Well, there you go! Thank you Ronald Reagan! Listen, I can't educate anyone about my positions in ten seconds. I'll just have to talk faster."

Gary Davidson had lined Monroe up on *Sunday Morning with Jack Mauer*. Davidson and his team selected a black suit for Monroe, with a solid red tie. Very presidential, but Monroe wanted to jettison it in favor of one of his lucky ties. He knew the old Britta tie would not photograph well though. He was surprised how nervous he was to appear live on national TV. He dismissed the superstition of having to rely on a lucky tie. The nerves were in no small part to his interacting live with Jack Mauer. Mauer was one of his favorite moderators.

They shuttled him to the studio early Sunday morning, with plenty of time to get him settled in. One of the producers greeted him and the team, and turned him over to a PA to organize the usual make-up and sound checks. Jack stuck his head through the door and welcomed him briefly, then darted off to prepare for the program.

The lights were intense as Monroe was shown to his chair at the desk, across from Mauer. The producers had given TPC a rough outline of the way the program was expected to proceed, but they emphasized that it was up to the Political Director (Mauer) to determine the course of the interview. Monroe expected as much and was on-board with that. He had rehearsed extensively with Kurt on a variety of domestic and international policy positions.

Monroe settled in and tried to relax, telling himself that this was only a chat with a friend.

"With us today is the Independent Candidate for President for 2020, Mr. Monroe Taylor." Turning from the camera to address Monroe, he began. "You won an 850 million dollar lottery. You have no previous political experience. And now you are running for president. Does this sound at all familiar to you?"

Monroe smiled, and his mind went blank for an instant. Live TV. A short pause elapsed in which Monroe thought to himself, *Maybe I should ask him to repeat the question. What the fuck am I doing here? Do NOT make this your Gary Johnson moment.*

"I'm sorry," he said. "Are you comparing me to Donald Trump?"

"Well, yes," replied Mauer. "It's not like this experiment in democracy hasn't been tried, and it hasn't exactly yielded a lot of political success. Why should the voters pay any attention to another rich white guy with zero political experience?"

"Because this particular rich white guy has a vision for America that is inclusive, and looks hopefully to the future rather than nostalgically to the past."

"What is that vision?" asked Mauer with a skeptical demeanor.

Why was his hero Jack being such a hard-ass? Monroe had a puzzled look on his face that came across like he was developing a thought. Kurt, Sam, Ted, and Sandra leaned in closer to a monitor in a nearby room and held a collective breath.

"My vision is to abandon a two-party political system that can no longer govern. My vision is to implement a cultural shift in politics, a sea change that brings intelligent debate of real issues into the public discourse, rather than fostering a not-invented-here mentality that rejects even good ideas that are introduced by the opposition party."

"Independents have run before. John Anderson in 1980, Ross Perot in '92, Ralph Nader, Bernie Sanders . . . None have been successful, although many will argue that the presence of an Independent in the general election will take votes away from a contender. You must have heard from the Democrats, who are going to be livid."

"It's true that Independents have been spoilers in some past elections. Voters should judge the candidate on the merits of their ideas though, rather than on party affiliations."

Jack looked up to the ceiling, formulating a question. "Are you more Liberal or more Conservative?"

"I'm more Independent. I don't even know what the Liberal or Conservative labels mean anymore." He was loosening up and took on the air of a favorite history professor.

"I remember reading an interview a long time ago about the cast from *West Wing*, and they were talking about their political views. One of the actresses said that she came from a very liberal family, as evidenced by the fact that her grandmother had been a stripper. So she said her family was very LIBERAL. Really? Does liberal mean permissive? I thought it had more to do with cherishing individual liberties.

"Same thing with Conservatives. Conservative implies being cautious about change or innovation. Is aversion to change a good thing? Somehow these terms have been corrupted by politics to mean that all Democrats are Liberals who are spend thrifts with loose morals, and all Republicans are Conservatives who are money-grubbing warmongers with high morals. And of course none of that's true. And if we don't break down these barriers to common sense, then our political system is going to fail. It has already started to fail."

"And so your plan is . . . ?"

"Concentrate on the large issues. Prioritize. Take care of the big things and the little things will take care of themselves. That's not new. But the way to achieve it is to solicit help from both parties and from experts."

"That sounds an awful lot like Ross Perot saying he will form committees of experts to solve the problems of the day."

"Is that really a bad idea? Is the alternative to ignore the advice of experts, because they are 'elitists'?"

"Okay, so drill down a bit for me. What are these 'big picture issues'"? He drew air quotes around "big picture issues." Jack Mauer appeared very skeptical and Monroe was having trouble understanding why he was having trouble convincing the man. And if Jack Mauer was skeptical, how was this going to play across the nation?

"Let's take the Three E's as an example: energy, the economy, and the environment. They are all inter-related. The economy cannot function without a robust energy sector. Energy generation creates pollution. Republicans will have you believe that environmental protection happens at the expense of the economy. Democrats will have you believe that the economy has to be sacrificed for the environment. But there are a lot of products and services that arise to address these issues. Air pollution control devices, sustainable energy solutions like wind and solar power. I'd like to see the nation pick from a variety of these methods, including mini-nuclear plants where appropriate. The electric utility grid is vulnerable, and if you want to bring this country to its knees, just let the grid fail. Just imagine. Without electricity, there's no gas to be pumped, no running water, no refrigerated food, no air conditioning, and no forced air heating. Look at Puerto Rico . . ." He was opening up a line of attack into the current administration's poor response and recovery effort after Hurricane Maria. Mauer cut him off.

"So you advocate what? A spending bill to improve the electrical infrastructure?"

"I advocate a holistic approach to solving problems. We have to recognize that most issues are interdependent, and throwing out catchphrases and pretending that there are simple solutions to major issues is simply not how the world works."

"Do you have an example you'd like to use to illustrate that point?" smiled Jack.

"How about 'Build the wall. And Mexico will pay for it!'" Monroe could not suppress a chuckle, which came out as a sort of snort. He felt immediately ashamed, because it was akin to giddiness. To the delight of his team watching in the next room, it looked on-screen more like derision born of confidence.

"Why not just run as a Democrat?"

"Here is the problem: the polarization that arises out of the two-party system prevents either side from compromising. There was a day when politics involved intelligent debate, discussion, and compromise. That all started to disappear roughly when Reagan got rid of the Fairness Doctrine, which required broadcasters to allow both sides of a story to be heard. And yes, I understand that in large candidate fields it got unwieldy, but inconvenience is a poor excuse for what took its place. The abandonment of Fairness Doctrine gave rise to a non-debate court presided over by the Limbaughs, Hannitys, and Becks of the world. And that is really nothing less than propaganda.

"If you were to draw a graph of population versus the spectrum of political views, with ultra-left wing on the left and ultra-right wing on the right, forty years ago it would have resembled a bell curve. Most Americans would be comfortable near the center, with few voters in the ultra camps. Today that curve is bimodal, with people being driven into tribes of Liberals and Conservatives.

The wedge driving them apart is the divisive rhetoric of politicians and political commentators. 'A house divided against itself cannot stand.'

"This notion about intelligent debate needs to be reinforced. There is an attitude among some voters that it's a character flaw to change one's mind. Isn't that the entire purpose of debate? To persuade the opposition to come around to your way of thinking? If you see an issue in a new light, and are persuaded to change your mind, that is a sign of reason. You wouldn't adhere to a false set of beliefs just to avoid being accused of a flip-flop."

"Monroe Taylor. Thank you for your time. After the break we will talk to the chairpersons of the Republican and Democratic parties. This is *Sunday Morning with Jack Mauer*."

The PA rushed over to disconnect Monroe's microphone and guide him off-studio. He stood and leaned across the desk to shake Jack Mauer's hand. Jack was gracious, if not affable, and Monroe did not know how to interpret that reaction. Monroe met the team in the corridor adjacent to the studio and they seemed generally pleased if somewhat reserved. Sandra grabbed each shoulder with her hands and looked into his eyes. "You have to stop bitching about Reagan!"

"Why?" he challenged. "What I said is true."

"Reagan is a saint to many of the voters you are going to need. You cannot alienate them."

"I'll clarify the message then."

.   .   .

10

BLAKE MRZOWSKI WAS TAPPING THE KEYS on his laptop beside Sandra. They were on the 8:00 PM American flight out of DC, bound for Des Moines. He was replying to an email from Gary Davidson about the signatures that were going to be required to get Monroe on the ballot. Iowa required only 1500 from ten counties. They already had those. Since hiring TPC, field offices had popped up across Iowa, New Hampshire, New York, and California accompanied by an advertising blitz in those states. Gary's multimedia approach appeared to be working, with lots of print ads in newspapers, supplemented by social media ads. They were now neuro-testing the next generation of targeted, issue-rich commercials for TV, and expected those to hit markets in the states that had the campaign offices. They needed to transmit a clear and concise message, and get people to recognize Monroe's name and face.

Monroe was on his way to a meet-and-greet to generate some personal buzz. To achieve that, he was starting a nationwide tour with the campaign staff. They were flying commercial until they accepted delivery of the Boeing Business Jet. They had decided to purchase a refurbished used jet rather than a new one, since TPC reckoned that there would not be a lot of resale value once they logged the million miles that would be required during a campaign. Whenever "Taylor One" was being maintained, they would just charter or fly commercial, like they were doing today. Flying commercial would be more inconvenient, but it would also reinforce the message that Monroe was one of the "people." Plus it would give him a chance to mingle, which he enjoyed.

Half of the traveling staff was on this flight, and the other half was scattering to other states. Ted was grateful once someone explained to him that there would be regular maintenance on the used jet. He was an anxious flyer.

They already had over five thousand signatures in Pennsylvania. Oddly, they got more in Pittsburgh's Allegheny County than in Latrobe's Westmoreland County, which was still a Trump stronghold. When told about the disparity, Monroe raised his right hand extending the first two fingers and said, "Verily, I say unto you, no prophet is accepted in his own country."

Ted scolded him. "You are about to walk into the first loop of the Bible Belt. You might want to lay off the smart-ass routine."

At that Monroe reached into his wallet and pulled out a twenty-dollar bill, and handing it to Ted said, "Here. Buy yourself a sense of humor."

They were over 60 percent of the way to gathering the signatures in New York, with 17 of the 27 congressional districts accumulated. They still needed nearly all of upstate New York, which was basically everything outside of metropolitan New York City. Theresa Stamford and Pat Metiore from *The Independent* were heading to Albany along with two TPC staffers to organize volunteers to gather the remaining signatures. Theresa was really embracing the role of Assistant Director, Field Department, and Sandra was impressed with both her willingness to accept assignments as well as with her abilities. Theresa and the campaign staff from Latrobe were now being handled through TPC's payroll.

Nancy had wanted to keep all of the money in one pot, and Sam had finally agreed after seeing the commitment and enthusiasm put forth by the crew from Latrobe. Ronald Le Quang also thought it made sense, and Sam generally deferred to Ronald in all matters administrative.

Ted and Monroe were also on the flight from DC. Monroe was studying a spreadsheet that Sam had provided of the cash flow. They were still not bringing in quite enough donations and Monroe was going to have to tap into his first year's interest to pay for the commercials that Gary wanted to run in four states. He was garnering about $40 million per year in interest on the principal that was set aside for the campaign. Since they switched from Albert to Blaise and Khalil, the returns were not exactly stellar. Some of that was due to a serious market correction, but he suspected that most of it was due to capital gains on the transfers. He did not have a lot of time to oversee it. He had Nancy and Fred and their teams for that.

Ted leaned over and said, "You know, you could save some money by not buying that jet."

Monroe leaned over to Ted and whispered above the white noise whoosh of the airliner. "You know, you can save us some money by bunking with Sandy."

"Hey! Shut up about that will you? I told you, she came on to ME!"

"Yeah. A hot forty-four year old coming on to you. After all, you're a specimen of male prowess." They both smirked, but for very different reasons.

Monroe was scheduled to speak at the Des Moines Chamber of Commerce breakfast meeting, at an agricultural industry exhibit at lunch, and at Francis University that evening. Kurt and Gary had him rehearse the speeches in front of a live audience with hand-held dials to see what phrases elicited what responses. Monroe knew that this was SOP, but he resented the hyperanalytics and the statistical nonsense. He preferred to read the audience and use his gut, speaking extemporaneously if need be. When Kurt reminded him that that was exactly the approach that had caused so much cringing across the media, Monroe had to remind Kurt that he was far more adept at it than the current resident of the Oval Office.

Kurt and Sandra and especially Phil had advised Monroe to deliver an anodyne speech about health insurance. This would be an important topic for the businessmen of Des Moines, since there would be many insurance representatives in the audience. Insurance is big industry in Des Moines, and they wanted to assuage an industry that had been buffeted by Obamacare and now the repeal of the individual mandate. Monroe ascended the dais at eight o'clock to polite applause. He began by explaining that he was sympathetic to both sides of the story.

"I know that insurance services are important to a lot of people in this room, and therefore they are important to this region. In fact, it is an important industry for the US. Three of the thirty companies on the Dow Jones Industrial Average are involved in health care.

"Who would want to be uninsured? Is not health care a universal human right? Who would deny health care to a child or the elderly? Or to those in need? Isn't the definition of a civilized society one which protects those who cannot protect themselves?

"My friends, these are not just rhetorical questions. They are questions that demand a sober answer. I would answer these questions like this: No one wants to be uninsured. Health care needs to be administered in a compassionate manner, with particular attention given to palliative care, to ease suffering and to minimize unnecessary costs and, ultimately, unproductive results. We have had government programs in place for years that help to address health care to those who cannot afford insurance. And we all recognize the imperfections of a bureaucratic system that oversees health care. It is inefficient, frustrating, and expensive.

"This is not a new problem. And other countries have had success in addressing it. Britain, France, Germany, and Switzerland all have health care systems that deliver good outcomes with reasonable costs compared to GDP. One argument frequently heard about US costs is that because the United States is an innovator in every aspect of health care, those costs are borne here and taken advantage of elsewhere. That's true. Would you prefer that we did not innovate? That IS a rhetorical question. Yet another driver of health costs is the enormous cost of liability insurance for malpractice. And the time has certainly come to enact tort reform to bring these costs down.

"Look, I'm a lawyer. Actually, I have never practiced law, but we all know that the exposure insurers face to medical malpractice forces premiums higher every year. And those costs are ultimately passed onto the consumer or the government.

"Health care is the only business I can think of where you purchase a service without ever knowing the price. You need a doctor, you go to one. He sends you a bill, and then you have a long discussion with your insurance provider. Over the phone. With a call center. And people with chronic conditions? I have no idea how they can be expected to keep track of the costs of serial procedures and doctor visits.

"And while we're on the subject, can I just point out that people with chronic illnesses who receive care from a team of doctors . . . How is that care coordinated? And how is their medication coordinated to avoid counteractive drugs? The answer, of course, is that unless they are lucky enough to have an advocate, and preferably one with medical training, there often is no coordination.

"So here is my simplified plan: One. Provide tort reform." There came some spontaneous applause and a few cheers. "Two. Provide health screening to prevent disease, according to the recommendations of the CDC. That would INCLUDE vaccinations for children and those vulnerable to transmittable diseases." A rumble of dissent arose from the crowd like motes of dust. Monroe plowed ahead. "Three. Provide major medical health insurance for all. Four. Make sure that preexisting conditions are not excluded from health insurance coverage.

"As a criticism of the preexisting condition clause of the Affordable Care Act, I hear people say that it defeats the whole idea of having insurance. The popular analogy is that in the auto insurance market, if you could wait until you had a wreck to buy insurance and then have the repairs covered, that's the same as being covered for preexisting conditions.

"This is a false analogy, and is wrong on several levels." Now some actual boos emitted from a section of the audience. Monroe raised a hand and pointed in the direction of the boos. "These are the same guys that cheered for the tort reform. They want to win ALL the time. Or maybe they never had a loved one face a prolonged illness. Allow me to continue.

"This is a false analogy because a car can be fixed. And if it can't, then you can buy another car. You cannot buy another body. The other point is that people who NOW have preexisting conditions may not have paid insurance before, but only because the insurance company would not insure them. You may develop such a condition in the future, at which point you have paid into the system for the coverage you deserve."

It wasn't a great reception and after the speech he entered the crowd to establish contact on an individual level. That part was more comfortable, and it helped to disarm the collective hysteria. Monroe actually began by plunging into the group where he received the most dissent. After thirty minutes, Sandra and Blake caught hold of him to inform him that he was on a tight schedule. They escorted him to a waiting car and he stepped inside to see Kurt, his head glistening with sweat as he swept from chin to neck with a coarse hand towel he had brought from the hotel.

"Well, not as bad as it could have been, I guess," crowed Kurt.

"When I walk into a lion's den," replied Monroe facetiously, "I look those lions straight in the eye. We are going to educate voters. And YOU better settle down before you have a heart attack. What is it out here? Thirty degrees? And you're here sweating like Chris Christie on a closed beach!" Then turning to Sandra, "Sandy, I want this guy on a no-red-meat diet from now on." Turning back to Kurt, "You're coming out with me tomorrow morning to go for a jog. Ted, you bring the defibrillator."

"You know I don't jog!" exclaimed Ted wryly.

"Then follow us in the car! Christ! Do I have to think of everything?"

The lunch event was a meet-and-greet at an agriculture exhibit at Hy-Vee Hall. A Monroe for President booth was set up with volunteers, and he headed straight to the booth to thank the volunteers, and amp them up for the upcoming campaign. Then he headed to the food court to meet some local dignitaries, including more than a few Big Ag reps. They seemed satisfied with his explanations of his proposed immigration policy. These guys from the heartland already knew what the conservative base had rejected in the last election: the crops are not going to come in with exclusively American labor. Period.

They went back to the hotel to refresh and recharge before the speech at Francis University at seven that evening. They were waiting for room service to bring dinner up to the suite of rooms they booked when Blake handed a cell phone to Sandra, who was on hers since they left Hy-Vee. Ordinarily Monroe preferred to dine publicly to garner additional recognition, but the schedule was tight tonight and Sandra had pressed hard for some private time. Ted gleaned that Tonya Jackson was on the other end of the phone. Sandra's forehead was wrinkling and her voice was getting agitated. She was throwing glances at Monroe, and then turned to find some privacy in one of the adjoining rooms. Ted followed her.

"What's up? What's wrong?" asked Ted.

"Two things," she said matter-of-factly, turning to face Ted. "Tonya says that a Pittsburgh paper has a lead on a story about 'Taylor money' financing Hezbollah. And she ferreted out a few of Monroe's dalliances."

Ted's eyes darted back and forth and he stammered a bit before explaining, "Oh! Well. It's probably nothing. Nothing at all. I mean the money thing is probably Khalil. It's a hundred percent innocent. And the women? Pfffhhh."

Sandra was glowering. Ted blinked and plaintively asked, "What?" She blew past him and marched into Monroe's room to confront him with this news. Monroe was hunched over a desk where Kurt was sitting with a laptop.

Monroe was dismissive. This was not a personality trait. It was simply a habit that had formed like a callus over years of having to deal with every manner of crisis at the paper. "The money thing is some misunderstanding with Khalil. He's solid. I'll straighten it out tomorrow." Sandra interpreted his attitude as detached and a little disrespectful. She continued to glower. "What now? I'm trying to prep for this thing tonight at Francis." He looked to Ted as if expecting some clue, or at least some acknowledgment of the possible need for assistance. Ted looked at him from behind Sandra with an expression that said "I wish I could help you Buddy, but I got nothing."

"Goddamn him," thought Monroe. "The sonofabitch has mixed loyalties!" Then aloud to Sandra, "The women are not a problem." Then sweeping his hand to the side, "Not that it's anyone's goddamn business."

"Monroe, you KNOW you ceased to have a private life the MOMENT you announced. We have been through this. Phil and Fuller and Tonya have already been combing through your past relationships and have not found anything. . . . uh, untoward."

"I'm glad they did not find anything 'untoward.' But yeah, I get it. No secrets."

"Then what about this girl in St. Lucia?"

"You bastard!" exclaimed Ted with a mixture of shock and glee. Sandra shot him a look over her shoulder. Ted retreated.

"Well, that was kind of impromptu," Monroe offered sheepishly. He ate dinner alone that night in St. Lucia, then stopped at the bar for a nightcap. Actually, he stopped at the bar because the three girls at another table stopped at the bar, and throughout dinner he made eye contact with one of them. Repeatedly. How the hell had she entered the picture? She was from France, an HR executive for a placement firm in Lyon. Well, he thought, *Le Monde* probably picked up the lottery story by now and she saw it there. Or online.

Sandra filled in the blanks. "A French online journal interviewed her. She sold her story to them."

"Aw, Christ. She doesn't have any proof. I don't even think she knew my name." As soon as he said it, he regretted it.

"She doesn't need any more proof than these," said Kurt turning the laptop toward them to reveal security camera stills from the hotel lobby. He had already started sniffing out the web while Sandra was talking. The picture was clear, not grainy at all, and showed Monroe with a slender black woman in a cocktail dress.

"Mmm. I wonder why she hasn't called," commented Monroe, trying to defuse the tension.

"'Cause she doesn't know your name," offered Ted.

"She does now," deadpanned Sandra.

"Well, look, she has no proof that anything happened. Does she? Does she?"

"Doesn't matter," said Sandra. "Like everyone else in this situation you will be judged in the court of public opinion."

"I say we ignore it." Monroe looked to Ted who confirmed with a nod. "That's it. We ignore it."

. . .

THE VENUE AT FRANCIS UNIVERSITY was the Buckland Center, a gymnasium that would have housed seven thousand people had there been a basketball game. As it was, there was room for another five thousand people. It was not the sort of crowd or venue that got Monroe very excited, and he turned to Ted and whispered that he wanted to have a word with Gary Davidson and Pat Metiore about their efforts in getting asses in seats. Worse still was that whoever was in charge of seating did not think to put the smaller crowd together. People were scattered all over the place, exacerbating the impression of anemic attendance.

After an explanation of why he was running as an Independent, Monroe launched into a brief overview of platform planks that by now were familiar to his campaign. He reiterated his positions on health insurance and immigration, and introduced a topic that had not been explored in detail in any of his previous interviews: America's place in the world.

"The United States has lost prestige throughout the world, and it's no surprise. President Trump campaigned on a platform that ridiculed President Obama's foreign policy for its policies and a perceived obsequiousness. If we are to be honest, the image of the US has been in decline since the early sixties, with a spike during the space race. At the end of the Second

World War, the US enjoyed the reputation of a world power. By now, we are struggling to get kids out of high school who can perform long division, who can hold a job, and construct a sentence with a noun and a verb. Not that school shootings help that situation.

"Ill-advised, if not outright unconstitutional, wars have been fought for dubious reasons. The toll on our nation is measured in lives lost or mangled, national treasuries that have been looted, and honor that has been tarnished.

"The United States is now in the unique position of having a leader who lacks support in his own party, who is reviled by the opposing party, and who inspires no confidence in our allies. How did we get here?

"At the end of World War Two, there were two superpowers; The United States and the Union of Soviet Socialist Republics. Europe was a fragmented conglomeration of nations striving to rebuild after the devastation of a war on all fronts. Asia was no better off. In September 1959, Soviet Premier Nikita Khrushchev visited the US. He visited New York City, Los Angeles, San Francisco, and Washington DC. But do you know what he wanted to see? He wanted to see a blast furnace in Homestead, Pittsburgh. And he wanted to see an Iowa cornfield."

The small crowd went nuts at this. There was a thirty-second standing ovation with feet stomping on the bleachers, and shouts of "USA! USA!"

Monroe raised his hands to tamp down the fervor, and laughed. "Easy . . . easy! Listen, that was fifty-eight years ago! A lot has changed since then! You're still growing corn, but there's only one blast furnace facility in Pittsburgh! Manufacturing has moved to Developing Nations. Thank God we still have the corn!"

Again the crowd went nuts. After another minute of pandemonium, Monroe continued his history lesson. Unlike the morning crowd, this one was amped for him.

"Since World War Two, the US has fought the Korean War, Cold War, the Vietnam War, the Grenada Invasion, the Gulf War, and the War on Terror. Two out of six ain't bad. I guess. Winning the Cold War was a big deal, but winning a war is not the same thing as winning the peace. The USSR fractured into its constituent nation states, and the destabilization created in that vacuum did nothing to secure a peaceful future for Asia and the Middle East. The Gulf War was a win, except for the antagonism created by having an American footprint in the Arabian Peninsula. But again, the same lack of follow-through created an opportunity for that vacuum to be filled by terrorists.

"Suffice to say some real errors have been made with regard to incursions into foreign soil in the past sixty years. These are bad enough, but then consider the political scandals like Watergate, Iran-Contra, and the impeachment of Bill Clinton. What followed after Bill Clinton is an out-of-control system, in which the pendulum has swung farther in the opposite direction every eight years."

"After the Lewinsky scandal, the voting public could not tolerate any affiliation with Clinton. Gore was too 'close' to Clinton, so the pendulum swung to George W. Bush, a man who was manifestly unqualified to be president. Once widely regarded as the worst president in history, Bush forty-three looks pretty good compared to the present occupant of the Oval Office."

Again, there were massive cheers.

"After eight years of Bush, the voting public could not tolerate another Republican, so Barack Obama was elected. The far right was intransigent, obstructionist, and so Obama's presidency was largely ineffective.

"That set the stage for the arrival of another manifestly unqualified candidate who is alleged to have run on a populist message. Luckily, 'populist' does not mean 'popular', because if what Donald Trump represents is a POPULAR message, then the United States is already is serious trouble.

"The election of 2016 may go down in history as outrageous, an anomaly, or the best thing in recent memory. Certainly it was outrageous. But depending on what happens next, it will either be an anomaly or eight years from now you may view Trump in the same light that we now view George W. Bush. What a world that would be.

"The new normal is to call the truth 'fake news' and lies 'alternative facts.' Because I have built a career in journalism, I can stand before you and affirm outright and without equivocation that I reject this. Facts are real. Journalism as now constituted is not without problems, and the fact is, the profession needs to be held to the highest standards. All the more difficult with people getting their news from unsourced platforms like Facebook, which brought us the Russian meddling.

"The United States needs to assert its position as a world leader. We cannot do that if our leaders are hapless, feckless, and hopeless. So get out and vote! You'll see voter registration tables set up outside the gym."

The event concluded with the campaign team meeting the crowd-at-large, and thanking the volunteers one-on-one. It was after eleven o'clock when they loaded into the vehicles and headed back to the hotel.

"What the fuck was that?" asked Ted at the briefing in the suite that evening. "Please tell me what the fuck that was, because I can tell you what it looked like. It looked like amateur-fucking-hour!"

"I'm so sorry," gushed Pat. "We didn't know that there were going to be so many empty seats. The online ticketing looked like they were going to be booked to 90 percent."

Gary defended Pat. "It's not Pat's fault. Fuller just told us that there appears to have been online reservations made by robots."

Heads lifted and swiveled around the table. "The fuck?" Ted was not one to mince words, but this was an especially visceral reaction. "Russians?"

"Too soon to tell," explained Blake. "Might be. Might be opposition. Might be a four-hundred-pound hacker on his bed."

"Fuller's on it. We'll see what he says . . ." Gary's voice trailed off.

"The speech was good tonight in spite of the crowd," Kurt stated. "You hit some home runs. We coulda used some of that footage if the background actually had people in it."

Monroe sighed and threw a fresh towel at Kurt. Ted cracked open a Michelob Ultra and passed it to Monroe. He raised the bottle to his lips and took a few swigs. Gary made a comment about the light beer, and reminded himself of the comment one of the ladies made about Monroe. He decided to broach the topic.

"Hey, Monroe, you're in pretty good shape . . ."

"For a man of his age," interjected Ted.

"No. Really. He's in great shape. We should leak some photos of him at the gym. It would create that vigorous, vital persona. Generate some buzz."

"Vivacious," offered Ted.

"Like Kennedy swimming with his kids?" asked Monroe sarcastically. "Or like Putin fishing? Do I need to go shirtless?" He thought it was a joke. "Or are you guys just being highly paid jerks?"

"Vituperative."

Sam and Blake were all over it now. "What do you bench press? How far can you jog? We should have him hit the hotel gym in the morning." Sandra was more circumspect, given the recent report from Tonya. Likewise, the Latrobe contingent laid off. Thinking of the editor that way was not just inappropriate; it was distasteful.

"You're kidding, right? First of all, hotel gyms are notorious for the crappy equipment. Second," there was a long pause.

"Yes? What's second?"

He hesitated. "I'm bashful."

"Virginal."

"Sandra has already busted me on that one. Get out of my room. I need a shower and some sleep."

"Vindictive."

"He can go all night like this . . ."

As they checked out of the hotel in the morning, Monroe advised Sam and Sandra to check their emails. Which of course was completely unnecessary as they both habitually opened emails before they performed their morning ablutions. Monroe had asked Khalil and Blaise to send a detailed report of his investments to him last night, and both had complied. Sam had already forwarded the reports to Fuller Thompson, who was already chasing down every line item.

They flew to Manchester-Boston Regional Airport the following morning for a day of driving around the lower loop between Manchester, Concord, Dover, and Portsmouth. Gary had pitched adding Kennebunkport to the agenda, but Monroe nixed the idea on the grounds that they only wanted this to be a brief meet-and-greet with some of the locals. Privately he confided to Ted that he did not need to see where the Bushes hung out. Even though he probably had enough money to buy the Bush compound, he did not want to give the impression that he was hobnobbing with the wealthy. He wanted to put his more common roots on display, and this trip was full of impromptu drop-ins to diners and shopping malls, and to surprise the volunteer offices that had been set up for a few weeks. It was time to energize the base, and Sandra and Theresa agreed that a surprise visit would give them a better picture of how things were really going on the ground.

On the drive from Concord to Dover they passed a farm with a large "Go For Monroe" sign along the highway. They stopped for a photo in front of the sign and Blake immediately uploaded the image of Monroe smiling with a gloved thumbs-up onto Instagram and Facebook.

"Iowa and New Hampshire," sighed Ted, shaking his head as he climbed back into the car. "How the hell!" Monroe looked wistfully out the window. They had had this discussion about the primaries many times over the years, and he realized there was no point in beating that horse, since the timing of the primary was a matter of state law, and nothing could be done about it.

In Dover, Monroe opened a creaky glass door to a storefront office on Main Street. Two middle-aged women and an elderly man all turned with annoyed looks toward the sound. "You have any money in the budget for a can of WD-40?" asked Monroe, feeling the action on the door. A kid came out from a room in the back with his head down, reading from a tablet. "Holy hell!" he blurted out, recognizing his hero. "I mean Mr. Taylor! Hey guys, it's Monroe Taylor!"

The rest of the entourage filed in, with Monroe holding the offending door open to prevent it from screeching with every rotation of a few degrees. The cold air blasted the flyers off a desk which caused one of the ladies to have to collect them. Ted and Blake helped her while introductions were made. Theresa whipped out a cell phone and called the landlord to get the door fixed. Sandra made some notes on her iPad while photos were taken with Monroe and the office staff. She was impressed with their enthusiasm, but less so with the furnishings and professionalism. She texted Alice, who was standing across the room, asking her to check the level of donations that were filtering through this outpost.

Monroe's cell rang a dull tone and he glanced down to see that Fuller Thompson was calling. "Hey Fuller, what's up?" He cast a wary glance at Sam and Sandra.

"Do you know who V.M. Techniek is?"

"Never heard of them, but I'm gonna guess it's a problem."

"They are a Dutch construction firm that is building schools in rural Lebanon under direction of Hezbollah."

"Well, that sounds like a helluva stretch to me then."

"Be that as it may, Ron Le Quang says you should have Blaise remove it from your portfolio, and instruct Blaise to be more careful in the future."

"Wait a second. You said Blaise. It's not Khalil."

"That's right. Khalil is clean. It's Blaise."

"Well I'll be damned. Just goes to show you." Fuller ignored the implication that he and everyone at TPC had laid the blame on the Muslim financial advisor. Monroe continued. "Ron knows damn well it will be impossible to ferret out where all of the money goes when investing in an international company, or in a domestic conglomerate for that matter!"

"He feels protective."

"Ron needs to stick to the legal aspects of campaigning. And leave the investments to the experts. But if he insists, I will ask Blaise to remove the stock from my portfolio, and then I will write a personal check to the government of Lebanon to invest in building a goddamned school!"

That last bit was a little loud and when he looked up Sam and Sandra were ushering the Dover staff aside and making pronouncements about their progress and energy in especially loud voices.

Fuller signed off with a good-natured chuckle. He had already emailed Gary to give him the details so that they could craft a rebuttal to the "Taylor-funds-terrorists" claim. They did not need a story like that to aggravate the already challenging need to raise funds for a multimillionaire.

• • •

BACK IN LATROBE MONROE WAS JOGGING at the latex-bound rubber track around the football field at Memorial Stadium. It was a warm morning, but he insisted on wearing a warm-up suit and sweatshirt. He felt like an idiot. There was a camera crew filming video, two or three guys taking still shots with telephoto lenses, and the usual crew of what he was now calling his "handlers". . . Ted, Phil, Sam, ABC, Sandra, Gary and Blake. When Franco DeMario showed up with Sheila Burns during his eleventh lap around the quarter-mile track, he trotted over to them.

"What the hell? Don't you two have a paper to put out today?"

"We heard the circus was in town."

"My God. What a clusterfuck this is," panted Monroe as he jogged in place to stay warm.

"I heard you were down here without a shirt," teased Sheila.

"It was discussed, believe it or not. I stood my ground. We ain't making a Chippendale calendar here. Oh wait. I can't say stuff like that anymore around employees in the 'me too' era."

"Oh wait," replied Sheila. "I can't say stuff like that either. Good thing we're out of earshot."

"Oh for fuck's sake," muttered Monroe.

"What's wrong?" asked Franco *sub rosa*, moving in close to Monroe.

"We are NOT out of earshot. Everything we are saying is probably being picked up on that parabolic microphone. Let me see what's going on over there. I don't know how many more laps I have in me. I'm sweating like a pig now and they want to get some shots at the gym."

Sheila called to him as he trotted away, "You wouldn't sweat so much if you shed some clothes!" Franco laughed and jabbed her in the arm with his elbow.

Ted was in conference with Sam, Gary, and Blake. Monroe jogged over to them, and slowed to a stop, sucking deep breaths. "Are you okay?" asked Blake, with a look of concern. "We're going for the impression that you are in shape, here, right?"

"He is in shape, Kid," said Ted, sounding more like a boxing trainer than a campaign manager. "He's just sixty years old and cranking out eight-forty-five miles."

"You guys need to collar the guy with the parabolic mike and make sure he didn't record anything untoward."

"On it," said Gary, and the others watched silently as he dashed into the end zone to speak with the sound crew. No warm-up and wearing Florsheims, and he looked like he was clocking a five-oh forty. Monroe turned to Ted and said, "I'll bet that guy never sweats."

"What was it you said that you are concerned with?" asked Sam.

"Nothing much. Innocuous. But if it was heard out of context it could feed a perception of insensitivity. Plus I said 'fuck.' Again."

"That will be twenty Hail Marys."

Monroe had been trying to curb his use of colorful language. He went through this periodically, usually whenever he was in a semiserious relationship with a woman, but now more earnestly. He was not a habitual curser. His vocabulary probably weighed in at around thirty-five-thousand words. He had frequent and regular bouts of vocabulary prowess with Ted, who, if he was being honest, probably had had him by another three or four hundred words. Ted was the kind of guy who read dictionaries over lunch at his desk. Monroe regretted that his toolbox was filled with so many words of the four-letter variety. And the stress of having to be managed by his handlers was getting to him. To the point where he was relying more and more on those particular tools. Those might come in handy in a debate with Donald Trump, but his campaign was built around the vision of elevating the level of discourse. The last thing he needed was to be seen as just one more hypocritical son-of-a-bitch. On national fucking TV. Goddamn it.

He started to peel off and doubled back thirty yards away. "I'm just not into it today. Let me hit the chin bar." A set of chin-ups always opened up his chest and relaxed his breathing after a jog. Blake and Gary followed him out around the west end of the stadium, past the memorial that described with bronze and granite authority how the first professional football game was played on this site. Ted and Alice followed behind, with Sandra wrapping up with the film crew.

"You know, what might work better is if you had some company on the track. It would improve your speed," Blake offered. He ran track in high school and college, and both he and Gary were in obviously good shape.

"Well, that's true Blake," answered Monroe. "But I did not realize we were intending on publishing my mediocre speeds. I thought all you guys wanted was a display of vigor. But hey, you're always welcome to join me. Just don't expect to engage me in a lot of palaver while I'm sucking wind out there."

Gary and Blake laughed. "We can try again tomorrow or Wednesday."

"Good. Because I really feel like we need to spend a little more time today on some foreign policy issues before we head to South Carolina." He reached the chin bar across the street, swung his arms several times and stretched out his hands in a bizarre twisting ritual. He leapt up to the bar and grasping it underhand, he angled his legs to keep his toes from dragging the cracked clay below. He dropped into a dead swing under the bar after the first rep. Then slowly he cranked out another, and another as Blake and Gary counted each rep, getting more and more excited with each rep.

"Eight! Wow, good job Monroe! C'mon! Fight for it! Nine! Look at this! Where's that film crew? Ten! Wow! Ten! Wait wait wait! Eleven! Phenomenal! Twelve! Twelve chin-ups!"

He eased himself to the ground and, grimacing yet satisfied, wiped his face with his sleeve.

Gary clapped him on the back and Blake went in for a high-five, which was reluctantly returned by Monroe. Monroe was really stunned at their sincere reaction. "C'mon guys. No one is winning the Nobel Prize because they can do twelve chin-ups."

"No, but I guarantee there's never been a President who could do even half that many. Okay. Maybe Jimmy Carter. Maybe Obama. But he smoked, so never mind."

TPC released a press kit that was engineered to lead to follow-up articles in health magazines and the lighter talk shows. Monroe allowed it grudgingly. The fact was he was proud that he was in good shape. But he took every opportunity with subsequent inter-viewers to lead the discussion toward issues other than exercise, his running pace, and the size of his chest and biceps. Predictably there were a number of caricatures in leading papers and memes online that were aimed at his brawn. More than a few made unfavorable comparisons to Arnold Schwarzenegger and Jesse Ventura.

"I told you this would happen," complained Ted during the next staff meeting in Falls Church.

Monroe rolled his eyes. "We aren't going to respond to this. It's just petty. I'm not crazy about it either. I never was. I want to return the focus to the issues."

"You ARE polling better among women, especially in the thirty-five to forty-five age range," said Sandra.

"Fu . . . Can we please just get back on task here?" said an exasperated Monroe. "Where are we on donations? What have we learned about the bone-up at Buckland Center? Why does this chick from Ligonier continue to call me?"

"Probably has something to do with your abs of steel," offered Alice with a smile to the cumulative amusement of the team.

Fuller Thompson spoke up, reasserting a level of professionalism. "The firm handling the reservations for Buckland was a third-party event specialist with offshore operations. A hacker exploited a security vulnerability and was able to install a rootkit that created bogus reservations. About 40 percent. Not enough to flag but enough to still look legit."

"So it was an overseas attack?"

"No, we determined that the source was domestic. Our external computer security consultant is going to handle reservations from now on. We just need to coordinate with each event center."

"Sounds expensive."

"Not really. We eliminate the mark-up of the third-party event planner and take control of that aspect, and avoid embarrassing situations like that in the future," interjected Sam. "It's a win-win."

Ted rolled his eyes and threw Monroe a glance that said *these guys know how to spin.*

"Well wait a minute," protested Monroe, looking around the table. "Who the hell was the bad domestic actor? Are we going to be able to ferret that out? I agree we have a solution, but I'd damn sure like to know who's fu. . . . Messing with us!"

"We don't know," explained Fuller. "They were very good at covering their tracks. No digital fingerprints. It was a very specific attack."

Ted was incensed. "You know what. That's bullshit!"

Monroe intervened, "Look, Monroe for President has enjoyed working with TPC. We appreciate what you bring to the table."

"Does anyone here think it's acceptable to get played by some hacker?" asked Pat Metiore. Sam shifted into a defensive posture in his chair. Phil Ainsworth looked stoic, Jenn Hensel, who abhorred conflict, folded her hands and looked down.

"We are paying you a fucking boat-load of money for two reasons," continued Ted. "One is your expertise in running national campaigns, and two is your stroke. Your juice."

"We need that juice," said Monroe shaking his head slowly. "I know Ron has filed with the states. I know Fuller is working on the hack. But we need results. I am not content to sit around and be wasted by the competition."

"You have one week to get this matter resolved," Ted said evenly. "We are heading to Columbia, South Carolina in one week, and I do not want a repeat of Iowa. You need to jerk a knot in this!"

"If you don't know who is responsible," said Jenn timidly, "can't you set a honeypot?" There was a brief silence while everyone looked around.

"Look who knows all about spycraft," said Gary Davidson.

"No, shut up," scolded Monroe, holding up his hand. "Go on, Jenn."

She hesitated, afraid of taking the spotlight. Fuller reluctantly joined the fray. He had been working on a honeynet with the third-party security firm. He doubted that Jenn actually knew that the term was applicable to computer security, but was impressed that she even thought about the concept. Poor unassuming Jenn. To the casual observer, no one would ever think she was given the credit she was due. But Fuller understood that the Latrobe contingent relied on her as a whip to get things done. She worked under the radar and things happened.

Now Fuller had to weigh revealing that he was, indeed, working on such a counterespionage tactic. The fewer people who knew about it the better. But now Jenn had raised the issue and he would look like an idiot for dismissing it. "We are examining a variety of measures similar to what Jenn suggests," he conceded. It wasn't much but it seemed to appease the Latrobeans. For now.

Sandra addressed the donations. "We've made some modest progress in the states that went for Trump. That's due to his poor approval ratings and the lack of a Democratic frontrunner. We've exploited the situation. But we have a short window of time before the Dems start to announce. On the other hand, Monroe enjoys an overall positive name recognition, with 23.5 percent favorable, 34.1 percent neutral, and 22.9 percent negative. The words most commonly associated with Taylor are 'Lucky, Rich, Wealthy, Conservative, Liberal, Pervert, Independent, Good, WASPY, Sexy'. In that order."

"Wait. What? Pervert ahead of Independent? What the fu . . . what the hell am I even paying you guys for?"

"No, relax." beguiled Sam. "That's an artifact from the first press conference in Greensburg."

"You know," explained Ted helpfully. "The masturbation speech. That's going right up there with 'Ask not what your country can do for you', and 'We will hang together', and 'Give me liberty, or give me a hand job.'"

Monroe was now beyond exasperation. He felt the heat rising into his face and his ears were actually tingling now. He turned to Ted who immediately apologized. "Sorry boss. Out of line." Jenn cocked her head sympathetically at Ted and reached out and patted him gently on the forearm.

Monroe excused himself and left the room. The remaining *Independent* contingent got up and left without ceremony. Phil turned to Sam when they were around the corner and said somewhat rhetorically, "Wow, that was some kind of coordinated effort!"

Sam looked at him. "Are they wrong? Did they say anything wrong? It's on us to reel this in."

Phil turned to Sandra. "I didn't wanna say anything in front of 'Mealticket,' but we need to dissect this pervert thing. Are they keying in on homosexual tendencies, this dalliance with the Algerian hooker, or the masturbation speech?"

"We've already analyzed that. The perpetual bachelor thing is a little weird to everyone older than a Millennial. The French girl is polling negative among whites older than sixty-two in the North, but is neutral in the West. The South, the Midwest, and the Evangelicals are having a conniption about it. Figures. They can vote for Trump, but our guy dates an Algerian girl and they're ready to crucify him. The Latin-versus-Anglo-Saxon-etymology-thing at the presser in Greensburg has actually tested neutral-to-positive across all demographics. College-educated voters seemed to like the wordplay, and less-educated voters liked the erudite put-down."

Ted snagged Monroe outside the conference room and whispered, "But that really was a funny bit about the masturbation speech!" Monroe massaged his forehead and conceded. "Yeah. It was pretty funny. And I do appreciate you all backing me up in there. But can we get on task here? I have about twenty things to take care of, and a million more to learn. But you all know I appreciate your loyalty."

Pat laid a hand on his shoulder. "Hey. You earned our loyalty a long time ago, amigo."

"That's right!" agreed Jenn, "long before you became a multimillionaire!" Then taking Monroe by the elbow and leading him to the safety of the coffee station, she called out to the group over her shoulder, "But that didn't hurt!" Everyone chuckled and Monroe smiled at Jenn's tactic that she employed in the newsroom when she felt protective. Monroe saw through it, but it was sweet and he could not resist allowing her to behave like that.

He poured her a cup of decaf, then filled his own GO FOR MONROE 2020 mug. "You know, what we need is a mindbender session tonight. Assemble the crew."

It was a long day before the *Independent* team congregated. Monroe was spending three hours every day reviewing foreign and domestic policy. Sam and Phil really did have some juice. There was a former Under Secretary of State for Political Affairs, a retired judge from the Fourth Circuit Court of Appeals, a professor of political science from the Harvard Kennedy School, and one from the Walsh School of Foreign Service.

Monroe had majored in History at St. Vincent but it was also his avocation. His home library was filled with nonfiction, including a prized first edition of all twenty-five volumes of Henry Smith Williams' *The Historians' History of the World*. His editorials were replete with lessons drawn from history to the point that the Letters to the Editor frequently made sarcastic observations about his reliance on that subject and gave him snarky nicknames like "Professor Monroe," and more playful ones like "Taylor the Younger." This background in history dovetailed into his affinity for world politics. The sessions with the subject matter experts would have been grueling but for his fascination with the topics. The open-debate format was lively, and Ted and Phil always sat in. They were often also joined by Kurt Bastille and Alice. Kurt would provide subtle advice to coach him and Alice was there for moral support. Others were invited on an open-invitation basis, since Phil and Monroe wanted there to be as many people as possible in the room. But the rest of the campaign staff had obligations, so their attendance was more sporadic. This afternoon the conference room had about twenty people in it, including a video crew filming a documentary for one of the cable networks.

Today's topic was Israel. The Under Secretary was discussing the new status of Jerusalem as the now-officially US-recognized capital. "It's my belief," Monroe commented rhetorically while the Under Secretary drew breath, "that Israel's treatment of Palestinians is one of the most destabilizing forces in the Middle East."

Ted's eyes grew wide and he looked up from his notes scrawled on a yellow legal pad. He had been down this road before, but he calculated that no one on the TPC team had heard this from the candidate. There was a pause as if the air had been sucked out of the room. Phil looked for Sam to get a clue as to whether or not he should temporarily shut down the documentary crew, but Sam was not in the room. He decided to let it ride, but he was really holding tightly onto the reins in case he needed to reel this in.

"In what way?" asked the Under Secretary.

"The 'Jerusalem Law,' the land grabs in the occupied territories . . . the walls. It all asserts their opposition to a two-state solution."

"Yet the US Congress passed the Jerusalem Embassy Law, requiring that our embassy be moved to Jerusalem."

"Which is really just a big nose-thumb at the Palestinians and the rest of the world. Even most American Jews were against the embassy move in the polls I've seen. But look, for all practical purposes, Jerusalem really is the capital of Israel. So other than securing religious and cultural sites for Muslims and Christians, I don't really care where our embassy is. The larger problem is getting to a two-state solution which would help eliminate what many perceive as a system of apartheid in Israel, and this incessant acquiescence to Netanyahu." He paused. "I guess that's two problems."

Ted observed the tension mounting and waved off Phil. "Look, this is not just a foreign policy briefing; it's essentially debate prep. Let's run with it."

"I'm not suggesting divestment or boycotts, mind you. But I do think there ought to be some serious discussions with Israel about how lots of countries view their treatment of Palestinians. And perception is reality. I'd love to speak privately and candidly to Prime Minister Netanyahu or the Knesset about it, because there is a lot about it that I don't know. I mean they had the unilateral disengagement from Gaza in 2005, but Israel still controls the infrastructure. There's a lot of work to be done there.

"And another thing," espoused Monroe. You could see he was getting animated. He shifted in his chair and leaned forward, his arm rising to make a point. Sam and Kurt watched in appreciation. Kurt despised the impotent crooked finger that Clinton used when he was making a point. It was obvious to Kurt that anyone who watched the tapes of JFK's speeches that Clinton appropriated that mannerism from him. Monroe was a natural public speaker. "I just love it when US politicians refer to him as 'BB.' As if they are so close to him. Like they are inviting him over for Shavuot to split a blintz."

Kurt walked over to the documentary crew and quietly asked them to take a break. His own cameras were still rolling. The crew's producer and reporter both sensed a story here and were reluctant to leave. There was a whispered conversation back in the corner, and Ted and Monroe saw Kurt shrug and return to his seat.

The Under Secretary had been enjoying his sessions with Monroe. There was always a lively exchange of information and he appreciated that Monroe was genuinely interested in subtle points of policy. He had coached a lot of potential politicians since his stint at State, but few of his previous students shared Monroe's enthusiasm and insight. Monroe's opinions regarding Israel were neither original, nor particularly insightful. But he wanted to see how much political courage Monroe had.

"As long as the Israelis continue to absorb land under dispute they deny the Palestinians ownership not only of personal property, but of their own state. And that destabilizes the region as much as anything."

Phil had had enough. He was not about to sit by and watch his candidate and meal ticket self-destruct over a political point that did not need to be made. He had already sent Kurt back to the crew to get them out of the room, and Kurt was instructed to shut off his own camera. "Monroe, that is going to sound a little anti-Semitic to people who are not as familiar with you as we are in this room."

"I disagree. Well, no, I don't disagree. It might sound anti-Semitic, but I am not anti-Semitic. Ted, am I anti-Semitic?"

"Seriously? You're asking the only Jew in the room if you are anti-Semitic? What if you were? Would I answer truthfully?"

"Point taken."

"But no. Not anti-Semitic . . ." his voice trailed off. The lack of additional qualifiers made it sound like there were other issues. Monroe waved his hand in a circle, prompting Ted. Ted laughed at Monroe, and turned to address the TPC contingent. "You have shots of him in all sorts of multicultural exchanges. But that crap was always staged. We don't have a lot of Jews or Blacks or Hispanics in Latrobe. But what you have yet to capture is that Monroe is genuinely inclusive. Just an observation.

"And for the record, he is not anti-Semitic."

. . .

13

TONYA JACKSON SAT IN A BOUTIQUE COFFEE SHOP near Monroeville Mall. She was back in Pennsylvania, and it made her skin crawl. She sipped on a caramel latte that was heavy on the latte and light on the caramel, and wondered how she could manage to live in places like Yemen and Suriname, yet here in Pittsburgh she wanted to vomit. Well, part of it had always been the thrill of being a case officer in a foreign land, and feeling like you were making a difference. Now as she surveyed the early spring landscape of western Pennsylvania and considered that she was just trying to keep another politician out of trouble, she was depressed.

The area was dismal. There were vacant retail spaces everywhere, gashes through hillsides that were not just devoid of greenery, but had actually spilled their rocky guts onto the roadways during the last thaw cycle and subsequent rainy season. Her mood was not improved by the flat tire she got when she hit a pothole and bent the wheel rim of the rental car. She would have changed the flat herself, but when she popped the trunk, there was no spare. She scolded herself for not checking before she drove the car out of TPC's parking lot where it had been delivered.

Fuller had dispatched her to Pittsburgh to collect intelligence on Amber Groves and another woman. Amber was the occasional companion of Monroe. Tonya was preparing a dossier on Amber in case the need arose. She would track her for a few days and get a feel for her habits, inclinations, tastes. Fuller needed to know if the relationship was going to pose any special problems that Sam and Phil needed to be aware of.

Denise Dexter was another matter. An occasional acquaintance who had worked for a short time at *The Independent*, she was now calling Monroe with suggestive declarations of her dormant passions. How she got his cell number was anybody's guess, but Monroe had assured Fuller that the number she dialed was devoted exclusively to business among the TPC staff. It wasn't like the guy was answering a personal phone since he won $850 million. Tonya was supposed to collect intel and learn where the soft spots were on Denise Dexter. Someone would need to push on those soft spots and get her to lay off. In the meantime, Monroe had burned through yet another cell phone. The leaks in the security were so pervasive that they assigned him a new phone every Tuesday morning. Blake himself programmed the contact data every Monday night. Oddly, the secure cells among Fred, Nancy, Blaise, and Khalil were always fine.

Tonya looked into her cup of coffee and wiped a hair from the side with a paper napkin. She nearly gagged. That weasel Fuller. He had sent a contract spook to Lyon to figure out what Mona Dupuis was all about. She could be having a quenelle right now with a delicate Cru Beaujolais. Instead she was wiping someone's hair out of a pretty crappy coffee. She uttered a disgusted snort as she considered that at least it wasn't a pubic hair in her Coke. She looked outside to see the tow truck cruising the parking lot. She picked up her purse and laptop bag and went out to direct the driver to her car. The driver was polite and dropped her off at her hotel before he towed the car to a shop where a new wheel could be mounted. Naturally the hotel had lost her reservation.

She burned a whole day in the hotel waiting for the repair. The car was delivered to the hotel the next morning and Tonya drove past Denise Dexter's house in Ligonier Township. It was out in the country so there wasn't really a good spot to ditch the car and go snooping in broad daylight. Out here, if someone saw you snooping, you were going to be visited by a state trooper. Or a coroner. Because she had scoped out the lay of the land from the comfort of her office at TPC, she had come prepared as a canvasser selling internet service. The local telecoms were always using third-party salespeople to comb neighborhoods to entice them to switch providers.

Pebbles pinged off the rocker panels as she drove up the long driveway. This was a far cry from Falls Church. These people really appreciated their privacy. She heard a dog going crazy inside as she got out of the car. She reached back inside the car and finding a stick of beef jerky in the console, rubbed it on her skirt. She rang the doorbell and tapped on the storm door. A pretty forty-ish woman answered wearing a tank top and yoga pants.

"Oh! I'm so sorry to have disturbed your workout!" Tonya apologized. "I'm with Fullcast and we are in your area to offer our fastest internet speeds and fiber-optic cable. Can you take a five-minute break to allow me to explain the deal?"

"Umm, sure. I was just warming down with some stretches. Won't you come in? It's freezing out there. Here, boy." She stooped to grab the dog's collar to guide it toward a side room, but it bolted and headed for Tonya, where it immediately buried its snout in her crotch and pawed a run in her pantyhose.

"Well . . . now we're friends!" Tonya laughed nervously at the shepherd-lab mix. "Very *close* friends." Denise apologized profusely and got the dog behind a door. Tonya had played it so that the dog had forced an obligation onto Denise to at least be polite, if not sign a three-year contract with an ISP she never heard of.

Tonya passed through the foyer and saw that the house opened up in the back, so that it appeared deceptively small from the front. She saw men's boots in the foyer and an assortment of ball caps on pegs around a mirror.

"So who is your internet provider now?" smiled Tonya.

An hour later Tonya had Denise's life history. She was voluble, affable, and it was not hard to imagine that there may have, in fact, been some romantic entanglement between her and the candidate. The boots were her brother's. He lived with her while he was going through a divorce. Denise was also divorced, no kids. She had worked at the paper in advertising sales for two years. She had a two-year degree from the community college, and claimed she loved to bake, though the kitchen was a mess. Denise was not the domestic type.

Tonya recognized a certain mania present as well, and so when Denise logged into her email to demonstrate how slow her service was, Tonya made sure to discreetly capture her user name and password keystrokes on her iPhone camera. It might come in handy, and would be easier to capture now than having Fuller hack in later.

She left with a bogus contract signed to a bogus telecom firm, and headed west along Route 30 toward Pittsburgh. The Turnpike would have been quicker but she needed to make a stop in Latrobe. Along the way she phoned Fuller. He greeted her formally.

"Hey, I just met with Ms. Dexter, and she seemed fairly normal . . . well, fairly normal for UP HERE . . . but vulnerable to such things. I captured her email log-ins, but you do realize that she probably got his contact data from a cellular, right?"

"Yeah, I've been through that with Monroe. He claims no involvement in reaching out to her. I sorta believe him. What's next on your schedule?" He knew exactly what was next.

"The Mole. And staking out Ms. Groves," said Tonya unenthusiastically. Amber Groves did not have as large a digital footprint on social media as did Denise Dexter. Fuller had already seen the beach shots of Denise online, the cursory review of her social media accounts indicating a party girl's pitiful slide into middle age. Ronald Le Quang had already drafted a letter to her warning that any future contact with Monroe might be considered harassment. But TPC did not want to push that button unnecessarily. Less was known about Amber Groves.

"I'll be up here in this hellhole for at least another coupla days."

"Thanks Tonya. Next time you get to go to France. The entourage will be back in the office next Tuesday, so let's debrief on Monday, okay?"

"K." She clicked off and turned her thoughts toward Amber Groves. She would begin surveillance as Amber left work today. Nothing TPC did was illegal. But Tonya recognized that it might appear to be unseemly to the average citizen. Her training and experience had conditioned her to pry into private matters in a clinical fashion. She knew what lines not to cross and she was exceptional at surveillance. She would stop by Amber's office to check what personal effects may be displayed and to see her in action. She would pose as a tech lobbyist for a fictional entity, trying to arrange a meeting with the County Commissioner's office. Allegheny County was always courting tech firms, so that ought to get her access.

She called the mole at *The Independent* and arranged to pick her up in a parking lot. The mole had bits of information regarding the financial health of the newspaper and an impressive network of Monroe's regional connections. She could not identify anything particularly nefarious, except for the usual corrupt government officials that Monroe had come in contact with professionally. There was nothing there that the opposition could exploit. They discussed shutting down the mole's employment, but decided to let it ride. The mole did not object. Besides, she was having fun being a reporter.

Tonya drove to the Allegheny County offices and found parking at a nearby lot. It was after 4 PM so local offices were already starting to thin. She walked a couple blocks to the Courthouse and passed through security. Taking the stairs to the second floor she entered the Executive Office vestibule and spent a moment surveying the area. Amber's office was beyond a set of double doors. Not quite the Holy of Holies, but still requiring a good reason to get beyond the doors. She turned and headed back to a coffee shop across the street and ordered another caramel latte. Maybe she would have better luck this time.

She had a view of the side door through which employees regularly exited. The place was emptying out in spurts and because there was a chance that Amber had left already, she phoned her office to speak to Amber on the pretense of arranging a Friday introduction. Amber was not at her desk, so Tonya punched "0" when the call transferred to AUDIX. The receptionist answered and informed Tonya that Amber was still in the office, but was away from her desk. She would be happy to schedule a fifteen minute meeting with her on Friday morning.

Tonya set up the meeting and waited another thirty minutes before Amber appeared at the exit. She had changed her hair color subtly from the photo Tonya had, but there was no mistake that this was her. Tonya expected her to drive home in the Honda Accord that matched the DMV records that TPC had pulled.

She considered for the umpteenth time that this sort of routine legwork could easily have been farmed out to some local detective agency, but she also recognized that discretion was perhaps the most important aspect of this job, and a local PI might prove unreliable in that regard.

Instead, Amber walked to a T-station at First Avenue and boarded the Blue Line. Tonya followed, watching her exit at the Boggs Station in Beltzhoover. Tonya headed to the next station, then caught a T back to downtown to retrieve her car. She headed back to the hotel to wait until dusk, when she would head over to Amber's house.

After dinner, she drove to Beltzhoover and ID'd Amber's car parked on the street. She circled the block and parked down the street and waited. The street was quiet, and after an hour, she quietly exited and took a walk around the neighborhood. No signs of Amber going anywhere. It was dark now, and plugging an infrared camera attachment into her phone, she thermal imaged the house. No grow-lights. Just images of Amber moving back and forth between the front living room and the kitchen. It looked like she was cocooning for the night.

It was now Thursday morning and Tonya considered what to do. She had done as much surveillance as the target merited, and her appointment with Amber was not until tomorrow. Yet this was turning into one big nothing-burger. She entered the County Courthouse and approached the receptionist.

"Excuse me. My name is Faye Williams. I made an appointment to see Ms. Groves for tomorrow, but my schedule has changed. I wonder if she has just a few minutes to spare today."

The receptionist smiled and quietly phoned the change request to Amber. "You can go right in." Amber's desk was stacked with reports and project calendars. About a dozen Beanie Babies lined a book shelf behind the desk. Tonya thanked her for accommodating her schedule, and launched into a bogus thirty-second elevator speech about her bogus tech company. Then she settled back and allowed Amber to talk, noting her body language, intonation, attentiveness, and the other personal contents of her office. There was a diploma from Indiana University of Pennsylvania, a framed photo of her parents, an autographed poster from the County Executive's last campaign, and nothing at all to link her to Monroe Taylor. Well, the chick was friendly and professional. Put-together and a big snooze-fest. Time to head back to Falls Church.

.   .   .

14

"GOOD MORNING COLUMBIA! How ya'll doing today? My name is David Evans, and I am here to welcome you to Campaign 2020! Eyes on Monroe Taylor!"

David Evans was a media front man hired by Gary Davidson to whip up the crowds. He introduced a few local dignitaries and celebrities who were sympathetic to the candidate, or at least curious. The South was polling behind the Northeast in support for Taylor, and the team wanted to dig in and spread the word. Not many well-known people down here had voiced their support of Monroe, and even fewer politicians were going to throw their support behind an Independent. South Carolina was no landslide for Trump, but like every other state except Maine and Nebraska, it is a winner-take-all state. With nine votes in the Electoral College, it is the first primary in the South. And even though they would not be running a primary as Independents, they wanted to get in early to steal as much momentum from the Republicans and Democrats as possible.

Turnout at this event was good but not great. They had learned a lesson from the Des Moines episode, and allowed no reserve ticketing until TPC's computer security firm ironed out the details. The story about the small crowds had been provided to the press, and Ronald Le Quang had filed a complaint against the hackers with the Iowa Secretary of State. Because each state administers presidential elections, similar complaints were being prepared for all the other states and territories.

Still the crowd was enthusiastic and Evans was working them over with his energetic style. A former DJ who had bounced around the AM dial, he found regional popularity as a game show host in Atlanta. When the show hadn't been picked up for national broadcast, he returned to radio as a talk show host, and took gigs doing stand up. He had crossed paths with Sam Balentine, who, like Phil Ainsworth, called him "Mr. Smooth." If Sam and Phil thought you were smooth, that was saying a lot. The crowd numbered around 2000, and 1999 of them were rapt. A music video started on a giant screen at the back of the stage while Evans made his exit. After a crescendo in the final chorus, the music diminished to images of a VFW company marching down a rainy street in a rural parade. The video had been produced by a couple of freelancers in Pittsburgh. Monroe trotted onto the stage and hit his mark to applause. He had forgone a podium, and now wore a miniature earpiece and microphone. Ted had kidded him, saying he looked like Mark Zuckerberg. "I'm not wearing a T-shirt, you moron," came the characteristically laconic rejoinder.

"What a great day to be with you in Columbia. And I am so happy to have such an energetic crowd here. You know every state is going to be important to our campaign. South Carolina is no exception. And I am going to ask for your vote. But we realize that I need to earn your vote, and the way to do that is to earn . . ."

"Monroe Taylor is a pervert who lays with whores!"

There was a commotion in the rear of the auditorium. A group of fourteen or fifteen protestors held up signs, some hand-lettered, others professionally done with the recent picture of Monroe without a shirt, and red flames licking around his image, the words "FLAMES OF HELL" superimposed over him.

Monroe rolled his eyes and extended his right hand in the direction of the protestors. "Well, I see the Westboro Baptist Church made it here all the way from Topeka, let's give them a big hand!" There was a handful of chuckles in the audience, but most of the audience had twisted around to see what was going on.

A brigade of police and security guards descended swiftly on the troublemakers. There was some scuffling. "Please!" called Monroe. "Let's not get anyone hurt! This isn't a Trump rally!" The crowd rolled with soft laughter, but Monroe was sincere.

"Look, this is the land of the free and the home of the brave. Everyone is entitled to express an opinion. That's a challenge we have always faced. And it's so much worse now, with the democratization of information. As a journalist, I can assure you that I am appalled at what passes for news. And as citizens, you should be too. We all should be. And I am not talking about 'fake news.' That's a story for later. We'll get to that in a minute."

He was off-script since the disturbance. This was supposed to be a speech about foreign policy. "A lot of people are now getting their 'news,'" he drew air quotes, "from social media. That's anathema to a journalist like me. You wanna talk about 'fake news'. . . . Unsourced. Unedited." He paused. "Gullible morons getting their strings pulled from Russia.

"You know, gone are the days when people got their news from reliable sources. There was a time when news came from Walter Cronkite or Roger Mudd or Harry Reasoner. Or the UPI or AP. And you could count on it being true. Factual. Sourced. Now any nitwit can email an article that 'looks' legit, and in a day or two it reaches a million people. And it doesn't just reach them, it inspires them. To take any manner of crazy action. Hillary is running a sex ring out of a pizza shop? Shoot it up! Antifa is going to disrupt the nation's food supply chain? Stock up on MREs! Obama's gonna confiscate your guns and ammo? There's a run on ammo at Dick's!

"Sounds like I'm busting on the Conservatives. Huh! Maybe the Liberals just don't have the strong messaging that the Conservatives enjoy. The truth is, I don't care much for the Democratic party either. And that is why I have chosen to run as an Independent.

"I mentioned 'fake news.' When President Trump uses that phrase, he disparages his antagonists in the media . . . of which there are many . . . and confers a sort of honor on his favorites. In particular, Fox News. Not that a lot of what passes for news deserves less than ridicule. You can watch local or network news shows doing stories about the unveiling of the latest iPhone, or some YouTube video about a lady who dresses up in a Chewbacca mask and wins her daughter a scholarship to a university, or hear about any obscure celebrity's 'baby bump.'

"These are serious times, people!" He caught himself sounding preachy, which was something that drove him nuts about Obama's deliveries. At least he said "People" and not "folks," like Obama. He paused and then dialed it down a notch. "A serious problem facing the constituency is the ability to discern fact from fiction. To discern news from noise."

"And if there is one lesson in life I have learned, it is that when things go wrong . . . and I'm talking BAD wrong . . . when things go wrong it's rarely due to one single cause. It's usually a whole host of causes that line up against you. And you don't stand a chance.

"So why are Americans so gullible? Why did they elect a reality-show personality? Why did every one of Donald Trump's massive rallies look like it was a WWF event?" He caught some movement in the front row and thought "what now"? It was Phil catching his attention by waving a hand quickly, but slightly, like someone with a tremor. He watched as Phil made the same motion with his head, quickly but nearly imperceptibly shaking it "no" side to side as he reached his hand to his throat in a slow choking motion.

Monroe hated these kinds of distractions because he ran the risk of losing his train of thought. Everything slowed down in his brain and he processed Phil's intent, his anxiety about losing his train of thought, which was doubly dangerous now because he was so far off-script, his public speaking lessons in college, law school, and the disruption drills that Kurt had run him through again and again. He knew that dead air was a killer, but he also understood that pausing for effect was sometimes an orator's best tool. As long as he did not look confused. He felt the ears heating up and in the same instant realized that Phil was objecting to the Trump rally comment. Worried that the next words out of his mouth were going to be "Why are Trump supporters such idiots, the same kind of people who believe that professional wrestling is real?" when he knew damn well that he needed to have some of those idiots' votes to win the election. So don't fucking alienate them already.

His thoughts collected, he forged ahead. "I'll tell you why. The dumbing down of America. A poor education system. The disintegration of the nuclear family. The collapse of standards of decency. The dismantling of journalism as a skill required to ensure a free press. And that largely due to the Fairness Doctrine I have spoken about so passionately.

"The problem is not the democratization of the internet. It's the inability of people to separate the wheat from the chaff. To tell the signal from the noise." He paused, because he felt like he was no longer connecting with the audience.

"Well, here's a hint: What you hear from politicians is noise. What you hear from me is signal!"

There was a dead silence in the crowd and Monroe reckoned that the signal versus noise analogy might be lost on this audience, except for maybe a few electrical engineers who would be too timid to start murmuring approval.

"Look, I was going to talk about some foreign policy issues that are really important, but I think it's also important to speak to some of these other chronic issues that are damaging the republic. Let's talk for a few minutes about why voters have a hard time distinguishing fact from fiction, truth from lies, reality from reality-show. . . . There was a time when education was a cultural priority in this country. It was during the Cold War. The US needed to develop scientists and engineers to combat the Red Threat. Now we rank behind Vietnam in math scores. Politicians are fond of ginning up support for education. Their knee-jerk reaction to education is to throw money at the problem. So we end up with standards-based education reform, arguments over school vouchers, and ultimately, an erosion of students' capabilities."

An uneasy groan rose from the audience. Sam leaned over to an obviously distraught Phil and said, "This is where we lose the teachers' unions."

Monroe heard the groans, saw the reactions of Sam and Phil, and ignored them. "I'm right. You know I'm right. Look at the dumbing down of the SATs in the nineties. They had to 're-center' them. Look at grade inflation. Look at the lack of discipline in the classroom. Look at the degradation of parent participation in education. And the disintegration of the nuclear family has not helped.

"I know this is an unpopular view. And it's not likely to garner any votes, but it has to be said: Discipline in schools is essential to learning, and parents need to be fully engaged in their children's education. People point to school shootings, and metal detectors, and arming teachers . . . it's way more than that. It's needing a cultural shift back to center. Dan Quayle took a LOT of heat for his comments about Murphy Brown having a child out of wedlock on a sitcom. But honestly, I don't think he was wrong. Tipper Gore took a LOT of heat for complaining about rock lyrics, and wanting advisories on records. But honestly, I don't think she was wrong. Now we have presidential debates where the participants are explaining that their penises are large and functioning fine."

He felt the heat rising again to his ears. "It's simply a collapse of the standards of decency. That's okay, I guess! But when I deftly deflect a completely inappropriate question about pornography, I get these nitwits from god-knows-where, stalking me across the country and protesting that I'm going to burn in eternal hell fire!"

The crowd laughed and applauded approvingly.

"And while we are talking about education, let me just say that while Barack Obama wanted to ensure that everyone has access to postsecondary education, and while Bernie Sanders wants that education to be free, remember this: the guys that fix your roof, pick up your garbage, and repair the roads don't need a college degree. There is a valuable working class in America . . . without which WE CANNOT SURVIVE! . . . that requires no postsecondary education! And oh, by the way, Bernie Sanders: you get what you pay for. If you give people a free education, you will shift the poor performance from high school to college. That data point will move. Not that it's not already happening, seeing as how Latin honors like *cum laude* and *magna cum laude* are now so common that more students graduate from college with honors than those who don't. Talk about grade inflation. But I guess that's where we are in America. Everyone deserves a trophy."

The crowd fell silent. Monroe couldn't tell if he was being preachy now, if he had them spellbound, or if he was merely deep in a shitpile of his own making.

"The grade inflation is interesting. It actually has its origin in the student deferments during the Vietnam War. Back then if your draft number came up but you were in college, the draft board granted a deferment. If you made a lousy grade in a class, one of your more sensitive professors might think, 'Gee, if I give this kid a D and he flunks another class, he could lose his deferment. He might be knee-deep in the big muddy after this semester. I'll let him slide with a C.' Yeah, that actually happened. And one thing led to another and now we graduate kids who can't find the State of New York on a map of the United States. Should there be an intelligence test to qualify to vote? Well, look at the last election, and you tell me!"

That was the money shot. The crowd was on its feet. Instant sound-bite.

"We have a lot of work to do, friends. There are a lot of serious issues facing us. Learn how to separate the wheat from the chaff, the signal from the noise. Don't get deflected by tweets from twits. Your palms should get sweaty when you consider what faces us. Active threats from foreign actors, states and otherwise. Lobbyists vying for their special interests. Citizens United says that corporations have the same rights as citizens, and Trump has not drained the swamp. Do you want a foreign government with a large shareholder interest in a corporation to spend money on an American election? I sure as hell don't.

"The evisceration of the EPA. You remember that the EPA was a Republican construct? Yeah. Nixon in 1970. Consider climate change. There are still deniers. People that believe that scientists are 'elitists.' Let me ask you something. If you need triple bypass surgery, do you want an elite heart surgeon, or do you prefer some hack? Maybe you want to confer with Sean Hannity. He seems to know a lot. The declining manufacturing sector. Walgreens replaced GE on the Dow this year. You understand that the Dow Jones Industrial Average used to be manufacturers and not pharmacies? Reagonomics. Trumponomics. Republicans love this notion of trickle-down economics. As though the *hoi polloi* should be damned satisfied that they get to feed off of the crumbs of the rich. The stuff that falls off their dining table. Hurry up! Scurry over there to get your share of the crumbs. What about a strong manufacturing sector that increases wealth across all classes? Wealth that trickles up? No realm has ever survived long without a middle class. The gap between the haves and the have-nots is just too wide. But bolstering the middle class has to be sustainable. The largest employer in the US cannot be the government."

The crowd was enthusiastic as Monroe's obvious passion drove him through his ad lib speech. The rally wrapped up around ten thirty that night. It got coverage on the cable news networks, and as the team gathered in the suite at the hotel, Kurt offered some additional coaching to Monroe. He had the ever-present hand towel draped around his neck. And even though the room was cranked down to 65 degrees, he mopped sweat from his head every five minutes. "Don't take too long on those dramatic pauses. It makes you look like you are floundering."

"I was floundering. I was speaking extemporaneously for the first ten minutes."

"And why were you doing that?" asked Sam. "It's not as though we don't have speeches prepared. There is a real danger in going off-script."

"Not with Monroe," defended Ted. "The guy does write for a living. Or he used to." Then turning to Phil, "So did we get any info on these idiots with the signs?"

"We will this time. Waiting to hear."

Fuller Thompson had hired a clandestine team as part of the security detail to track down disruptions at public events. Posing as reporters, they tracked the protesters to the police station, and then followed two of them home after they posted bail. Then they downloaded the data to Fuller and Tonya to dig for digital fingerprints on the internet.

What they turned up was no surprise. There were a lot of posts to ultraconservative message boards, and an evangelical message board from a website that exhorted its readers to commit violence to further a fundamentalist agenda. That one raised Fuller's eyebrows. It wasn't too far removed from some of the radical Islamic websites that Fuller had hacked during his tenure at CIA. He traced the IP address to a location in Fayetteville, Tennessee, picked up his cell phone to call Tonya, and then put it down.

Tonya was feeling imposed upon and he decided to cut her a break. He did not need to send a black girl with a bad attitude into southern Tennessee to collect intel on a bunch of radical ultraconservatives. He decided to sub this one out.

. . .

A "BREAKING NEWS" BANNER SPILLED across the bottom of the screen as the anchor intoned about a new source who had just gone public with incriminating evidence that Independent presidential candidate Monroe Taylor has exhibited erratic, and VIOLENT! behavior. A bevy of similarly minded journalists piled on with sympathetic insider knowledge, agreeing that "This guy is clearly unfit to be president," "How could anyone expect this nobody from Podunk, PA to be a serious candidate," and "Just look at his history of deviant sex! Shouldn't there be a constitutional test for STDs for candidates?"

The main story centered around Stan Garrett, whose portrait was flashed on the screen interspersed with scenes from an interview he had done late last night on cable news, claiming that a professional disagreement led to Monroe punching him in the face, breaking his nose, and effectively preventing him from pursuing a career in front of the camera. Garrett had been an award-winning journalist whose integrity was impugned. Besmirched. His reputation ruined, and his facial features altered when this maniac boss, who had INHERITED his position from his daddy, felt threatened by a real journalist, and sucker punched him. What a coward!

The host of the morning show smirked in reply to each of the answers from the five guests. They were responding to softball questions he took two minutes to ask. It was like watching congressional hearings; the senator gives a speech berating someone before he finally gets to the goddamned question.

The screen showed the host talking to one of his gorgeous co-anchors, saying, "Tracy, now we learn that Taylor gets his information from *Playboy* magazine! In his interview with Jack Mauer he referenced an interview about a *West Wing* actress that he read in the magazine from October 2001!"

"Well, Brian, we know he loves his pornography." The screen cut to the cover of the alleged magazine. "The feature of that issue was 'College Girls Nude'!"

"I could just kill that son of a bitch!" uttered Monroe.

"Well, that's not gonna improve your reception with the media," joked Ted lamely.

"I wasn't talking about THAT nitwit," spat Monroe, pointing at the TV host. "I meant the OTHER son of a bitch. Garrett!"

"Well. There goes your infamous temper again. Maybe you wanna take a nice long jog this morning."

Monroe's disposition was normally flatlined at equanimous. Lately he had been feeling irritated. His message was not getting out there. He felt ineffective and some self-doubt had crept into his consciousness. In truth, it was more than some self-doubt. He was now wondering why he hadn't taken everyone's advice and just taken the money and run. He was into the campaign to the tune of $122 million and change. Some donations had accrued, but not enough to be sustaining. Trump never had problems getting dupes to donate to a billionaire. Why was he having such a tough time with it? Well, for one thing, Trump knew how to play to the crowd and whip up the fanatics. Monroe, on the other hand, expressed more interest in clarifying his positions and educating the public.

It wasn't helping that he felt that TPC was dropping the ball when it came to filling the venues, raising money, finding the source of the asymmetrical attacks on his campaign. Or even something as simple as keeping the momentum going. He was feeling frustrated. Had been for some time now. This was definitely not the way this was supposed to play. And he knew he wasn't alone in his feelings. Ted was his gut check, and to a lesser extent, Pat, ABC, and Jenn. They thought that the last confrontation with Sam and his team was adequate to redirect the timbre of the campaign, but now here he was fighting off another attack. That they should have seen coming. It wasn't as though he hadn't revealed every damn detail of his private and professional life during the vetting.

The vetting was peculiar though. He felt like maybe they were just going through the motions. TPC was getting paid. They had only their reputation to protect, and after all, what is that for a political consultancy? If it doesn't work out, you just file for Chapter 11 and regroup. Maybe close up and rename yourself. It wasn't as though they had to convince the RNC or DNC that he was a viable candidate. He and Ted had discussed this *ad nauseum*. They finally had decided that if he was serious about running (he was) then he needed to trust the most suitable consultant (TPC) and roll the dice. No one ever became president by being timid.

"Let's have a sit-down with Sam and Phil. ASAP. I'm going to grab Kurt and Blake and Gary and go for a jog."

On the road, they had settled into a routine. TPC felt that it wasn't safe for Monroe to be out alone. He had not qualified for Secret Service protection since he was not a member of a qualified party. In fact, because the campaign did not want to give the appearance of failing to qualify, they had preempted the process by going on record to decline protection. They had hired retired state troopers as a security detail wherever they traveled (when the occasion called for it), but there had yet to be a permanent security detail established. Ted thought it was a mistake since Monroe was an easy enough mark simply due to his wealth. Being a candidate presented other security risks as well. Monroe balked. He wanted to be able to press the flesh. One compromise was that whenever he went out for a jog, someone from TPC would join him. Having the imposing figure of Kurt along was enough to discourage anyone. The problem was, he was good for a mile and a half tops, and was done. Monroe and Gary and Blake were just getting warmed up by then.

"Why so quiet, Monroe?" panted Gary.

He didn't like being sullen. It was not part of his nature. "This news report about Stan Garrett has me playing defense. Again. I have a meeting with Phil and Sam at eight-thirty. I'm hoping they have a plan."

"I see." Silence. "It's not as bad as it seems. Never is. We'll be setting up a press conference to respond."

"Well, see, that's the goddamned problem, isn't it? We respond. When we ought to be in front of these things." Another twenty strides in silence, except for the audible exertions from Kurt, jogging alongside them with the ever-present towel draped around his neck. You had to give the guy credit. He was trying. Blake spoke up.

"Is any of it true? I mean, any part of it? That's the critical thing here. Bending a truth to develop a narrative that fits the intent."

"Of course part of it is true. I pushed the bastard down. I never broke his nose though. And remember . . ." He paused in mid-sentence to wipe his face with his shirt. It was already humid at 7 AM in Columbia. "I'm a news guy . . . I know how a truth gets bent."

Phil and Sam entered the suite, followed by Ted and Sandra. "I'll get right to the point," began Monroe. "TPC is costing me this election. I'm 122 million into this, and I don't feel like we are making much progress." Blake and ABC slipped through the door, and into the fray.

Sam stepped up, always on point. "Gary has a plan for that. You're going on local TV for an interview this morning. Kurt has already worked up some responses for expected questions that he wants to rehearse with you."

"Look. Guys. I am not interested in Kurt's anodyne responses to expected questions. I'm a big boy. I was in the room when Stan fell down and broke his crown. I pushed the bastard, remember? I can fend for myself. What I don't get is why we are reacting instead of leading. This thing with Garrett is just the latest. It's a metaphor for this campaign. We talked about leading. About getting in front with our message."

"It needs to fucking change," interjected Ted. "Pronto."

"No, it needed to fucking change a month ago! I feel like a goddamn punching bag!" Alice had a look that verged on tears. Ted started to usher her out but she shook him off. She had a will of iron, but she was sensitive too. This was a personality conflict that often occurred to her in the newsroom. But it was a long time since she had been this rattled. It must have been the timbre and volume of Monroe's protests.

For what seemed like the millionth time, he was seated in a local TV station with a crew scurrying around him to prep for an interview. He was quite facile with these by now, even though the occasional interviewer would try to trip him up. A few of them thought they could break out and make a name for themselves, but he had been able to dispatch their tentative attacks with ease. Most, however, were quite professional, and if not exactly professional, then at least polite. The national guys were gruffer, more detached, and chasing market share in the quickest, crudest ways.

Ted, Kurt, and Gary were chattering with him, but his mind wandered. He glanced around the studio and considered the corresponding roles in his newsroom. There were a lot more moving parts to a televised production than to a newspaper, and he stroked his chin and wondered how his professional arc would have been different if his father had been involved in the nascent television broadcast industry.

The host for this segment was Lori Spalding, a stunning blonde in a red dress designed to caress her hips. She had greeted him warmly but professionally earlier, and when she got on set with him, she asked if he was ready, did he need anything, there would be a brief intro and then she would start into the interview with topical questions. Gary had primed her with a list of proposed questions (the local journalists loved it when an advance press guy made their jobs easier) and according to Gary, Lori was not likely to go off script.

"Good morning Columbia, and welcome to WZBY's Outlook news program," she announced in a velvety broadcast voice. "Today's guest is newspaper publisher and Independent candidate for president, Mr. Vaughn Monroe Taylor. Welcome to the show Mr. Taylor."

"Thank you. It's a pleasure to be here."

"Your campaign has been interesting for a number of reasons. First of all, you announced your candidacy after claiming a winning Powerball ticket. So I imagine that fundraising is not as critical for you as it is for other candidates."

"Fundraising is always critical to any political campaign, but you are correct, a substantial amount of my personal assets have been set aside for this effort. In our case we use fundraising as not only a gauge to determine how successful we are as a campaign, but it also plays a crucial role in energizing the base, getting the name recognition, and sustaining the campaign both financially and psychologically."

"How much more difficult is it to get poor folks to donate to a millionaire?"

"It's very difficult. However we ask that people donate what they can without hurting themselves. The Trump campaign spent something like $322 million, of which only $65 million was his own money, so it's clear that people are willing to finance wealthy political candidates. We feel good about our chances because we feel our message is stronger."

"And yet your message has been overshadowed this week by some new hard hits."

He did not know if she had finished with this new line of questioning, or if she wanted him to volunteer information. The lawyer in him wanted her to ask a direct question. He waited her out.

"Just today we have a report about one of your former employees who says you physically attacked him."

"You are speaking of Stan Garrett, a former contract employee of my paper, *The Latrobe Independent*. Mr. Garrett worked for us briefly awhile back, and he was terminated for cause."

"He says you punched him. Broke his nose."

"There was, in fact, a brief physical altercation in which Mr. Garrett fell over a trash can. At no time did I strike him in the face, and the damages to him appeared to be largely to his ego. The damages to me were largely to my reputation, and so when he filed suit against me and *The Independent*, it was settled out of court to the satisfaction of both parties. Further, there was a nondisclosure agreement that prohibited the release of the terms of the settlement."

"So it seems you have a bit of a temper? You let your fists do the talking at times?"

"No, Lori," he smiled patiently. "As I said, at no time did I physically strike Mr. Garrett in the face. However, I have been known to defend myself and anyone I recognize as incapable of defending themselves. And while I certainly do not condone physical violence, I recognize, and the American people should too, that it is sometimes necessary in the defense of one's interests."

"And what about news of this *Playboy* interview?"

"Let me just clarify, Lori. I READ an interview in *Playboy* about the cast of a TV show. I was not interviewed by *Playboy*. Jimmy Carter was interviewed by *Playboy*."

"But the cable news is stating that this is further evidence of inappropriate behavior for someone seeking high office."

"Again, I read an interview in a magazine."

"You did not look at the pictorials?"

Fuck. Here we go again. "No doubt I did, Lori. Like many males, I appreciate attractive females. But what I remember about that issue happens to be the interview."

"Others have probed the similarities between you and Donald Trump. You both inherited family businesses, you both possess great wealth, neither one of you held public office before announcing your candidacy. What makes you any different from Donald Trump?"

"I maintain an appreciation for the Constitution and the rule of law. I maintain a historical perspective, yet I am not nostalgic for some mythical past. Rather, I am hopeful for the future. Furthermore, without thoughtful, intelligent leadership, my fear is that America's future is tethered to superstition rather than to vision and science and a sustainable working class.

"It is true, I have a lot of new wealth. But I have also worked hard my entire life."

"But what are your differences?" she interrupted. "Your REAL differences?"

Monroe concealed his exasperation. As he formulated a response, he considered that his ability to communicate orally matched his ability to communicate in written form. Which was considerable. Yet here was Lori Spalding rejecting his answer, searching instead for a more powerful contrast between Candidate Monroe Taylor and President Donald Trump. He looked at her earnestly, and in a steady voice with no sarcasm, said, "The difference is, I am not an idiot. Nor do I believe that the presidency is about self-aggrandizement. I do not speak in sound bites, or parables, or word salads of indiscriminate, incomprehensible thought.

"As I said, I have worked hard my whole life. I have no sense of entitlement. Clearly, Donald Trump does. He has always had a sense of entitlement. He comes across as a bully. A big baby. Choose your epithet. It's clear to me that he never has his clock cleaned. I worked my way through college, and then law school. It's true that I took over control of my father's newspaper when he died suddenly. And what he left me was in pretty good shape. But that is not why I am grateful to my dad. I am grateful to him for instilling pride in performing a job well, for teaching me a middle-class work ethic. For inculcating a love of knowledge. Donald Trump brags that he doesn't read books! There's a role model for America!"

"So who in your esteem was a great president?"

"I look at Teddy Roosevelt and national parks, FDR and his leadership through the depression and World War II. Lincoln stitched the country back together in four years.

"Now we're mired in Afghanistan for seventeen years," he uttered parenthetically. "But if one looks through a historical lens, then these icons . . . sometimes even they don't look so great." He added, almost as an afterthought. "Jimmy Carter was a good man. At least he had an energy policy. Then along came Reagan."

"Yes," she smiled. "A lot of Southern Conservatives admire Reagan."

"You misunderstand. I don't admire Reagan. I think that while he certainly assisted in winning the Cold War, he caused long-lasting harm by dismantling Carter's energy policies. He caused lasting harm by eliminating the Fairness Doctrine. Which led directly to the polarization of Conservatives and Liberals. Now no one can have a good idea. Congress is gridlocked. And the cable news networks are locked in ratings wars for the souls of their 'bases.' It's completely unhealthy. There is no room for intelligent debate. For persuading the other guy to see your point of view. And really, isn't that the art of politics?

"And speaking of winning the Cold War, without a plan to win the peace after the war, it led to destabilizing the region. To the point that now Russia is trying all kinds of asymmetrical tactics to recover its influence. Invading Ukraine, tampering with our elections, and god knows what else."

"I want to get to your foreign policy positions, but can you elaborate on what you mean by viewing through a historical lens?"

"Teddy Roosevelt is revered as one of the giants among presidents. He established the national park system out of his love for the outdoors. He was a sickly kid, yet he strengthened himself and made himself into an image that back in those days could be considered a 'real man.' And that was his self-image. He was a frontiersman out west and a big game hunter in Africa after he left the presidency.

"On one of his hunting expeditions in Mississippi, he hadn't shot anything. The bush beaters and hounds trapped and clubbed a mangy bear, and tied it to a tree for him to shoot. Roosevelt refused to shoot the bear, because he felt that was not sporting. A political cartoon of the day showed him sparing the bear's life, and that spawned the invention of the Teddy Bear. And that was kind of misleading because instead of letting the thing go, he gave orders to put it out of its misery. So someone killed it with a knife and they dined on bear that night. Our sensibilities today don't permit beating game out of the bushes and cornering it only to be slaughtered. At least mine don't, but then again, I'm not much of a hunter.

"Another example . . . actually, there are many . . . are presidents who had several extramarital affairs. Many, like FDR, Kennedy, and Clinton, had major successes. But their reputations are tarnished by these revelations, either during or after their term of office.

"And this raises another important issue," he said, so animated that he was almost rising up out of his seat. "The president is a human, with all of the personal foibles that humans are endowed with. The American people need to remember that we are not electing a saint. We are electing a leader who may have to make terrible decisions to kill people ten-thousand miles away. Some of them innocent. Those are not the actions of a saint. And so while I think the character of a candidate is very important, this reliance on 'men of faith' really amounts to a religious test, and is completely inappropriate."

"Okay, what about your foreign policy views? Can you elaborate on those?"

"Sure. First of all, I encourage everyone to look at our website, Taylor2020.us. All of the planks to our platform are there, and it's a very easy site to navigate." Monroe shifted forward in his seat, and from the studio wings, Kurt noticed that this was the natural response to stimuli that interested Monroe. "But to answer your specific question would take more time than we have, so permit me to give you the highlights. I believe in engagement. I prefer it to isolationism. I've never understood why countries pull their ambassadors when they have a disagreement. It seems to me that the best way to resolve problems is to maintain open channels of communication."

"So you agree with President Trump's meetings with Kim Jong-un and Vladimir Putin?"

"I agree with engagement. Look, no one . . . even Trump . . . can be wrong ALL the time. The kowtowing to Putin is unsettling. Do you remember when the internet went nuts over Obama bowing to certain world leaders? I'm no apologist for Obama, but what I perceived was a show of respect. The ultraconservatives went crazy and called it his 'apology tour.' What do they say now when Trump . . . in Helsinki, with Putin standing beside him says 'the United States has been very foolish'? What do they say when Trump asks Bill O'Reilly if he thinks our country is so innocent? When he puts more credence into what Putin tells him than in his own intelligence community? They defend those statements and actions.

"But yes, I agree that engagement is more productive. Even with North Korea. I don't subscribe to this notion that by meeting personally with the President of the United States, legitimacy is granted to a despot like Kim Jong-un. It's not like kissing the pope's ring or getting the blessing of the Metropolitan. And any luster that was accorded the Office of President of the United States was already corroded a week into Donald Trump's term."

"Well, Mr. Taylor, we are running out of time. Thank you for the history lesson. Have a good day, Columbia! And remember, WZBY's Outlook is BUSY LOOKING OUT for you!"

. . .

"MAYBE WE NEED A CHANGE IN LATITUDE for a few days," offered Ted, rubbing his eyes with both hands. "I'm just spitballing here . . ."

"If you wanna take a break, I think it would be more productive to spend a week out on the west coast," said Phil, lowering a tumbler of Johnny Walker Green. The single cube of ice clinked pleasantly against the thick glass of the Lismore tumbler.

"That's a good idea." Sam shifted in his club chair. "We haven't visited LA or Las Vegas in weeks. We need to spread it around."

They were having a late-night head session, just the five of them. It started out as plans for an impromptu planning session over happy hour drinks. Then David Evans had invited them to take advantage of his membership at an exclusive country club outside of Columbia. David was such a nice guy, thought Ted. So smooth. Like Phil. Ted was tired. Spent was a better word. Enervated was the word he would have used had he needed to spar with Monroe. But he had downed a few Johnny Walkers and was having a little trouble concentrating.

Alice and Sandra came back from the ladies' room and took their seats in the small circle in the club room. A mahogany-paneled room with a mash-up of oriental rugs and original impressionist paintings, it was cordoned off, reserved for members of the club who had particular needs, and particular stroke. David Evans had both. The room was pleasantly dark and empty but for the party of five and the discreet attendants, who kept the napkins fresh, the drinks cold, and the crumbs off the tablecloths. The acoustics were terrific, thought Ted, who knew all about acoustics as a kid who worked his way through college as a DJ, and as a reporter who appreciated the nuance of picking up stray conversations in echoic rooms.

Sandra had pressed for weeks to get back to the west coast during the weekly staff meetings. The political climate would be friendlier, and there were fifty-five electoral college votes up for grabs in California alone. They had concentrated on the early primary states first, including Nevada, with minor excursions to California, Arizona, and Oregon, but those had been short visits to get test footholds. Monroe needed to really follow through now to raise money, energize the grass roots, and show face. Social media was great, but as Gary had stressed in the introductory meeting in Latrobe, it only goes so far. You still need print and broadcast, and the best way to do broadcast was to get out and make speeches. And because Monroe detested social media, meeting real people and showing face were always an easy sell.

Monroe had retreated to his room to review some details about his domestic policies. Judge Andropoulos, the retired Fourth Circuit Court of Appeals jurist, and Dexter Manfred, the PoliSci professor from Harvard, were in town to double-team him. Manfred had just appeared as a panelist on one of the evening Liberal cable news shows. He was introduced as a political coach for Taylor, but gave a good accounting of Monroe's qualifications. More than that, he made the host sound like a crybaby when the usual complaint arose about an Independent stealing votes away from the Democrats. The three of them were hunkered down with Kurt for the night, leaving Sam to reconcile with the Taylor campaigners from Latrobe. He appealed to Ted for a head session. Had Monroe been able to join them, it would have been a more relaxed mindbender with his intimates.

"We are already strong on defense. We are already strong on energy independence, R & D, and the economy. I know our position on abortion is still immature. But I want to hit this homeless situation hard. It ties into the economy and the 'tired of winning' BS."

"There's also gun control, crime, race, urban sprawl, climate change, the environment, cryptocurrency, the digital economy, IOT and privacy, and about a hundred other more important things," rattled off Manfred, with no trace of hyperbole.

"Yeah Dex, I know it. And I am passionate about all of those things. That's why we are sitting here at ten thirty while everyone else is out getting hammered and laid."

"Ouch." The judge was not a prude.

"He's thinking about his forty-two-year-old bride," joked Dexter.

"C'mon, let's finish this so we can enjoy a nightcap. I can't unwind until everything is taken care of."

"Well, Monroe, my man, you must not have unwound in a very long time!"

"True. So, every time I . . ."

"So, you're doing it again," corrected Kurt.

Monroe looked at Kurt, nodded once, and restarted. "Every time I drive into Pittsburgh I see homeless people standing at the exit ramps with cardboard signs, saying they are hungry, veterans, please help, god bless you, et cetera. Granted, some of them, maybe a lot of them, are just professional panhandlers. But in a civilized society, there ought not to be homeless people." The three others nodded silently. "What I propose is to enforce the vagrancy laws. Evaluate and process these people, and get them to a safe place where they can be assisted. I'm not talking Club Med here."

"You mean incarcerate them."

"There would have to be a temporary incarceration period while they are being processed."

"You can't say 'processed.' You make it sound like you are turning them into Soylent Green."

"Right. We'll stick to 'evaluate.'"

"What happens to them after evaluation?" asked the judge. The others had heard Monroe's plan before. This was the first time for the judge. "This has the smell of family separation and detention all over it."

"No, Dino, It's not like that. What I want to do is provide safe, clean, and reasonably comfortable accommodations for these people while they transition back into society. IF they are able to transition back into society."

"So what does that look like?"

"We convert military bases that closed under BRAC, unused commercial and industrial sites and the like, into living quarters. We hire social workers . . . who are always underpaid and looking for jobs anyway, to help evaluate and transition them. And whenever possible, we teach them a trade if they have the aptitude. The 'residents' perform menial jobs . . . custodial, groundskeeping. And here is the best part: these sites can be repurposed for mass housing for people displaced by natural disasters. Think Katrina. Or forest fires."

"Rising sea levels," added Kurt.

"Right. Or the big one when it hits California. I heard twenty years ago that when it hits, the casualties would fill every hospital bed in the free world."

"So everyone rounded up learns a trade? Gets free health care? Gets evaluated, tested, educated?"

Monroe turned to Kurt and joked, "Why does he get to say it?"

"Because he's using it as a conjunction and not as a placeholder."

"Duly noted." Then, turning back to the others, "Everyone gets all of that. And I think the program pays for itself with the labor we get to maintain these facilities. And we have to explain that whenever we move into brownfield sites, or even—wait for it—Superfund sites, we perform ALL of the environmental clearances that OUGHT to be done anyway. For me it's a win-win."

"And the workhouses? Are they still in operation?" mocked the judge.

"I know, I know," conceded Monroe. "The opposition will make it sound all Dickensian . . ."

"I like it!" exclaimed Dexter. "There's a humanitarian need being filled, it helps the environment, and it provides a refuge for future emergency relocations."

"I like it too," admitted the judge. "But selling it as a humanitarian effort is gonna take some polish. Otherwise it sounds like a pogrom."

"Don't forget the boost to the construction and environmental industries for cleaning up these places. There's a lot of economic benefit to this too."

"Alright, sir," drawled Dino. "I believe you owe me a nightcap." They retreated to the hotel bar.

• • •

"HEY BUDDY, WE'RE GOING TO SUNNY CALIFORNIA!"
Ted was wearing his Ray-Bans and a fedora. He was going for
the Blues Brothers but was coming off as a bookie.

"What the hell?"

"You know, the place with all the forest fires and earthquakes
and guys with pierced nipples and purple hair?"

"Shut up and look at this!"

A red banner floated across the bottom of the TV announcing
"EXCLUSIVE: TURMOIL WITHIN TAYLOR CAMPAIGN."
Ted stood with arms akimbo in front of the TV, a look of utter
disbelief as the host (same one as yesterday) exclaimed that
"unnamed sources embedded deep within the Monroe campaign
stated that the chances were good that a reorganization of the
campaign management would be announced."

"Brian, this is just the latest evidence of a campaign in free-fall.
First they whine about the lack of attendance at their rallies." The
camera cut to Brian, nodding and smirking. "Then they blame
their management team. I mean, it looks like amateur hour in
the Taylor camp. It would be comical if it wasn't so pathetic!"

"Absolutely," said Brian. "But what do you expect? This is just
the latest manifestation of the liberal media's attempt to discredit
a legitimate, conservative agenda, by running one of their own

liberal-media-fake-news-mongers! Just look at this guy's credentials. HE HAS NONE!"

The panel smirked knowingly, party to an inside joke that they were eager to share with the fawning masses.

Monroe's bottom lip curled inward, he had the countenance of a rabid pit bull. Had he been alone, he would have searched for something to break. His phone rang and he picked it up from the desk. The caller ID spelled out DENISE DEXTER and his inhibitions fled. He wound up and dashed the phone against the wall, pieces of plastic and silicon scattering in a cloud. Ted silently fetched a broom from the linen closet and started to sweep up the pieces.

"Careful you don't step in these. They're sharp." There was a short pause. "Let me guess. Was that a former employee?"

A knock on the door announced the arrival of Sam, Phil, and Sandra. Ted leaned the broom in a corner, opened the door and ushered them inside. Monroe rolled his head and his eyes, in a "what now?" look of total exasperation. He took a deep breath, trying to regain his composure. The TPC contingent lined up sheepishly. "We have a leak," said Phil.

"You think?" Monroe was back in control. He was never proud of losing his temper. He recognized that it was a personality defect, but it did not happen often. He thought briefly about what the hell Denise Dexter might be pestering him about this time, but quickly dismissed the notion. He had bigger fish to fry.

"Gary, Kurt, and Blake are prepping a response now. It will be the usual sort of 'we aren't going to comment on internal matters . . . the campaign is functioning as a team, and Monroe Taylor views the campaign as a dynamic process, much as he does the presidency, responding to challenges foreign and domestic.'"

"What's Fuller got?" demanded Ted.

"This fundamentalist organization in Fayetteville is a shell organization. It's really just a PO box, a website, and a cell phone. In reality, it's a Super PAC with really deep pockets, founded by Harlon Michaels."

"Well, I don't guess that surprises anyone," said Monroe. A billionaire with the resources and interest in exercising influence over politics, Harlon held sway over a broad swath of the right wing, including neocons, paleoconservatives, and especially evangelicals. "Fine. Let's get to Bryan tonight for a meet and greet. If I'm going to be in the cross hairs of these bastards, I'm going to the source. We've been neglecting Texas anyway."

"What about California?" asked Ted.

"The purple hair and pierced nipples can wait another couple days," intoned Monroe. "Unless there's another natural disaster between now and then. But all of the disasters I'm seeing lately are of a more personal nature."

Harlon Michaels' compound was outside of Bryan, Texas. Born and raised in Waco, he attended Texas A&M, and spun off an agribusiness after five years in private industry. His empire included industrial agriculture, farm machinery, real estate, fertilizers, and biofuel. The headquarters for Michaels Industries was in Bryan, near his beloved Aggies.

Sam and Sandra wanted to take a more cautious approach, issue a statement about the leak, and stick to the schedule. "No," argued Ted. "I like this approach. You have to eat a frog, you do it fast. Besides, we go to A&M, let's pay a visit to the Bush 41 library. The Bushes hate Trump almost as much as I do. It will be a good visual, and send a nice 'fuck you' to Harlon Michaels in his own backyard. I like it. I love it!"

Taylor One touched down at George Bush Intercontinental Airport early that afternoon. They stayed downtown at the Hilton

Houston North. Gary had already arranged an interview with the local ABC affiliate to be taped for viewing the following day. A press release was issued announcing a speech in Bryan the following day as well. The Aggies could not be reached in time to get permission to speak on campus, and while the Bush library welcomed visitors, there was no time to set up anything more official than a simple visit to the Presidential Library and Museum. Gary turned it into a photo op which Monroe didn't mind since he had always regarded Bush 41 with respect, if not adulation.

Monroe and his entourage spent the next day in Bryan and College Station, glad-handing the locals and visiting the local campaign office. He was heartened by the enthusiasm of some of his young supporters, and offered career advice to more than a few of them who expressed some interest in either journalism, law, or politics.

A conference room had been rented at an events center in Bryan, and coverage appeared to be excellent. Gary was willing to accept some of the credit, but everyone recognized that the publicity from the cable news reports about Stan Garrett and the chaos within the campaign had backfired on Harlan's Super PAC. All it seemed to do was stir up renewed interest. The room was abuzz with an excitement that had been eluding Monroe. When Gary and Sam drove up they saw the parking lot crammed with cameras and sound equipment, reporters taping intros, and an assortment of Taylor supporters as well as protesters.

Monroe was in back, behind the dais with Ted and Kurt huddled around him. His speech was up on the teleprompters, having been edited overnight by Kurt. Even though the speeches were actually written by Monroe, Kurt and the TPC communications team always edited them. They had developed proprietary software to integrate with the teleprompters, providing timing, cues, phrases, and words to emphasize. It was almost like a musical score, with accents, crescendos, and diminuendos. Monroe generally eschewed the frills, preferring to rely on the text only. He had complained to Kurt that the supplementary notes were distracting. Kurt realized that Monroe really did not need the cues, that he was a natural orator. So they generally stuck to the text only.

This was not a rally, so David Evans was not along to whip up enthusiasm. Monroe hopped up to the dais and welcomed the crowd. By now he was accustomed to the clicking and whirring of cameras. Kurt had seen to that.

"I want to thank all of you for coming out on relatively short notice. As you have probably heard, our campaign operates like a well-oiled machine, and we generally like to plan things out to the nth degree. However, in light of the nature of the job for which I am applying, we also know that we must react to dynamic and fluid situations. So when Harlon Michaels' Super PAC claimed that our campaign was falling apart, we wanted to prove to him that, in fact, we are in great shape, we are achieving our goals, and we are a united team.

"But really I misspeak. To be accurate, Harlon's Super PAC hasn't claimed anything. They have worked back channels to insinuate themselves into our campaign, with attempts to sabotage us. They have operated silently, providing anonymous sources to news organizations who feel threatened by the success of our campaign. And so in that sense, we feel vindicated by the legitimate threat they feel we pose to their worldview.

"I'd like to acknowledge my team, starting with my longtime friend and associate Ted Polanski; Technical Political Consulting's Sam Balentine, who has done an outstanding job orchestrating his team, Sandra Pease, Phil Ainsworth, Kurt Bastille, Gary Davidson; and my other associates from *The Latrobe Independent*, who have done such a fine job applying their excellent skills to the complex tasks required in mounting a national campaign: Alice Conway, Pat Metiore, Tom Loughery . . . stand up and take a bow . . . and Theresa Stamford, who never travels with the group because she works so hard assisting Sandra in the Field Department.

"All of these individuals will be accessible in person or via phone to answer any questions the media may have after this press conference. And you will find them to be candid, committed, and confident in our chances in this race. We would not be doing this if we did not possess something akin to a religious fervor. Not just a willingness. No. Rather a need to put ourselves out there in the public to provide an alternative to a lack of cohesive vision, a lack of exemplary leadership, a lack of moral fortitude.

"We don't have the time, and I don't have the stomach to go into all the things I see wrong with the current administration. I would rather explain to you some of the visions we see moving forward in a Monroe administration."

Monroe outlined his programs for intelligent defense spending, developing high-speed and commuter rail systems, and the benefits those would have for the economy. He hit the trickle-up economics sound bite while the cameras clicked and whirred. There was an outburst from the back of the room when protesters crashed a rope line and chanted "HOMO MONROE!"

"Hey," shouted Monroe over the commotion, "any time your boss wants to have an intelligent debate about issues, I'd be happy to arrange that!"

He turned back to the audience. "Speaking of debates, I really hope we will be able to satisfy the Appleseed criteria and be able to participate in the presidential debates. Current polling suggests that we will. You know, I do not rely on polls to shape my opinions. But they are important to campaigns because that seems to be the only way to capture the attention of the voting public. And in order to participate in the presidential debates, a candidate has to be on the ballot in enough state ballots to win a majority in the electoral college, and poll at least 5 percent nationally. Participation in the presidential debates is a big deal for our campaign. We feel we can change hearts and minds in a debate setting.

"On the other hand, I recognize that politics is so polarizing that a lot of people wouldn't care what happens in a debate. They simply pull the party lever. I've been struggling to understand why people do that, because it is antithetical to a democracy. For a democracy to work, people need to be thoughtful, engaged, and informed. Not tribal, prejudiced, and ignorant. This is exactly why Congress shall make no law abridging the freedom of speech, or of the press.

"Now is President Trump wrong when he says that the media are the enemy of the people?" The crowd consisted of professional reporters, so it was a rhetorical question.

"Yes, of course he is. But he is not wrong about claiming that news media is biased. I hate the blanket 'fake news' mantra. I detest it. But the fact is, news is not what it used to be, and the level of discernment among the voting public is nowhere close to where it needs to be in order for a free press to function as a tool for an effective democracy. It is up to us to educate the voters about what constitutes journalism. To source stories. To avoid hyperbole and exaggeration. Because let's face it: there is no need to sensationalize. The truth is bad enough."

Monroe took questions following his remarks.

"Are you saying there are no dissenting views within your campaign?"

"I am saying no such thing. Of course there are dissenting views! Disagreements are healthy. They spawn debate, which ought to be a good thing. I run this campaign the way I have always run my business. With an open mind. No one has an exclusive right to good ideas! And that's the way a Taylor administration would be run."

"You've written some op-ed pieces about how candidates should be forced to inform the voters who would be in their cabinets. And yet you have yet to choose a running mate. Any word on how that search is progressing?"

"Thanks for that question. The answer is no, we have not yet focused on a running mate, but we have a list of people under consideration. I won't go into specific names, because I don't want to put anyone on the spot or exclude some very qualified candidates. Our immediate goal is to get the public informed about the major planks of our platform. But yes, I still believe that a president owes the people the names of his cabinet before he is elected, so we don't end up with a bunch of nitwits and incompetents thrust upon us."

A chorus of reporters shouted out, nearly in unison, "Who are some of those nitwits, sir?"

"Ulysses Grant had a really terrible cabinet, but in recent memory we could start a list that begins with James Watt and ends with Rick Perry." He thought about his disdain for Condoleezza Rice and Janet Reno, but he correctly predicted a shitstorm of negative reaction to naming women, so he kept quiet.

"Mr. Taylor, if you hate Conservatives so much, why don't you run as a Democrat?"

"Thank you for that trenchant question. The fact is I don't 'hate' Conservatives. What I hate is this ultraconservative agenda that accuses anyone who disagrees as being less than American. And that includes Harlon Michaels and his Super-PAC. That kind of thinking allows for no debate. It assumes that you are always right. It takes a special kind of arrogance to think like that, if thinking is even part of that philosophy. It's asinine.

"And the reason I will not run as a Democrat is really very simple. I am not a Democrat. I can think for myself . . . independently . . . and so I don't feel a need to subscribe to one party's views. I can pick the best of both, or develop my own. And so should you."

· · ·

SMITTY STEPPED into Franco DeMario's editor's office and closed the door behind him. "Guess who I saw getting into a car with a black chick?"

"I dunno. Monroe Taylor?" Franco deadpanned. Monroe did have a reputation with the ladies, and a few news cycles ago were all about him with Mona Dupuis.

"Little Miss Perfect."

"Ronni?"

"None other."

"Why is that so remarkable?"

"'Cause this black chick happens to work for TPC."

DeMario knit his brows and considered. Ronni Davis was a likable young thing, and she was doing a pretty good job in the newsroom. Met her deadlines, good writing, very stylish and squared-away. But he could not deny that there was something weird about her. The regulars picked up on it too, but when they made snide remarks, Franco had attributed it to jealousy. He heard someone wonder aloud how she could afford designer bags and shoes on the lousy cub reporter salary she was making. It was a valid point. A background check showed that her family did not come from money. Where was the money coming from?

"Okay, spill it! I got very little time for bullshit today, Smitty."

"Well, no one can figure out where she's getting her money from. I see her getting into a car with a black girl for like ten minutes. Could be a source for a story she's working on, could be she's selling bath salts or cocaine on the side. Either way, I'm running the out-of-state plates and I find out it's a rental car for TPC in Falls Church."

"Naturally you took a picture of the two of them."

"And the black chick was ID'd by Alice as one 'Tonya Jackson,' who works in TPC's 'Research Department.'" He paused for dramatic effect by making air quotes. "Which is a euphemism for 'Intelligence and Counter-Intelligence.'" He had no idea that it was a euphemism for anything until Alice mentioned it to him.

DeMario wrung his hands, considering what his next move should be. Maybe they should advise Ted and Monroe. But advise them of what? Smitty was a bit of a conspiracy theorist. He should probably have some proof of malfeasance before he raised the alarm. If there was even any malfeasance involved. So far all he had was Ronni Davis dressing better than she should be and meeting with a girl from TPC. Maybe Tonya Jackson had interviewed her for information about *The Independent* and background on Monroe. Simple as that. If Tonya Jackson knew anything about espionage or even journalism, she would have asked one of the long-time associates of Monroe to get the real poop. Not the new girl.

"Awright. So what do we do now?" Franco asked rhetorically.

"I think we need to dive a little deeper. We get her iPhone. Check her contacts. Hack into the little bitch's laptop."

"Jesus. Easy, Tiger. We can't go off half-cocked and get into legal trouble."

"What legal trouble? TPC is the one spying on us!"

"Allegedly." Franco was amazed at how thoughtful and smooth he felt since he had moved behind the editor's desk. It was as if the desk was some kind of talisman, conferring editorial insight and managerial wisdom upon him. He was smart to consider the legalities. To rein in Smitty. To keep the presses rolling. To keep these idiots he worked with from running amok, which they surely would without his sagacious oversight.

Franco slept on it for a night, then convened a secret meeting with Smitty, Sheila Burns, and Dave Barlow, the county reporter and Franco's confidante. He laid out the suspicions that Smitty had and led them to a plan he concocted to separate Ronni from her iPhone. It involved some complicated setup with a meeting, then calling her out of the meeting on a pretense, and hoping she left her phone behind. They all thought it might work. They also discussed hacking into her laptop. Naturally, she took it with her every night. But Barlow knew a guy who knew a guy, who could probably do the job. They decided to make discreet inquiries.

They scheduled a small meeting that afternoon to review plans for a story about local playgrounds. Ronni was tapped as the feature reporter. She already had a good rapport with the city officials, so she would be a natural choice. About five minutes into the meeting, Sheila entered with an urgent request for Ronni, the pretense being an email to Blaise Conrad about the paper's finances for the fiscal year-to-date. Something to do with Monroe's investments and Sheila was having trouble attaching the PDF, and since Ronni was so knowledgeable about techy stuff, could she please help before Blaise left his office for the night in London?

Sure enough, she ditched her iPhone on the table to the amazement of Franco and Smitty. Smitty stood watch by the door while Franco turned the iPhone on, and was prompted to enter an unlock code. Fuck.

"Try 1-2-3-4-5-6," suggested Smitty. To his credit, Smitty had already anticipated such an obstacle, and had gotten the last and first six digits of Ronni's SSN, phone number, parents' phone number. And birth date. None of them worked. Hers was locked by fingerprint. No dice.

"Here she comes!" Smitty told Franco in his ventriloquist's voice, his lips hardly moving.

They would have to go to plan B. The guy who knew a guy.

. . .

19

"WE GOT A PROBLEM."

"We HAVE a problem. Didn't they teach you anything in journalism school?" Ted was on a bad cell connection with Franco DeMario, the Acting Editor.

"You're br——n- -p," crackled Franco.

"Goddamnit," muttered Ted. "You'd think this thing was supposed to be a convenience. HOLD ON!" he shouted as he marched outside to find better reception. "Okay, what's going on?" He woke up in a good mood. Monroe had nailed his speech last night in Bryan, Sandra and he were enjoying discreet encounters, the stocks in his IRA were outperforming the indices. It was an enigma, but even with that incompetent buffoon in office, the market was up.

But now it sounded like Franco was having a meltdown. Why didn't he just email me, he wondered. Can't these idiots back home run the paper without me and Monroe there to hold their hands?

"Are you sitting down?" asked Franco with more drama than Ted thought the situation might deserve. "We got a spy in the newsroom. The new girl we hired to fill in for the campaign staff. Ronni Davis. We think she's a mole for your campaign consultants. Smitty caught her talking to that spook from TPC in the shopping center parking lot."

"What spook?"

"Tonya Jackson. The spook for TPC."

"You did NOT just refer to a black girl as a 'spook'! Jesus Christ, Franco!"

"Holy fuck! She was with the CIA! A spy! Goddamnit, Ted! I meant 'spook' in the CIA sense! What the fuck is wrong with you?"

"Alright! Calm the fuck down!" There was a long pause. "How did Smitty even know about Tonya Jackson? She flies pretty under-the-radar."

"Alice sent a whole packet of info for us to track the campaign with. There was an org chart from TPC, we started a database here. Smitty sees the new girl get into a car with a black chick, he gets suspicious, runs a license plate check, finds out it's a rental to TPC, and so we all get suspicious."

"Why would he get suspicious to begin with?"

"Well, Jesus Christ, Ted. We're all reporters here. We sniff out stories. So he and I check the org chart and find out that Tonya is working for Fuller Thompson's Research Department. Alice ID'd her from the photo Smitty took. So we managed to separate Ronni from her cell phone, but no go. It's locked. But we do find some stuff on her laptop about TPC. A LOT of stuff. She has a whole freakin' dossier on all of us. Especially the 'MAN.'"

"How the hell did you get into her laptop?"

"Barlow knows a guy," he explained mysteriously. To Ted it sounded like Franco was putting on airs. "Don't worry. He guaranteed it would be untraceable. Oh, and one more thing. There's a lot of stuff in there about Denise Dexter."

"What kind of stuff?"

"Like gossipy stuff that we already know about. Some other stuff in there too that even I didn't know about. Like her brother."

"What about her brother?"

"Like he's kind of a sleazeball."

"Well, Jesus, we all knew that. Denise is just barely this side of respectable." He paused. "Listen. Let's don't do anything hasty here," Ted cautioned. "I'll let Monroe know, and you should also probably get hold of Fred During."

He hung up and dreaded talking to Monroe about this. The poor guy had enough to worry about already. He decided to sleep on it and catch Monroe in the morning.

The next morning Ted was awakened by a gentle rapping at his door. Disoriented he stumbled out of bed and shuffled to the door. *Who the heck is it at this hour?* It was still dark, which it always was when he rose, but god almighty, this felt very early. He glanced at the digital clock on the nightstand and saw 4:28 AM. As he peered through the peephole he saw Alice and Pat standing in the bright corridor. He uttered a silent prayer of thanks that Sandra hadn't spent the night with him. "Hold on a sec," he mumbled as he crawled into a pair of slacks and buttoned a few buttons of his shirt. He unlatched the door, which sounded excessively loud in the echoic hallway. His hair was swept up over his scalp in a bad Mohawk.

Alice and Pat looked worse than he did. Like they hadn't slept at all last night. Alice croaked, "We got a problem."

"What the hell is going on with you people," he asked, thinking that there must be a confederacy of morons employed at the paper. "Yeah, I know. The mole. Franco told me. Now go to bed."

Pat shot a look at Alice, who returned the look and gaped at Ted. "How the hell did Franco know?"

"Smitty saw her get in a car with Tonya."

"Wait. What? Saw WHO get in a car?"

"Whatshername. The new girl. Donnie, Dory, Denise. . . . What the fuck," he started to laugh. He was so tired that he was punchy. "Leave me alone. Let me sleep." He was doubled over now, peals of laughter erupting from deep within, and tears running down his face. Pat regarded him with curiosity and started to giggle, but Alice was not amused. She was tired too and brushed past Ted, filled the coffee carafe with water and started to brew a pot until the commotion died down.

"Listen, Ted. Who are you talking about?"

He had regained his composure. "The new girl at the paper! Why the fuck can I not remember her name? She's the mole."

"Ronni Davis?" offered Pat.

"Yeah, that's it!" he exclaimed pointing at Pat. "Oh god, I needed a laugh like that! Now off with you! Vamoose!"

"Not so fast *mi amigo*," said Alice. "Those leaks are coming from Blake. He's the mole!"

"Blake? No way! That kid is solid!"

"Yes, Blake! He was in the room when you and Monroe blew up at TPC. The only people that were there were me and you, Sam, Phil, Sandra, and Blake. It can't be Sam or Phil, they're principals in the company. And Sandra never leaves your side. Where is she by the way?" ABC looked around the room. Well, so much for discretion.

"Hmmm." Ted considered that it was Blake who had been providing the secure burner phones to Monroe. And Denise was still getting through. He ushered them out of the room and instructed them to get some sleep.

This was bad. Very bad. He sat in the darkness on the edge of his bed. Oh god, he felt like he was having a panic attack. What if it's a heart attack? Should I call someone? His stomach felt so full. The Texas barbecue had lain in his gut all night. Ted was part Jewish but not observant, and so when the gang went out last night to a local barbecue joint, he felt no compunction about wolfing down a sampler platter of coleslaw, brisket, pulled pork, and chicken. Chased it with about a quart of iced tea, and followed that up with a few drinks at the hotel bar with Sandra and Phil. Now he had this to contend with. He got up and went to the bathroom, propping himself over the sink. He felt like maybe he should have a glass of water, or swallow a Pepto-Bismol caplet. They were in his toiletry kit hanging behind the door, but he was too woozy to turn and retrieve them. He started to heave. He was angry for allowing himself to have such a visceral reaction to an administrative problem. He thought maybe the laughing fit had triggered this. Damn Alice and Pat! He'd be sound asleep now if it wasn't for them. Instead, here he was worried about whether he was going to have a subconjunctival hemorrhage.

He could not fall back asleep so he showered and dressed even earlier than usual and rapped on Monroe's door. Monroe opened the door and turned back into the room to finish his preparations. "How's it goin', Dude?" He turned back to Ted, who was wearing the Ray-Bans again. "What is it with you and those glasses? We're not going to California yet."

"We have to talk about a few issues, and I think you should clear your schedule for a couple hours." Ted removed the glasses to reveal a massive hemorrhage of his left eye.

"Jesus Christ! What the hell happened to you? You get in a fight?"

"Yeah, I went nine rounds with Tobie's Texas Bar-B-Cue last night. I feel like shit. After we chat, I'm gonna have to lay down and recuperate."

"You look a little paler than usual. Sit down. Why don't we call a doctor? Or get you to a doc-in-a-box?"

"I actually wouldn't mind seeing a doctor. But we need to talk."

"So you said. We can talk while you go to the doctor's." Monroe called Phil, who arranged for Blake to take Ted to an urgent care office nearby. Blake stopped by a moment later to let them know that one of the bodyguards, a driver, was already waiting for them under the *porte cochère,* in a rented Toyota Highlander Hybrid (in the mandatory black reserved for politicians and VIPs). There was a moment of mild confusion as Ted fumbled for seating arrangements, primarily due to the unexpected presence of Blake. Blake rode shotgun.

"So what is it you wanted to chat about?" asked Monroe in the back seat with Ted.

Ted turned his face to him to reveal a wan look. He wanted to convey that he could not talk with Blake in the car, but the effect was the same, with Monroe nodding, understanding that the effort would be too taxing. In the next moment, Monroe thought, *Jesus, I could be doing about a million other things right now. I thought he had something important to discuss.* And then an instant later, *Jesus, what an unmitigated ass I can be sometimes. My best friend might be having a heart attack and all I can do is worry about the impact on my schedule.* Then aloud, "We probably should have called an ambulance. Ted shouldn't be walking."

"It's not a heart attack, Monroe," Ted wheezed. "I'm just dehydrated. Something I ate." He sounded convincing. Which led Monroe back to considering his schedule. He was relieved when they pulled into the urgent care parking lot following three minutes of uncomfortable silence.

The triage nurse took his ID, clasped a plastic ID band on his left wrist, and sent Ted to an exam room. Monroe followed him in while Blake texted Sandra and Phil to let them know what was going on. They would need to send a surrogate to the breakfast that was scheduled, and Sandra would probably be concerned for Ted.

A female Physician's Assistant, pretty and petite, entered the exam room. After a quiz of his last night's activities and a review of his vitals, she drew blood and left the exam room to Ted and Monroe. "Okay . . . finally I can talk to you." Ted seemed a little slow yet lucid, surprising Monroe and immediately relieving some of his concern for his friend. "Ronni Davis is a spy for TPC, and Blake is a fucking mole for Harlon Michaels."

"Whoa." Monroe was again concerned for the well-being of his friend. "You okay, buddy?"

"Yeah," croaked Ted. "It's why Denise has been able to get through to you. Blake's been programming your phones."

"Okay. Relax. None of this is important right now."

"Listen. I'm not that sick here. You need to pay attention. Call Alice and Pat if you think I'm delirious. And Franco. They have the evidence. I wanted to tell you a little smoother, but this bug hit me and we haven't been able to peel ourselves away from Blake."

"You're sure about this . . ."

"I am. But call ABC and Franco . . ."

"And what about Ronni? How did you crack that?"

"Smitty saw her get in a car in Latrobe with Tonya Jackson."

"Who IS Tonya Jackson? I mean, I know she works for Fuller, but I've never met her. Never seen her."

"You never met Tonya?" Ted asked incredulously. He paused and considered. "Listen, brother, better you haven't met her. She's a looker and you don't need that kind of distraction."

There was a knock and the door opened. It was Blake. "You guys need anything?"

"No, Blake, thanks. We're all good in here."

"A ginger ale or coffee or anything?" He appeared genuinely concerned.

"No, Blake. Thank you." Blake nodded politely, smiled and closed the door.

"That little shit. And there I was all impressed that he quit American Political Consulting just to come to work for the consultant that won the bid to run my campaign. I'm a sucker!" Monroe recalled Ted commenting on how Blake's transition to TPC augured well for the campaign.

"Take it easy, slugger. We all got played. These guys are pros, remember?"

"Goddamnit! We're supposed to be more sophisticated than that! Where's my professional skepticism? What if this was a foreign operative infiltrating the government?"

"Isn't that what the FBI and CIA are for?"

"Yeah, well isn't that what Fuller Thompson is for? Or are they in on it too? Jesus Christ! This is a fucking nightmare!" Monroe hissed, as he ran his hand through his hair.

"Well now you just sound like an irrational conspiracy theorist." Ted sat up, feeling better. There was another knock and the PA entered.

"You've really dehydrated. Your electrolytes are low, and you probably got a case of food poisoning. I'm going to prescribe Lomotil for diarrhea and Lorazepam for nausea, and I want you to stay on a clear liquids diet for a day or two to give your gut a rest. Then transition to BRAT for another day before you take solid nourishment. I can give you an IV to get some fluids into you quickly. That will make you feel better almost immediately, but it's up to you."

"No, we're all good. We have things to do. I'll grab a Gatorade at the convenience store."

The PA shook Ted's hand, and wished him good luck. She turned to Monroe and shook his hand. "And good luck to you too, sir, in your campaign!"

Monroe looked at Ted and said, "Well, that augurs well!"

. . .

TED EASED INTO A CHAIR BACK at Monroe's room. They had debated about bringing Pat and ABC into the meeting, but Monroe decided that he did not want to confront TPC with a show of force. So it would be an intimate meeting. Sam and Phil knocked and Monroe let them in.

"How did you find Ronni Davis?"

Sam replied without hesitation. "Ronni is an asset recruited by Fuller to collect intel within the organization."

"And by 'within the organization' you mean inside *The Independent*."

"Monroe, she's a dust buster. She's there to identify any liabilities that the opposition may be able to exploit. It's SOP, and I understand she's a pretty good reporter." He looked at Phil who nodded his assent.

"Alright, it's SOP. Has she sucked up any dirt on me?"

"Turns out that except for a few, ummm, dalliances . . . which all seems to be within current social norms . . . if not the letter of the law . . . you're respected by your peers and revered by your employees."

"That's good to know. Now how about Blake?"

Sam shifted uneasily in his chair.

"Is he one of yours too?" asked Monroe tersely.

"No, no, no!" protested Sam. "I mean, YES, he is obviously an employee of TPC, but no, his TPC-sponsored activities have only been intended to assist with the campaign."

"Why is he still ON the campaign?" Ted was becoming impatient.

"Fuller has been tracking Blake," admitted Sam.

"For how long?" asked Monroe, shifting his weight forward like he always did when he was engaged in a topic he found interesting.

"Several weeks," answered Sam, weakly.

"So you haven't fired him because you still don't know who is pushing his buttons!"

Ted already had Fuller's phone icon up on his phone. He touched the icon and put Fuller on speaker. The desktop helped to amplify the conversation.

"Hi Ted, it's Fuller here."

"Hi Fuller. We have you on speaker with Monroe, Phil, and Sam. Sam tells us that you have been watching Blake Mrzowski."

"This is a conversation I would rather have in person, gentlemen."

"Are our communications compromised any more than we already know?" asked Monroe.

"No, sir," replied Fuller. "It's just that due to the sensitive nature, I would rather be in the same room."

"Be that as it may," continued Monroe. "What is the story with Blake?"

"We're sure he's the source of the leaks about discord in the campaign. . . ." Sam winced visibly at the word "discord." "And we know he is responsible for giving your personal contact data to Denise Dexter. Beyond that, I really don't have much else." It was Fuller's nature to hold back. Monroe's journalistic sense was sounding klaxons though, and he could tell there was more to the story.

"You're going to try to turn him, aren't you?"

"We've thought about that." Fuller smiled, understanding that Monroe realized that sometimes setbacks presented opportunities for those in counterintelligence. If the presidential thing didn't work out for Monroe, maybe he would be interested in working with Fuller. But no, the guy was a billionaire. Fuller continued aloud, "But we are not exactly sure who he is working for. They are covering their tracks very well."

"Surely you have gotten into his computer!" Ted speculated.

"I'm not going to answer that." Ted and Monroe exchanged glances. So they HAVE gotten into his laptop. "Suffice to say that there is a paucity of contact data, as well as anything that could be used to exploit his allegiance to his handlers."

"So he's not surfing porn sites . . . Huh! I thought the internet was invented for that!" Monroe raised a hand to tamp down Ted's sometimes inappropriate sense of humor.

"The kid is squeaky clean," assured Fuller.

"No one is that clean," retorted Monroe. "Who is the scariest guy we have?"

"That would be Kurt," answered Phil.

"No. Blake and Kurt are tight. Fuller, how soon can you join us? Can you interrogate Blake in a semi-threatening way and get a confession? Or let's say an 'admission.' Maybe that will be enough to turn him against Harlon Michaels."

Fuller reminded them, "We don't really know if it's Harlon Michaels' Super PAC behind Blake. It might be someone else. Russians . . ." his voice trailed off.

"It's Harlon," Monroe said with conviction. Then considering, "but if it isn't we need to find out who."

California seemed like it was never going to happen to the chagrin of Ted and Sandra. It wasn't as if they were planning to hit the beaches or tour the homes of actors. They were antsy about getting feet on the ground in the state with the highest number of electors. Sandra felt like they were behind schedule with the campaign, even though she knew they enjoyed a stunning presence there on social media and internet platforms. The traditional media coverage in California was expensive, but there was a lot of buzz, owing to the odium that was accorded to Donald J. Trump. Odium was insufficient for their purpose though. Both she and Ted knew that they needed to show Californians that Monroe Taylor had concrete solutions to problems, and not meaningless slogans like "BUILD THE WALL" and "LOCK HER UP." Well, they had more urgent matters. Monroe was hell-bent on facing his detractors here in the heart of conservative America. And so even before they left for Texas, TPC had scheduled a town hall meeting in Lubbock. It was a toss-up between Plano and Lubbock, but since Plano is largely a suburb of Dallas, Monroe and TPC opted for Lubbock, since it also leaned heavily conservative, but was isolated enough to be considered rural. They did not want to be seen as playing to only the major cities. And that ruled out Dallas.

Taylor for President booked the exhibit hall at the Lubbock Memorial Civic Center. When Taylor One pulled into the gate at Preston Smith International Airport, they were greeted by supporters waving placards at curbside. Monroe surged into the crowd and met a few of the local campaign office managers and other volunteers. After pleasantries the volunteers assured him a full house for tomorrow's town hall.

"I hope you didn't pack the theater with only supporters!" Taylor shouted over the cheers. "I'm viewing this as an opportunity to change minds!"

Ted turned to Sandra and deadpanned, "Not to worry."

The entourage got to the hotel and checked in. Blake quickly unpacked his laptop on the blonde laminate desk, plugged in the charger, and logged on using the fingerprint swipe as his cell phone vibrated and played the first notes of Copland's *Fanfare for the Common Man*. That was Ted's ringtone. He answered and Ted asked if he could drop by one of the suites upstairs. It was extremely urgent, and would only take a minute. "Sure," Blake replied earnestly but uncomfortably. He hung up his garment bag, ditched the suitcase on the folding stand, grabbed a bottle of water out of habit, and then feeling his gut rumble, he returned the water to the minibar. He headed up to the suite, rapped twice, and was startled when Monroe opened it immediately. "Come on in, Blake," intoned Monroe evenly. He motioned to a dining table that was bare. At the table sat Sam, Phil, Ron Le Quang, and Ted. They were quietly chatting. The presence of Ron made Blake's mouth go dry. He thought of the bottle of water as he took his seat across from Monroe.

As Blake sat down, Fuller was lifting Blake's laptop from his room.

"Blake," began Monroe, his elbows resting on the table and his fingers templed before his mouth. "We have reason to believe you have been contacted by the opposition." Blake started to object, but Monroe raised his palm toward him to silence the incipient protest. "We're going to ask you some questions, and then Ron is going to ask you some more questions. Ron will then make a determination as to whether or not we should get the authorities involved. What I want to know is, how long have you been working for Harlon Michaels?"

"I don't work for Harlon Michaels!" rasped Blake. "Why would you think that?"

Ted considered that while the response was pretty convincing, the act needed a little work. Blake was clearly stressed, and any polygraph styluses would have been dancing if they were monitoring his vitals. "Look," started Ted. "We have you dead-to-rights. You're the one who has been leaking embarrassing details to the press, you're the one who has been passing Monroe's mobile phone numbers to Denise Dexter. What else have you been up to? You might as well admit it, because we're going to find out."

Blake remained silent but not quite stoic. Monroe was not surprised. He had figured that the threat of legal action imposed by Ron Le Quang would have little effect if he was being handled by Harlon's crew. They had pockets as deep as his own. But Blake did not strike him as the type that would be deceitful. Unless his radar was way off on this one, Blake just did not come across as a Bible-thumping, ultraconservative, right-leaning operative. And his acting skills were just not that good. He looked like he might piss himself. Or worse.

"Blake, I'm very disappointed." Monroe spoke softly, reminding himself of Al Pacino in *The Godfather*. Michael talking to Carlo before they garrote him in the car. He pushed the risible similarity out of his mind. "I had you pegged for a man of loyalty. Someone I could count on. I'm rarely such a poor judge of character. Ted and I were really taken by you leaving your job at APC to come join our campaign. I guess that was part of the master plan. Harlon got to you back then through APC. Are they in on it?"

"When did Harlon's people approach you, Blake?" asked Phil.

"You might remember signing a confidentiality agreement with us," suggested Sam, a look of disgust on his face. Sam was particularly pissed. This infiltration was a reflection on his organization. On him personally. He had already pressed Ron to bring in the authorities. He was not about to have his firm tarnished like this. This was like a fire in a coal mine. Deadly.

CHAPTER 20

"Alright, I think we're done here," sighed Monroe dejectedly, getting up. Sam, Phil, Ted, and Blake rose. "Not you," said the still-seated Ronald to Blake. The four others exited, nodding to Fuller, who was waiting outside with Blake's laptop tucked under his arm.

Ronald Le Quang was not a trial lawyer, he was a procedural lawyer. But he could be a regular son-of-a-bitch. He turned now to Blake Mrzowski and regarded him much as a hyena would a wildebeest carcass. "Mr. Mrzowski, you are in serious trouble. We have you facing both criminal and civil charges. I am certain you have the advantage of the deep financial pockets of your handlers, and that may help you in a civil judgment. But whatever the Michaels cabal has told you about white-collar prisons, I can assure you they sugar-coated it. That is," he hesitated, "IF you are convicted of something innocuous."

"I told you already, I do not work for Harlon Michaels!"

"We have a forensic accountant foraging through your expenses. Tonya Jackson is conducting a background review of your calls. Fuller Thompson is examining your hard drives and the secure server. I assure you that none of these incursions are illegal since the cell phones and laptops and servers are owned by TPC. Further, I assure you that whatever we find will be used to cast you in a most undesirable light before the District Court. We intend to, quite literally, make a federal case out of this."

The door was unlocked by a card reader and clicked open to admit Fuller Thompson, looking serene. He greeted Ronald warmly and smiled unctuously at Blake.

"Hello, Blake," began Fuller, sounding so calm and friendly that Blake understood it meant that Fuller had uncovered something. "Welcome to Lubbock." He set up the laptop and powered it on.

173

"You need anything? Some water? A Dos Equis? Glenlivet? Hemlock? You wanna phone a friend? Use one of your lifelines? Maybe you want to call Harlon's lawyers. Though I can't imagine why. We certainly do not have the authority to place you under arrest. But we do have the authority to press charges. Ronald, what's the name of that nice young Special Agent you spoke to this morning? Darryl Something . . ."

Blake rolled his head and blurted, "It's PDS! There's a liberal Super PAC called Progressive Democratic Socialists. They asked me to keep an eye on Taylor when I was with APC. They're afraid he's going to split the left and give Trump another term. Goddamnit! I need a rest room!" he pleaded.

They excused him and looked at each other. "What's on that laptop?" asked Ronald.

"Nothing I can find," whispered Fuller. "This was a total bluff. I've never seen anyone fold that fast. I could have kept him going for hours. We DO have him on violating the NDA. Let's see what else we can get out of him."

Blake returned, his rep tie loose around his open collar, his face flushed. He walked slowly to the couch, sat down, and got up again to go back to the bathroom.

"What the hell did you guys do to him?" asked Fuller. Ronald shrugged nonchalantly. "We should probably at least follow the Geneva Convention."

The toilet flushed, and they heard water running in the sink for about a minute. Blake returned and sat back down on the couch. The room felt unnaturally hot to him. It was. Under Fuller's instructions, everyone else had been advised to dress casually. Blake was known as a clothes horse, very professional. An hour before Blake was summoned, Ronald had set the temperature to eighty-five degrees. Fuller had also seen to it that Blake had a couple of bran muffins and creamy coffee for breakfast on Taylor One. The others had distracted him with enough tasks to keep him occupied until he was summoned.

"Who approached you?"

"Jonathon Stengel at APC. He's tied in with PDS."

"Is he your handler?"

"No. He's sort of like a facilitator for PDS. The handler is, I don't know who the handler is. It's all very cloak-and-dagger. I pass info to files on a secure site."

"What kind of info? Audio? Video? Text?"

"It's mostly text files, but sometimes . . . well, you already know . . ." his voice trailed off weakly. "I guess it doesn't matter now."

"Do you have a codeword for being discovered?"

"Yes."

"What is it?"

"'I'll be taking some time off.'"

"Wow, that really is a good one, Blake. You are a workaholic. Have you had any time off since the campaign started?"

"Not much."

"You'll be getting some now. But don't tell your handler."

·   ·   ·

DAVID EVANS HAD FLOWN OUT to Lubbock to host the town hall. No one mistook him for a moderator, since he was firmly entrenched in the campaign and in the employ of Taylor For President. The format was going to include opening remarks by Monroe, followed by questions from a panel, as well as questions from the audience. It promised to be exciting TV since the panel included local conservative media, and Lubbock boasted a conservative majority. The national cable news organizations were present as well as network coverage. They prayed their silent prayers for newsworthy sound bites as they ran through their sound checks. Maybe the candidate would commit some unforgiveable *faux pas*.

The Lubbock Memorial Civic Center's exhibit hall seats three thousand people. TPC had ensured that there was a legitimate number of tickets available for the throng ringed outside at dusk. Sam and Phil were determined not to be subject to the humiliation that greeted them in Des Moines. Camera crews were interviewing skeptical voters snaking through the parking lot. There was already a buzz of excitement in the area as Ted and Monroe pulled up after an early dinner. "Sam must be giving away free beer," cracked Monroe weakly.

"We should be so lucky," countered Ted. He was gentle and a little concerned for Monroe. He hoped there would be no unforgivable *faux pas*.

They exited the black SUV at the rear of the Civic Center and entered a back door flanked by two stocky, but retired, state patrolmen with buzz cuts and sunglasses. TPC had been beefing up the presence of bodyguards for three reasons. The first reason was that because Monroe was not a party candidate, the US Secret Service was not on the hook to provide protection. The second reason was that they felt exposed to the lunatic fringe that had been protesting the campaign events. And the third and best reason was that it provided a visual indicator to the media and the crowds that he was a VIP. Someone who deserved protection. Monroe and Ted had bought into all three reasons. The retired troopers were all very fit, and very professional. They had been screened to promote a professional image and provide an intimidating appearance. They exuded confidence, and were not averse to bringing order to chaotic situations. Monroe had learned all of their names, and Phil had taken the extra step to provide background about their families so Monroe could make polite inquiries of them.

David Evans was schmoozing in the corridors outside the dressing rooms backstage where the on-stage talent were having their makeup applied. He rapped on Monroe's door jamb and saw Ted leaning against a counter stacked with makeup. In a barber's chair was Monroe, sitting patiently with a barber's striped apron around his neck. A technician was applying a light foundation to his face while another was testing the wireless microphone that he would wear tonight, clipped to his lapel. The sound tech was uttering staccato syllables softly into the mike while other invisible techs in control rooms inside the arena and in various sound trucks parked outside monitored their frequency responses and tweaked their sibilant levels. Kurt was in the auditorium control room monitoring the technicians.

Evans was quietly impressed with how cool Monroe appeared. The guy really did have a natural talent for media coverage, and coupled with his inside understanding of how journalists thought and how he had perfected his craft, it was small wonder. Still, thought Evans, this is the national stage, and Monroe was taking it in stride.

Monroe was chatting with Ted and Phil about some of the anticipated topics.

"That's what you get when you don't preview the questions," opined Ted to a facetious complaint that Monroe had just made. "This is gonna be like improv night at the Funny Bone."

"I'd feel better if your simile had been 'open mike night at a coffee club.' But no. You have to cow me with a comedy club comparison." He paused and looked around moving only his eyes, as the tech sprayed some glue-like product on his hair. "What! No one caught that alliterative turn?"

Evans motioned to Ted to be careful about where he leaned. His light gray trousers were perilously close to some dark-colored eyeliners that were lying open on the laminate countertop. He turned to Monroe with a confident smile.

"Okay, Champ, you'll go on in about forty-five minutes." Evans was the only person in the campaign who could conceivably get away with calling the candidate anything but "Monroe," "Mr. Taylor," or "Sir." He cultivated a familiarity with even casual acquaintances that naturally put his audience at ease. His mere acknowledgement of your presence was enough to lift the spirits of the most indifferent of personalities. "I'll be on in about thirty minutes to warm up the crowd, then I'll introduce the panel, who will make brief statements regarding their qualifications and interest in participating. By which I mean, they will state for the record to what right-wing fanatical organizations they belong. Then I will introduce you. You'll be off stage but you'll be able to hear everything that is being said, and if everything goes as Gary has planned, you'll also be able to watch it on the monitors and listen through your earpiece. So there ought not to be any surprises other than the questions you haven't previewed. Piece of cake!"

"Mmm. Glad to hear it. Thanks for the vote of confidence, David. Break a leg."

"Toi, toi, toi!" replied Evans, knocking on a wood desk. He exited into the corridor, slapped a cameraman on the back and shook his hand, and took his place offstage to examine the energy level of the crowd. He felt the familiar tickle on his neck and shoulders that preceded moments of professional and entertainment excitement.

The lights dimmed a few times, signaling that the event was about to begin. David trotted up the stairs on stage left, and paused, realizing that something was out of sequence. The panel was already on stage at their table, and he heard a microphone click followed by a basso-profundo voice saying, "Ladies and gentlemen. Please rise for the National Anthem."

Offstage, Monroe started and then stopped like a deer in the headlights. The incipient roll of the snare drum had already started, and if he sprinted now he would be too late. He turned to Ted beside him and uttered "Goddamnit!" into his live mike.

Fortunately the sound techs had the mike's output level adjusted low in case he sneezed or made comments prior to when he should be heard. The only people who appeared to hear the

Independent Candidate swear at the start of the National Anthem were those in the control room, and half a dozen random people clustered about him who would have heard him without the microphone.

David placed his hand over his heart and stood at attention while the cameras rolled and a recording played a rousing rendition of the *Star Spangled Banner*. What the cameras could not capture was Ted and Monroe offstage, their hands over their hearts, standing at attention. Monroe sorted through the jumble of thoughts that now fought for his attention: "Who am I going to fire over this?" and "This is a really good recording of the National Anthem. I wonder who did it?" and "If this town liked me, they would not have played a recording. They would have had their high school band here playing live."

David thanked the crowd for coming out to meet the candidate, and he assured them of an interesting evening. He thanked Lubbock for its hospitality, and proceeded to explain that his own personal connection to North Central Texas was important to him because of his southern upbringing in a conservative family in rural North Carolina. Though his reputation was cemented farther east, he was less well-known west of the Mississippi, and he was compelled to provide some additional details from his childhood that engaged the crowd and was designed to relax them. He was one of them. After a couple anecdotes, he took a more serious tone and described the failure of American political discourse. He explained that the audience was in for a treat, because tonight they had access in a town-hall format to the most exciting presidential candidate this campaign cycle. He introduced the panel.

"From the local FOX affiliate, the lovely and talented Stacy Arnheim; from the *Lubbock Standard-Bearer*, the incomparable

Tom Flanders, and from Panhandle Media Group in Amarillo, the hard-hitting Clay Stuyvesant."

The three panel members were all well-known to the audience. Each made a brief statement thanking the city and David and the Taylor campaign for the opportunity to participate in the town hall. David laid out the rules of engagement for the audience and then introduced Monroe, who was overcompensating for his earlier outburst by strolling almost too casually to the stage. He turned to the audience as he walked and smiled and waved.

The crowd gave up polite applause with a few shouts of "YOU GO MONROE" which were followed by chuckles. "At least you didn't protest," he began self-deprecatingly.

"The reason I am in Lubbock tonight is because it is one of the most conservative regions in the United States. I don't like preaching to the choir. The president is fond of rallies that are stacked with his supporters, and they adore him. I am happy to walk into the lion's den and try to tame them with reason rather than slogans."

There were a couple of boos. "Go ahead," Monroe raised his right arm gesturing in the direction of the boos. "Go ahead and voice your dissent. But please follow the rules tonight because we have a lot of ground to cover and I want to address as many of your questions as possible."

Stacy Arnheim began, "Mr. Monroe, you have been an outspoken critic of President Trump. Because your platform contains many left-leaning planks, why don't you simply run as a Democrat?"

"It's true that I have been an outspoken critic of the president. I hope I am THE MOST outspoken critic of Donald Trump. Donald Trump is the reason I have sacrificed my fortune to run for the highest office in the land. For two years I sat around seething about how poorly he has done, but without a background or head start in politics, and without a war chest, I felt powerless, as so many Americans feel powerless to effect change in a lethargic and ineffective government.

"But I reject your assertion that our platform leans in any direction. Have you read our platform policies? We want a strong defense. We want safe communities. We want a robust economy. We want to do all the positive things that both Republicans and Democrats want to do, but are incapable of doing because of their religious adherence to party politics."

Stacy followed up. "Yes, sir, I have read your platform position, and it certainly seems to be highly critical of the Republicans."

"Again Stacy, you are correct, but not correct enough," retorted Monroe. "I am critical of the president. The government is flawed in many critical ways, but the reason I stand before you tonight is Donald Trump." More boos. "The Republican party has changed course under his rudder."

Clay Stuyvesant adopted a skeptical expression and requested a clarification. "Mr. Taylor, we understand you hate the president. But you claim to have equal disdain for the Democrats, even though you seem to be much fonder of their policies. And of Obama and Hillary for that matter."

"Another great question. Thank you. Listen, I am no apologist for Obama. I feel that he could have done so much more, but we have to look back at the hand he was dealt. There had been an economic collapse under a lame-duck president, the national debt was skyrocketing on account of the War On Terror, the bailouts of the auto makers and the banks. He was faced with an absolutely obstructionist Congress led by Mitch McConnell. They hated him and the hard-line Republicans in the House and Senate were determined to defeat him. The Tea Party held up budgets and shut down the government. That's no way to lead.

"But could he have done more? Yes, I think so. What's going to be his legacy? First black president? The guy who got Bin Laden? I would have liked to see him engage more across party lines.

"Now you also asked me about Hillary Clinton. Like too few Americans, I approached the last election with an open mind. I wanted to withhold judgment until I got a better feel for the candidates. Did you watch the debates? Clinton destroyed Trump in every one of them. She came across as 'presidential,' which the media wonks are always so wrought over. What was clear throughout the election cycle though, was that there were so many Americans who just despised Hillary Clinton. And what was equally clear was that had she, in fact, won the election, Congress would have obstructed her as bad as or worse than they did with Obama. So I'm not sure the country would be any better off with her."

"LOCK HER UP!" shouted someone.

"Yeah. Here's the problem," continued Monroe in a casual tone. "An untethered Donald Trump is no better than an obstructed Hillary Clinton. Probably worse, but we can let history decide. Those slogans that he promotes are mindless, divisive, and contrary to common sense." There followed a prolonged chorus of boos, shouting, and whistles. This wasn't going well.

Monroe paused and then held up his hands and began speaking again, in a voice loud enough to be heard over the decrescendoing tumult. For an instant, he felt like he was trying to reason with a mob armed with pitchforks. He suppressed those emotions, realizing that this was another in a string of make-or-break moments for him and the campaign. "Look, disagree if you want. That's a right granted to you by the First Amendment. The same amendment that Donald Trump attacks and undercuts with every tweet, every rally. Go ahead and give away your freedoms.

Watch them erode. Watch the Bill of Rights be torn up before your eyes. Ladies and gentlemen, I cannot let that happen. Not because I hate Donald Trump. But because I am an American. I will defend your right to disagree with me. When Trump disagrees with a particular news report, it's 'fake news.' I'm here to tell you that some news is fake. Like anything that comes out of Sarah Huckabee Sanders' office. Like anything on social media planted by Russian trolls. But I also want to let you know that any serious journalist, politician, or student of American democracy must embrace a free press. It's called 'accountability,' and you better start to hold your president accountable. So yeah. Lock her up, build the wall, those are a lot easier to digest than, 'We the people of the United States, in order to form a more perfect union, establish justice, insure domestic tranquility, provide for the common defense, promote the general welfare, and secure the blessings of liberty to ourselves and our posterity, do ordain and establish this Constitution of the United States.'

"Forgive my lack of perception, but I just do not see Donald Trump forming a more perfect union by sowing division, nor establishing justice by not calling out neo-Nazis in Charlottesville, nor insuring domestic tranquility by attacking the media, nor providing for the common defense by alienating our allies, nor promoting the general welfare by eviscerating the EPA and racking up even more debt with harebrained schemes like the wall and a 'Star Force.'

"By the way, my dad fought in World War Two. The Greatest Generation would not be amused to see a president who has any sympathy for neo-Nazis. Neither do I for that matter, and I can't hold a candle to my dad."

Some of the people in the front row were taken aback by the intensity of Monroe's expression, and the sincerity in his tone.

The cameras had zoomed in on him and the monitors inside the Civic Center had picked it up also. Viewers at home also got to see the reaction of a few people in the front rows. They looked thoughtful. The crowd fell silent, and then there was some applause from a few supporters who did not need to be convinced. Their applause was joined by some of the more thoughtful attendees. It was not a roar of approval, but it did seem to stem the tide of disapproval, and that was enough for Monroe and Ted and Phil to take as a solid win.

David Evans moved in to moderate some questions from the audience. First up was a fiftyish lady in conservative dress. She was soft spoken and had a typical central Texas lilt to her voice. "Hello, my name is Constance Blakely, and I am a professor of economics at Texas Tech." There was a chorus of "GUNS UP" from some stalwart Red Raiders.

"Let's hear it for the Second Amendment," joked Monroe to some appreciative guffaws. Half the crowd thought he was a supporter and the other half, knowing his opposition to the NRA, was in on the irony.

Constance Blakely hesitated, looked around anxiously until the noise died down, and continued, clearly uncomfortable that she has been interrupted. "My question is, what do you have against President Trump's trade policies?"

"Thanks for that question, Constance. The president's tariffs really amount to a tax, and that tax is ultimately paid for by consumers of those goods. I had a contractor in Pennsylvania tell me the other day that he was working on a project that had the first stick of US-made stainless steel piping that he had seen on a job in years. He used that to illustrate that the tariffs are working. We're using American steel. Well, the reason they are using American steel is that the cost of foreign steel is matching what American steel costs. It's not that any new pipe mills have been built. It takes years to design and construct a steel mill. Those tariffs did not create any new jobs. Except for the US Steel blast furnaces in Granite City that started up. Which put a thousand or so people to work, and created temporary engineering and construction jobs. Great. That's good. But weigh that against a TWELVE. BILLION. DOLLAR. Emergency aid package for farmers who were hit by retaliatory tariffs. And poking our allies in the eye with a stick. That's a seriously bad move. The US needs our allies."

A burly man with thick forearms and a patchy beard was next in line. He was wearing a red MAKE AMERICA GREAT AGAIN hat and an XXL Carhartt T-shirt that was straining at the seams. He took the mike from one of the moderators in the aisle and said, "America is the greatest country on earth, and President Donald Trump is the greatest president! We don't need no allies! What we need is a WALL!"

A chorus of "USA! USA! USA!" thundered through the hall. Monroe crossed his arms and chuckled. Offstage Phil turned to Ted and said incredulously, "He actually looks like he's having fun up there! Jesus!"

His arms also folded, Ted turned to Phil, and keeping his eyes on the stage, assured him, "He is. That's our man!"

"First of all, America does need allies, especially today. We have military bases in over seventy countries. Those all require some level of cooperation with the foreign country and local support. Second, America cannot defend our interests in the rest of the world without our allies. It's just impossible. There are simply too many threats. So it is in America's interests to maintain relationships that have been forged with the blood of Americans. It does no good to antagonize Angela Merkel, or Justin Trudeau, or

Theresa May, or Emmanuel Macron, or Shinzo Abe, or Malcolm Turnbull. These are important alliances because of geography, trade, and democratic governments."

Tom Flanders from the *Standard-Bearer* interrupted, "Scott Morrison is the Prime Minister of Australia now, Mr. Monroe. Malcolm Turnbull left office in August 2018. As a candidate for president, I would have thought you'd be more current in your foreign affairs."

A smattering of catcalls called attention to the one-upmanship.

"Well, of course you are correct Mr. Flanders," conceded Monroe, turning to address him. "However, Trump and Turnbull did have a contentious relationship. And speaking of contentious relationships, I do not consider the European Union to be a 'foe.'"

"Third, I would want to get some feedback from citizens of border states. And actually all of the states heavily dependent on agriculture . . . but the reality is, a wall is not going to keep illegal immigrants out. US agriculture is heavily dependent on migrant farm labor. Americans are not gonna pick produce. It's been proven time and time again. The way to handle illegal immigration is to ensure that the standard of living in poor countries south of the border improves, and ensure that US employers hire legal, documented labor, so everyone is paying their fair share of taxes and Social Security so that access to public services can be funded.

"Sure, you can build the wall. For seventy BILLION dollars. And Mexico is NOT paying for it. You are. And it can be tunneled under or climbed over. And even if it keeps out all those 'filthy immigrants,' what then? Who's going to harvest the produce? You? Your teenaged son? I don't think so. You'll end up paying two dollars for a tomato. Or plowing under fields of rotting produce. Or importing vegetables from Peru. I guess we could always put a tariff on foreign vegetables too though.

"Finally, nice hat. I always thought America was pretty great to begin with. There is plenty of room for improvement though, right? I mean the US is behind Slovenia in math, science, and reading, which, if you're Melania Trump is good news/bad news. We're something like twenty-fifth in health care access and quality. Number one in incarceration though, so . . .

"But honestly, I felt like the criticism of the whole MAGA thing was unwarranted. There were people who were saying that it was dog-whistle politics for racism. I just don't get that. That's a trumped-up criticism. The media doesn't have to have apoplexy over every single thing the guy does. The truth is bad enough."

Tom Flanders addressed Monroe. "Mr. Monroe, some of us heard an untoward comment from your side of the stage during the playing of the National Anthem. Could you elucidate your patriotic views?"

Oh for Christ's sake. Here we go. His ears felt hot, and he knew the blood was rising. He hoped the makeup might camouflage his reaction. He thought if he moved, the air motion might cool him off and the motion might make it more difficult for the high-def cameras to pick up the crimson now rising to the rest of his face. Yeah, right. He moved anyway to the side of the stage where he entered.

"You mean from over here?" he asked, gesturing offstage. "Yes, you probably heard me voice some disappointment over the planning that did not permit me to be onstage while the National Anthem was playing. I would have appreciated the chance to show my respect. If you'd like to join me, Mr. Flanders, we could regale the crowd with all four verses of the National Anthem. Although I have to admit, I do not have a very good singing voice. But I do know all the words. The third verse is particularly haunting, as it recalls the horrors of war.

"Incidentally, I am in favor of a law that prohibits singers at sporting events from embellishing any portion of the melody of the National Anthem. It's a beautiful, moving song as written." That drew massive applause, whistles, and cheers throughout. It was clearly in jest, but everyone understood there was a kernel of truth to it.

"That should shut the little cocksucker up," remarked Ted to Phil.

"I should say so, but I'm afraid Monroe is a little bit pissed over that lack of planning," admitted Phil.

"I should say so," replied Ted dryly.

Another question came from a fortyish man wearing a suit. "Good evening," he said in a resonant baritone voice. "My name is Joshua Jacobs, and I am the pastor of the First Baptist Church in Wilburn, Texas. There has been some coverage of your religious beliefs, but not enough to satisfy our Christian communities. I would like you to expound your views on religion, and what role it plays in your daily life."

"Thank you, Reverend. There has not been much coverage of my religious views because in the United States, there is no religious test for public office. Period. I am not ashamed of my upbringing as a Roman Catholic, but my personal religious views are entirely separate from my views on public policy."

Clay Stuyvesant weighed in. "Follow up, Mr. Monroe. The question is really how your religious views affect your daily life, your decision-making, and your ability to lead and make policy."

"Again, my religious views are personal."

"Do you go to church?"

"I occasionally attend mass."

"How is the voting public supposed to judge your ethics? You claim you are ethical, yet you attend religious services only occasionally. At least John F. Kennedy said he wouldn't be taking advice from the Vatican!"

Monroe was flummoxed. He wanted to throttle this jackass. He started to formulate a reply that began with "Look, . . ." but he recalled Kurt's observation that sentences that began with "Listen" or "Look" made him sound like he was pissed off. Which by now he was. But he realized that he needed to reel it in too. On camera, he appeared to hesitate a couple times as he wound his way through an appropriate response.

"Religion is a personal matter. The right to practice any religion is guaranteed under the First Amendment. My ethical views are guided by traditional Judeo-Christian concepts and Western philosophy. But fine. You asked about my religion and so I will tell you plainly.

"There are some people who convert to a religion. I don't know how many, but it has to be less than 1 percent. Wouldn't you agree? There are not many Christians who wake up and decide, 'Oh well, I think Shinto is for me after all.' Not many Jews who convert to LDS after reading the Book of Mormon in a hotel room. It happens, but not very often. One's religion is largely an accident of birth. You're probably going to become what your parents are. Or you may convert to a religion if you happen to fall in love with someone from a different religion. Those are personal decisions, left to individuals, and there is no mandate or precedent to practice any form of religion as President of the United States.

"Leaders must often make terrible decisions. The decision to send troops to war. Decisions that will affect the health and welfare of citizens. There ought to be some level of ethics in that decision-making process, but the overarching guideline needs to be to preserve, protect, and defend the Constitution of the United

States. The President of the United States needs to make decisions that will sometimes run counter to the New Testament."

Stuyvesant was unconvinced and undeterred. This was going to be his sound bite. "Mr. Monroe," he drawled unctuously. "You are an unmarried man, and we have seen considerable evidence of some pretty unsavory behavior in your social life. It seems to me that these are ethical matters that speak volumes of your character."

"Mmm." Monroe shook his head. "Do you really want to go there, Mr. Stuyvesant? The religious right has traditionally voted for Conservatives. That's a lock the Republicans have, right? Family values. Christianity. Evangelicalism. The moral high ground. And yet Evangelicals voted overwhelmingly for Trump! By what yardstick are they measuring ethics? Morals? I mean, 'Let he who is without sin cast the first stone,' but give me a break! You're going to compare my social life against a man who was recorded saying he grabs women by the genitals? Who has been accused of sexual harassment? Who has yet to release his tax returns? Why has the religious right been so quiet about such obvious turpitude?"

Phil pressed close to Ted and hissed, "Please, please, please don't go with the 'fornicated, urinated, illuminated' line. Just shut up already!"

Ted looked at him, annoyed.

David Evans stepped in. "We have time for one or possibly two more questions. Yes sir. You there. Please state your name and your question."

A handsome, middle-aged, but youthful-looking man in a western shirt and a cowboy hat reached for the offered microphone. "Thank you. My name is Brett Simmons. I am a builder in Lubbock. I've been listening to these explanations and excuses all night, and it makes me about sick. Obama was a weak president who bowed to the Muslims! Donald Trump is STRONG! Obama and Clinton were weak! Donald Trump won! Hillary lost! Get over it, Snowflake!"

The crowd reaction was mixed, with many approving hoots and guffaws, and a nearly equal number of ambiguous boos.

Monroe took the measure of the man before him before replying. "Mr. Simmons, I'm not here to defend Hillary Clinton. It's true she lost. We all lost that night. We had a choice of two candidates who were divisive in their own way. Clinton because she is married to Bill Clinton and had all of his baggage, and Trump because he was ill-equipped to lead this country. I get that some people simply hated Hillary Clinton, just as there are some people who were 'never Trump-ers.' I am a bit of a historian, but I am here tonight because I believe in the future. I'm not wringing my hands about the past.

"You mentioned Obama bowing to the Muslims. That's often cited by ultraconservative wing-nuts as his 'apology tour.' Those same people say that such actions diminish the prestige of the presidency, and humiliate the US. Yet these same people are silent when Donald Trump embraces and heaps praise on Vladimir Putin and Kim Jong-un.

"Yet I give Trump credit where it is due. I do not believe that meeting with despots grants legitimacy. I believe in engagement. I have never understood this legitimacy argument. I'm just trying to illustrate the double standard.

"Listen," Monroe concluded patiently. "I'm not trying to run a negative campaign. But it's impossible to overlook the damage being done to America by Donald Trump. Any luster accorded the Office of the Presidency has been corroded by Trump. I wish it were otherwise."

"What about Benghazi?" demanded Simmons defiantly. Another chorus of cheers.

Oh for Christ's sake! What is it with these idiots and Benghazi? Aloud, he said, "What about Benghazi?" And immediately he realized the unfortunate parallelism with Gary Johnson's Aleppo comment and quickly moved on.

"Any loss of life like that is, of course, tragic. For those of you who need a refresher, on September 11, 2012, there was an attack on two US government facilities in Benghazi, Libya. There were two State Department employees killed, including Ambassador Stevens, and two CIA contractors killed. It was a tragic loss of life and in the immediate aftermath one of the reasons for the attack was purported to be an internet video that was alleged to be critical of the Prophet Mohammed. That was a bogus idea that was floated by the administration, and there was a lot of confusion about whether Clinton declined a request for increased security there, or whether Obama issued a stand-down order to prevent a rescue, or general negligence by the administration.

"And after six investigations by Republican-controlled congressional committees, no cover-up or accusation that was leveled against Hillary Clinton or Obama, or any senior official for that matter, was found to have merit.

"I already said I am not here to defend either Hillary Clinton or Barack Obama. I have issues with both.

"But while we're at it, thanks for bringing up another important point: Why does the United States rely on contract security firms to protect assets overseas? If there aren't enough highly skilled Marines to go around, let's get more! Why are for-profit companies and individuals getting rich off of providing security that ought to be provided by the armed forces?"

Evans wound up the event by thanking the audience, the panel members, and the television viewers. Monroe posed for photos with some of his local supporters. There were quite a few more than anyone expected. One elderly man approached Monroe with an outstretched hand and explained, "I was dead-set again' ya when I came in tonight, but ya made some purty good points! I'm still gonna vote Republican though!"

· · ·

"CARLA, I THINK YOU DESERVE HARDSHIP PAY for having to sit through that last night!" The host shook her head slowly, a sad, sympathetic display of disbelief for her colleague.

"Yeah, Samantha, it was really tough to stomach, to handle it. The whole thing was staged like it was some kind of Broadway production, like 'Hamilton' or something, and this Lubbock audience just was not falling for it."

"Yeah," sneered the hostess derisively. "It was pretty clear from the outset that an East Coast liberal was not going to put one over on the hardworking folks of Lubbock, Texas. That was like trying to mix oil and water!"

"Certainly, Samantha. Taylor's answers were so stilted. He tries so hard to impress his audiences. We've seen this behavior again and again, where he talks like some kind of elitist professor. Like he is so intelligent and superior, trying to speak over everyone's head. Many in the audience complained afterward about his vocabulary."

They showed a clip of several of the attendees of the town hall meeting being interviewed. One woman in a MAGA sweatshirt was asked what she thought of the candidate. "He ain't one of us!" she cautioned. "He seemed like a pompous a—," the word was bleeped from the interview. "That's what we love about Donald Trump. We understand him! He's one of us!"

The next interviewee was a youngish guy with a wispy goatee. He shook his head slowly from side to side and chuckled,
"'Elucidate' and 'turpitude' . . . heh. I mean, he just came off as
kind of a jerk."

Kurt changed channels, trying to find a more sympathetic station. Seated around a glass desk covered with coffee mugs and laptops
was a panel of five or six wonks, dissecting Monroe's performance.

". . . did pretty well expounding on his views regarding foreign
and domestic policy."

"And Steven, it was a hostile crowd, right?"

"Yes, Mark, in fact, Taylor acknowledged that he felt like Daniel
entering the lion's den. And unbelievably, this event was completely
unscripted. It takes some real intestinal fortitude to walk into a hostile
venue like the Lubbock Civic Center and try to tame those lions.
Taylor's remarks were often reinforced by biblical references, which
we have seen him do from time to time. And with the conservative
crowd, last night they were probably particularly well-timed."

"That's what I'm talking about!" exclaimed Kurt to Ted and
Phil, who were waiting for Monroe to get off the phone. Kurt
pumped his fist and paced in front of the TV, tiny beads of sweat
glistening on his head.

Ted looked inquiringly at Monroe as he pocketed the cell
phone. "That was Fred During. I'm getting sued by Denise Dexter
for sexual harassment."

Phil immediately dialed Fuller Thompson and said, "It's on."
Then he called Sam and told him the news. That started a chain
reaction that forced Gary Davidson to draft a response to the
lawsuit for the media.

Gary was downstairs in another suite. He shot an email out
to his team to call an emergency meeting. The email to Blake
bounced back with text that said:

"Your email was not delivered to the following recipients: *blake.k.mrzowski@taylor2020.us*

Reply text:550 User 'blake.k.mrzowski' Unknown"

"What the hell," mumbled Gary. Then shouting, "Kate, get me Blake! And get the guy who does our IT stuff!"

"Blake usually takes care of our IT on the road, Gary."

"Well, get him down here on the double! We have a problem! We have a few problems."

Had Ronald thought Blake was a flight risk he would have sworn out a criminal complaint. As it was, Blake had decided to cooperate so he remained at the hotel in Lubbock with minimal supervision. Blake's phone played the first notes of the theme to *Mission Impossible* in Fuller's coat pocket. Fuller had confiscated the phone. He turned to Ronald, and glancing back to Blake said, "that will be Gary, I guess, panicking about Denise Dexter." He sighed, and looking at the incoming call realized that it was Katherine Frachette, one of Gary's minions.

"Hi Kate. This is Fuller Thompson. Blake is indisposed at the moment." Pause. "No, he won't be available for quite some time. I'll explain to Gary in a few minutes."

Fuller politely excused himself and exited the room, leaving Ronald Le Quang to monitor Blake. He took the prudent but unnecessary additional precaution of repositioning one of Monroe's security detail officers outside the room with a pass key to enter if necessary.

"What are you doing here?" asked Gary, his eyebrows knit together in a look of incredulity. Gary was a high-energy guy, not prone to fits of rage or impassioned pleas. The knitting of his brow was evidence enough to Fuller that he was having a really bad day.

"Relax, Gary," comforted Fuller, his slender hand pressed on Gary's shoulder. They hardly ever worked together, their skill sets being so different, but Gary found the gesture oddly reassuring. Fuller applied his calming dispassionate voice to lull Gary into believing that everything was going to be alright. "I know about Denise Dexter, and we are going to take care of it."

The calming technique wore off instantly. "Take care of it? How in holy hell are YOU gonna take care of it? This is a PR matter, and. . . . Where the hell is Blake, anyway?"

"Let's step outside." The room was full of campaign staff, hotel staff refilling the minibar, and several other people that Fuller could not identify. He escorted Gary into the hall and explained how Blake was compromised. Gary listened raptly, interjecting grunts of disbelief at all of the appropriate places. Fuller cautioned him that because he was trying to turn Blake to gain counterintelligence, Gary was now obliged to keep quiet on the matter. He also reassured him that Denise Dexter had been under investigation by his team, and that they had actually discovered enough compromising information about her to discredit her claims.

Once Gary had settled back behind his laptop, he received a call from Phil, requesting a brief meeting with the candidate. Gary hightailed it to Monroe's suite. "Alright," exhaled Monroe. "Let me give you the lay of the land re Denise."

Ted silently debated whether he should make a "lay of the land" gag about Denise, but prudently restrained himself.

Monroe brought the TPC team up to speed with his views on Denise. He explained that Denise was a former employee, and they had enjoyed a close friendship for awhile, but his work drove them apart. She had a few issues with some of the other women at the newspaper, and there had been some unspecified but nasty cattiness. She left to find other employment, but they stayed in casual contact. Her brother was a real dirt bag, and she was in a chronic state of financial peril on account of his bad decisions. Fuller took note that this explanation dovetailed into what he and Tonya had uncovered, although Monroe either chose not to mention or did not know about the brother's many failed businesses or his alcoholism. Fuller also noted that it was more than likely that Monroe was familiar with Denise's status as a party girl.

"Now where is Blake? What did you get out of him?"

"Blake is being questioned by Ronald and me. He has admitted to spying for an organization called 'Progressive Democratic Socialists,' and the pretext is that the Left might use information to keep you from becoming a spoiler. Ronald threatened him with criminal action, and I am trying to use that to turn him so we can gain counterintelligence."

"Fuck that noise," snarled Ted. "We need to fire that little son of a bitch!"

There was some reactionary movement by the TPC team, but Monroe agreed. "No. Ted's right. I'd never be able to trust him inside the organization. I don't care about the intel. I want his ass gone. And I want the threat of criminal and civil damages to be held over him for an extended period so he stays out of our hair. I'll deal with Progressive-Social-whatever-the-hell-they-are myself." Then as an afterthought, "Or through Ron and Fred. I've had enough of that kind of BS."

"Okay," Fuller relented, "but the guy is really being cooperative. I don't mean that you should take it easy on him! No, no, no, no! I mean he is practically soiling himself with fear. He'd be very easy to coerce. He's quite vulnerable."

"Nah. Cut him loose."

. . .

23

"THIS IS APPALLING!" MONROE WAS SHAKING HIS HEAD as he wove around the bodies lying on the ground. "What the hell is wrong with this country?" he asked rhetorically as he stepped off the curb to avoid another of the motionless figures that lined the sidewalk.

"See, this is exactly what I was talking about with the homeless problem. The economy is doing so goddamned good, and I'll just bet you these poor bastards are sick of winning!"

They were in San Diego for the first leg of their push through the Golden State. "Well, at least these guys had a better idea. I mean what's the low in San Diego? Fifty-five? Maybe? I mean if I was one of those guys begging in Pittsburgh, I'd be walking to make Key West by winter." Ted was always ready to cast a practical eye on problems.

They were taking advantage of the time zone change and so decided to burn the extra hours and energy by taking a stroll through downtown. They grabbed an impromptu dinner downtown after checking into the hotel, and determined to take in the sights. Included in those sights were mounds of homeless people reclined on the concrete, some huddled under hoodies, a few in sleeping bags, and some others off the streets in common spaces, forming small communities of tarpaulined derelicts.

Society's detritus, pathetic souls swept aside due to poor choices or plain misfortune.

Ted walked ahead, unaware that Monroe had paused to talk to one of the guys who was alert, and who had made eye contact with him. "Hey Dude," the bearded mendicant rasped. "You got a fiver you can spot me?"

"Sure." Monroe dug into his pocket for a bill. As a rule, he never gave money to homeless people, since he figured they would just blow it on booze or drugs. And if the fellow was going to put it to a more legitimate use, it would be like bailing out the Titanic. *Ah well. Whatsoever you do to the least of my brothers. But damn! We need to get these people some help.* "What's your name, Brother?"

"Jesus," croaked the guy. He wasn't Hispanic, and he didn't use the Spanish pronunciation. Maybe that was his *nom de rue*.

"Well, Jesus, what's your story?"

"Same as so many of the other brothers on the street. Navy vet. Fourteen years in. Medical discharge. Hooked up with a chick here in OB a few years. Kicked me out coz I couldn't keep a job. No dough, no point in leavin'. San Diego's got a good vibe and I got nowhere else to be. Thanks for the fiver, Dude!" He nodded.

Ted had hurried back, frantic that Monroe was encountering some of the local color without any protection. Monroe had abandoned the bodyguards for the evening against everyone's advice. Ted had assured them that they would steer clear of trouble, and though they were not quite incognito (Taylor 2020 ads were everywhere on TV) Monroe was confident that he would not be recognized. Plus it had been awhile since he flew under the radar, and he wanted to sample the local culture. Well here it was.

They had been to LA and Sacramento earlier in the campaign, right after they purchased Taylor One. But this trip was the one Ted had looked forward to.

"I don't understand why you are so jazzed about going to California," groaned Monroe. "It's cold and it's damp. Or is this your big chance to be discovered by some big-shot producer?"

"No. This is my big chance to enjoy some Napa Valley wine." He left out the part about enjoying the wine with Sandra at a series of B&Bs she had selected. It would have been inconsiderate for him to mention it to his friend in any case. Ted was actually worried about Monroe's monk-like abstinence since the campaign began. The guy was private, but wow, how could he be that private? And keep such details from his confidante and best friend? He was away from Amber, and Denise had been out of the picture for some time now. The chance of him connecting with anyone on the campaign trail was practically zero given the schedules and the lack of alone-time. Still, it's not like that stopped other candidates. Or presidents.

They stopped into a bar for a nightcap before heading back to the room. It was a sort of open-air karaoke joint, pretty packed for a weeknight with everyone enjoying themselves. A younger crowd (most were, at this point in their fifth decade of adolescence, observed Ted). Ted was listening to a girl render a passable impersonation of Pat Benatar. "See?" he chided Monroe. "Eighties rock is still a thing out here! No wonder I love California!"

"Eighties rock is a thing with the chick that's singing," retorted Monroe. "No one else is paying her any attention. And the reason you love California is so you can spend some quality time in Napa with Sandra."

Ted considered his friend. He looked remote and a little downcast. How could a guy who won a lottery be depressed?

Monroe drained his glass of Guinness and announced that they needed to get back. He had a full day tomorrow.

He was up at 5 AM and out the door with Kurt, Gary, and Fredo, one of his bodyguards, who had replaced the now-absent Blake in the jogging retinue. As usual, Kurt packed it in after a mile (the hills were killer) and the remaining three jogged down to the waterfront, skipping around errant and too-frequent bodies on the jogging path. He was back in the hotel in an hour and out the door to meet with some business leaders for a breakfast downstairs in one of the ballrooms at 8 AM.

Sandra and Pat Metiore had done a fantastic job in scheduling the events for the California trip. They knew that there was going to have to be a concentration on redirecting votes from Democrats to Monroe, and Gary had bombarded the major markets with radio, TV, and especially social media messages targeted at Democratic voters. The west coast was not going to swing for Trump so there was no use in pursuing that tack. What they needed to do was convince them that there was a viable alternative to the traditional Democratic candidates, platforms, and ideology.

First up was the San Diego Chamber of Commerce. While they were enjoying coffee and fruit cups during breakfast, Monroe took the podium and laid out his plan for helping the homeless across the country. It was the same plan he had rehearsed with Dino Andropoulis and Dexter Manfred that night back in South Carolina. Two weeks ago it seemed like a good idea. Stepping over broken veterans on the sidewalks here it seemed like a national emergency.

The Chamber received the plan enthusiastically, and lots of people who greeted him afterward mentioned that they especially liked various aspects of the plan: the environmental benefits of cleaning up sites to prep for the arrival of the homeless, providing shelter as a contingency against the next disaster, providing economic benefits by rehabilitating abandoned sites, and ultimately, salving the collective conscience by helping the destitute. And to Kurt's sublime satisfaction, not once did he refer to "processing" the homeless.

As the campaign meandered its way north from San Diego, the conservative news outlets were mercilessly hammering Taylor. They were laying into him harder than ever since the town hall in Lubbock. Nothing was out of bounds. There were renewed attacks on his love life (do we really need another president who can't keep it zipped up?), innuendo about his sexual orientation (the guy has never been married), renewed criticism about his temper (Stan Garrett is a credible, award-winning journalist), his lack of experience (Trump was a titan of business), his insecurity (did you see the humiliating pictures of him at the gym?).

"I am sick of this bullshit!" Sam announced to an internal TPC staff meeting. "We are going to bring in a pit bull. Someone who can counterpunch without getting the Candidate's hands dirty!" They had holed up in Santa Monica for the night. Everyone from the core team (except, of course, Fuller and Tonya, and the internal staffers) was along for the media blitz.

"You know, he should really start to announce who is in consideration for VP," offered Kate Frachette. "He's mentioned several times how candidates ought to let the voters know who is being considered for cabinet-level positions. If he doesn't announce a VP soon it's gonna look like we're dragging our feet and not serious."

"Point taken," interrupted Sandra. "Plus if we had a Veep we would have a pit bull."

"Well, obviously that's where I was going with the VP thing," added Kate, annoyed. It had been a long day. A series of interviews was scheduled for tomorrow, and Gary and Phil had lined up some photo ops for curious celebrities over the next two days. The coordination had been hectic, but they were accustomed to that. Something else was going on, and Phil knew what it was. They needed to fill in the utility position vacated by Blake.

"Where do we stand on finding Blake's replacement?"

"We have it narrowed down to three or four people."

"Well, hell. Hire them all. Why are we dicking around here? It's not like we don't have a thousand people already!"

It was hyperbole but in truth the ranks of TPC had swelled in proportion to the number of volunteers stumping for Monroe across the country. Even though there was considerable blowback from the Conservatives, there had recently been a groundswell of support through the Midwest as TPC's media machine hit the airwaves and social media. Donations were at a new high over the past two weeks, since they had hit Houston and Lubbock and thrown the gauntlet at Harlon Michaels. If it wasn't exactly an army, it may have been a brigade that had fanned out over the country.

The good news was that Monroe Taylor had become an obvious irritant to the Conservatives. The evidence was the thrashing that the right-wing media were giving him. That meant that the Trump administration was paying attention. It also meant that Monroe 2020 had inadvertently employed the same strategy that Trump had been using since he announced his candidacy: any publicity is good publicity. Monroe was not thrilled with the notion, but he was enough of a media guy to recognize that it worked once, and could work again.

The next morning Monroe brought coffee and donuts to a volunteer office in Santa Monica. "Brought" was really not the right word. He arrived with the van that delivered the donuts. This office was a far cry from the one in Dover. The campaign headquarters occupied four thousand square feet of a ground floor storefront on Wilshire Boulevard. It hummed with a level of activity that thrilled Monroe, evocative of press time. He smiled and walked closer to the crowd of volunteers, who upon recognizing him broke into a chorus of shouts and applause. Of course they had been expecting him.

A young blonde woman in tight slacks and heels jockeyed for a closer position. The bodyguards stepped up, more to prevent anything untoward from happening than to prevent any perceived physical threat. TPC and Monroe himself were on high alert for avoiding any notion of inappropriate contact. He and Ted and Phil had discussed such matters at length. Months ago, he had met with the staff of *The Independent* to review new policies that seemed prudent following the Me Too movement. The difference was that the meeting at the paper was basically a perfunctory review of a policy that no one was going to observe, but there it was: on the record. At the meeting with the campaign staff, everyone pledged fealty to the guidelines. Or pretended to . . . Ted wasn't quite convinced.

The blonde girl grasped his cautious, outstretched hand with both of hers, and introduced herself as the office manager. "Welcome to Santa Monica, Mr. Taylor!" she gushed, all teeth and hair. "We're all super-excited to meet you! Let me introduce you to the staff!"

It was hard to not be impressed with the level of enthusiasm that the volunteers exhibited. There was one TPC staffer who oversaw the efforts of Southern California from this office, and Monroe made a mental note to meet this guy and offer his heartfelt congratulations on his organizational skills.

Phil was assured that there were five times as many volunteers outside the office, canvassing neighborhoods, shopping centers, and public spaces. Upon hearing that Ted creased his brow and interjected, "Wow. That's great. But it sounds like we could really do something to improve the economy if there are that many people available to volunteer on a weekday."

"Soooo," chanted the office manager, "no one is going to object to improving the economy, but many of our volunteers are retired. But the campaign also has a lot of support from millennials too." She bent over a laptop and quickly brought up a bar chart of registered voters by age, party affiliation, and current polling data. It showed that Monroe held a slight lead among voters aged 18 to 26, 27 to 35, and 55 to 65. Independent voters across the board were showing an even split between Taylor and the assumed Democrat nominees. The charts were provided courtesy of TPC's latest website which Monroe generally shunned. He had told Phil and the gang that he did not want to be distracted by the "latest" polling numbers, just as he had always said he would not use polling in his campaign.

But practicality overruled his decision. While he did not use polling data to massage his policy beliefs, he was convinced to use it to help target his message to those who needed it most, to provide the metrics that TPC relied on to gauge successes and failures.

Ted was jazzed about the reception and the results when he got back in the SUV for the return drive to LAX to board Taylor One. Monroe was more reserved and circumspect.

"Jesus Christ!" exclaimed Ted, his hands spread wide in an attitude of supplication. "What's it gonna take to cheer you up, Buddy?"

"Why are you so excited? Because 'Little Miss Thing' told us we are doing great against Donald Trump in the heart of liberal America? Of course we're gonna look good here. I acknowledge we need to pay homage to the fifty-five electors in California. We're gonna need them. But let's not get complacent. We don't have time to relax. Besides, what's going to keep those fifty-five electors from voting Democrat?"

"Well 'Little Miss Thing' was running a pretty efficient operation." He looked around furtively, but without purpose: there was no one else in the car. "And she was pretty easy on the eyes . . ."

"She was pretty," sighed Monroe in a sad, monastic sort of resignation.

"Maybe we should bring her into the national campaign," offered Ted.

"Maybe we should leave her alone. Get behind me Satan! What's the next stop?"

"We're flying into SFO to meet with some Silicon Valley tycoons in Palo Alto tonight. Then on to Sacramento tomorrow to pay homage to the new governor and the other state pols."

The meeting with the Silicon Valley leaders was more to Monroe's liking, since he was comfortable discussing his forward-thinking ideas with them. He tried to steer clear of the social media hype while there, but during a cocktail reception he got sucked into a discussion about the responsibility of platforms like Facebook to adhere to journalistic principles like fact-checking. Monroe had listened patiently to an inflated twenty-something named Dake Ayoubi pontificate about how important social media platforms are.

"Like the Arab Spring protests. Many of those were organized using digital platforms that people around here developed."

Monroe was compelled to step in.

"You're right about there being some value in communicating events. But people who use these platforms as news sources have a reasonable expectation that the news being reported is reliable.

Otherwise, you are only proving that Trump is right when he talks about fake news. The democratization of the internet gives every crackpot a soapbox. And that's not just wrong. It's dangerous. Ignorant people are too easily influenced. News isn't sourced. Radicals believe their beliefs because other radicals propagate those beliefs.

"Imagine how the Arab Spring protests would have worked out if a hard-line Fascist had lured protesters into an ambush. Truncheons and tear gas and bullets. It's a double-edged sword, and it's only a matter of time until someone leads a lot of peaceful protesters like lemmings."

Dake Ayoubi looked at Monroe vacantly, trying to process "lemmings."

Gary Davidson was standing beside Ayoubi, and grabbing him gently by the elbow, led him to the juice bar to freshen up his kombucha. Gary leaned in to Ayoubi, whispering confidentially, "Monroe really appreciates the enormous knowledge base influencers like you have. I'd love to set aside some time with you and a few of our senior-level advisers to talk about leveraging our synergies."

The team debriefed late that night in Ted's suite.

"That was a productive evening," announced Phil. "We picked up a bundle of pledges."

"Thanks for the redirect back there, Gary," offered Monroe. "I appreciate you bailing me out."

"You looked like you might go nuclear," observed Gary. "It was an easy call."

"Who was that asshole?" asked Ted.

"That 'asshole' is Dake Ayoubi. He's an influencer on Twitter. He's the Communications Officer for TechStrom, and they're killing it."

"Well, your 'influencer' doesn't know a lemming from a lemma. And how are they killing it?"

"They rolled out a new social media platform that is going to be like a cross between virtual reality and instant messaging. Of course, they haven't made any profits yet."

"How is a company worth anything if they don't make a profit?" scoffed Monroe. It was a rhetorical question. He knew that answer was in the future ad sales, data and metadata collection, and other incursions into the privacy of the users. At this stage it was just a giant research project that was well-funded by risk-takers.

"It's just a giant R&D . . ." explained Gary until Monroe's hand tamped him down. "Right. Well, it's not about US Steel anymore. You've said it yourself. Look at the Dow Jones."

"Well, the next war may have battles fought in cyberspace, but there will still be battles that need armor and artillery."

They flew to Sacramento, leaving Ted and Sandra to peel off to do some independent campaigning in Napa. On the flight from SFO, Monroe looked out a window to see a dense, dark haze to the north. He recognized it as one of the many wildfires that have been plaguing the state.

The California Democrats were polite, if not warm. Their reservations were understandable given the typical allegiance to party politics. Monroe had remarked about the fires in one of his meetings with some of the state legislators. One of them predictably brought up the specter of climate change. Monroe played devil's advocate by asking her if she felt that commercial thinning of the forests would help.

"Well, there are already a couple billion board feet of timber harvested annually. And that's overseen by CalFire."

"Oh yeah! The guys that aren't sweeping the forest floors! I'm no lumberjack, but that sounds like a lot of trees."

She chuckled good-naturedly. "Yeah, I don't know, it's probably ten or twenty million trees." She shook her head slowly and said, "Can you imagine? Raking the forest floor. As if there's some giant lawn bag. . . . If you win, you should put that in your budget for Interior!"

"California is a beautiful state. But it has its share of problems, huh? Wildfires, earthquakes, drought. . . . It's the earthquakes that worry me. You may be too young to remember, but when Bush 43 was debating Gore in 2000, they kept arguing over how much money each was going to return to the American people. There was a budget surplus and neither one could pander enough to give money back to taxpayers. And I'm sitting there watching this—reporting on it—and I'm thinking, 'What if China invades Taiwan? What if the big one hits California? Where does that money come from? Wouldn't it be better to hold on to a surplus?' And of course those fears were unfounded. Instead we had 9/11. And now we have a national debt of what? Twenty trillion dollars? I mean there was a national debt in 2000 too, but it was something like six trillion. And I still worry about the big one hitting California."

She reached out and touched the sleeve of his jacket. "I do remember. But thanks. For the compliment and the concern."

.　.　.

24

TED LIFTED HIS RAY BANS from the bridge of his nose to examine just how bright the reflection off the sand was. He uttered an involuntary grunt, and settled down on a lounge chair with the newspaper and a mug of coffee. The beach towel had shifted and the back of his bare leg met with the powder coat on the aluminum frame of the lounger, which had been absorbing infrared radiation from the rising sun all morning. He would have been wiser to have accepted one of the shaded chairs that Monroe had offered. As it was, the searing sensation that passed through his epidermis caused enough of a reaction that not only was his next utterance also involuntary, but so was the reflex of his right hand launching the coffee out of his mug, with portions of it crossing all the way across to the shaded side of the pool, to the immense displeasure of Sandra, Monroe, and Phil, who all made similar utterances.

"Who invited this yahoo, anyway?" asked Monroe to Phil as they mopped sugared coffee from their faces and arms.

"Don't really know. Thought he was with you."

"You know, there's no such thing as a healthy tan," reminded Sandra, amused. "What with the holes in the ozone and everything."

"Thank you for your concern. But I'm half Middle-Eastern," Ted replied. "So the swarthiness protects me.

"In theory," he added, contorting himself to examine the first degree burn branded on the back of his upper thigh.

"Good thing Sandra talked you out of wearing your Speedos, Buddy! The damage could have been a whole lot worse!"

"Yeah, thanks for that also," he hollered sarcastically across the pool deck.

"Nice of you to join us in any case," said Sam, opening the sliding door with a vodka and tonic in one hand. "Finally," he snickered. The rest of the group suppressed chuckles, but they weren't really suppressed at all.

Ted accepted the ribbing good-naturedly. He pretended like he was mildly offended, but he was really enjoying the attention of being the goat this morning. He knew he would be joining the retreat later than the rest, having flown in from Latrobe late last night on a charter jet. Taylor One had preceded him by a day, and was secured in a private hangar at Southwest Florida International Airport in Fort Myers. He had needed to return to Latrobe after his layover with Sandra in Napa Valley. There was a lingering doctor's appointment, a meeting with his lawyer back home, and he wanted to check in on the paper. Monroe was also having some issues with one of the tenants of his office building, and he had asked Ted to drop in and have a look around. The whole thing took a week.

What Ted hadn't counted on was how late he would get in. Working on the campaign was for him a real treat. It was practically first-class service all the time (at Monroe's expense and insistence). But some of the hours were taking a toll. Hence the doctor visit. He had been feeling fatigued since his laughing fit in Houston. His doctor thought it was really just fatigue, but doctors these days never just *think* something. That provokes liability. Nowadays tests are required. So he had submitted to a whole battery. There were the standard lipids and metabolic panel, but also mono, Lyme, lupus, a chest x-ray, and an EKG. He felt like he needed a vacation just to relax from all the tests. Now he was just catching up, and off to a bad start. His charter landed at Fort Myers at 3:40 AM. Luckily TPC had arranged for one of the drivers to meet him. He decided to sleep in, and everyone staying at the beach house had paid careful attention to remaining quiet until Ted started to stir around ten thirty. No one on the TPC team knew anything about Ted's health concerns; not even Sandra. He shared that info only with Monroe.

The trip to Fort Myers was agreed to by the whole team. Monroe had wanted to treat them to a short getaway to reward the loyalty and performance of late. His popularity was rising, and the gang back at *The Independent* had even started to frame the magazine covers that featured their CEO and owner. Implied was the fact that even when trying to relax at the beach with a pina colada in your hand, the talk would be about the campaign. It was a small price to pay.

The beach house was a newly constructed four-story affair, with an infinite pool overlooking the gulf on the third floor. Monroe had spent time on the Gulf Coast on occasion, and he enjoyed the wide beach offered here. There was a restaurant within walking distance that offered live music in the evenings, interrupted by one of the locals heralding the last rays of the setting sun with a blast on a conch shell.

Monroe had rented four consecutive houses, forming a sort of complex to comfortably provide for the quotidian needs of the fifteen people that comprised the getaway.

Sam sat across from Monroe and toasted him. "Thanks for doing this, Monroe. It's very kind of you to invite us all on your vacation. I'm kind of surprised you didn't just buy a place like this down here."

"You know, it is tempting," Monroe paused while he drew down a pineapple juice laced with rum. "But I figure that the sea levels are going to continue to rise faster, and if the beach erodes or there are more frequent severe weather events, then it's a bad investment. I have the capital to buy something like this, sure. But I can't bring myself to invest in something that might not hold its value over my lifetime. I'd rather just rent and let someone else absorb the risk." He leaned back and gazed over the beach.

He enjoyed the downtime, in theory, but throughout his life he'd always had a hard time relaxing. How could anyone truly relax, knowing that there was so much left to do? And while you're wasting time not getting anything done, even more things are entering the queue on top of what you are already not doing. *God,* he reflected miserably. *This is exactly how I felt in St. Lucia.* Then in the same instant, *at least I got laid there.*

"What's up? You look like you're a million miles away," said Sam.

"Nah. It's fine. I think I'll walk the beach for awhile."

"Make sure you take security," Sam cautioned. Then yelling to Phil, "Hey Phil, can you raise Terry and get someone to accompany the Candidate?"

"Wait a minute. Are those guys still out back?"

On his way back from an early morning jog, Monroe had seen a couple of burly guys on the security detail standing conspicuously in the access road behind the house. They were actually drawing attention to the environs and occupants.

"Get them inside for Christ's sake. For one thing, they look ridiculous. They stick out like a sore thumb. And more importantly, it's inhumane. Get them some drinks and a sandwich. They're more useful in here anyway."

Phil acquiesced. The two hulking rear bodyguards were invited in and sheepishly took up posts inside, scanning the beach with binoculars and making rounds through the house. Satisfied, Monroe hit the beach alone. He ambled along the water's edge, listening to the surf, the gulls, and the people. He was pretty incognito, wearing a flimsy long-sleeve shirt, a nondescript bathing suit, a wide-brimmed hat, and wraparound sunglasses. He was transitioning into public life but he occasionally appreciated the alone time. No one seemed to notice as he trudged along the beach, alternating between the soft sand higher up and the firmer wet sand closer to the water.

As he returned to the house an hour later he noticed a man and a woman on the beach in front of the house. The man had trained binoculars on the house, and was talking in low tones to the woman. Monroe sauntered over to them. "Hey there," he greeted them. "What's going on?" He mustered a nonthreatening voice. The approachable voice he had trained himself to use as a reporter to dispel any essence of threat. The one he used to inspire the confidence of eyewitnesses.

"Oh!" exclaimed the woman. "My husband thinks there's someone important staying in this cluster of homes. Might be a movie star or someone."

"No kidding! Well, you know how hard it is to ID a movie star. I mean when you see pictures of them on vacation in the tabloids without their makeup, and their guts are all hanging out over their swim trunks . . ."

"Yeah," the guy laughed, not taking his eyes from the binoculars. "Babe, look." He handed her the binoculars and put his sunglasses back on. "That's one of the bodyguards we saw this morning out back."

The woman took the binoculars and looked. They were a good two hundred yards away. "Yeah, that's him. He's got that bodyguard build and broken nose. Here," she offered the glasses to Monroe. "You wanna look?"

"Sure. Thanks." He took the binoculars and saw Fredo staring back at him with his own binoculars. Monroe waved.

"Whoa, whoa, whoa, what the hell you doin', man?" asked the guy. "They'll make us!"

"Yeah, it's okay. I'm staying there. My name's Monroe Taylor, and I'm renting that complex for the week. Needed a getaway. Thanks for the spyglasses." He handed the glasses back to the lady and shook their hands. "Nice to meet you. Enjoy your stay on the beach. Oh, and listen. I am running for President of the United States, but I'd kind of appreciate it . . . sort of a personal favor . . . if you'd keep the identity of the occupants here a bit of a secret for a few more days. I'll be out and around later on. We're working on a few ideas here and trying to decompress without the commotion of campaigning. But I'd love to buy you a drink at the tiki bar some evening."

He turned and strode up the beach under the watchful eye of Fredo Martinez. Fredo turned to the crowd and warned, "Saint's back. He's making some friends, looks like." A couple of objections rose from the group.

Sam smoked some tri-tip roasts out on the pool deck that evening. Monroe pitched in with a romaine and mandarin orange salad, and Ted prepared the baked potatoes and accoutrements. The mood was festive but relaxed, and Monroe was finally feeling like he was able to unwind a bit. He'd had a couple glasses of Malbec, so that helped the cause. There were fifteen people gathered around the ample tables once the sun went down and dinner was served. With this many wonks and political hacks around, there were not many lulls in the conversation. But in the relative calm between exclamations of brilliance and proclamations of how delicious the meal was Monroe glanced around the tables and sighed, considered how lucky he was to be in this position, and mouthed a silent prayer of thanksgiving for providing him with another close family of colleagues that he could call friends. He reflected on the many times he had gathered his employees at the paper together for celebrations, congratulations, or just mindbender sessions to decompress.

He missed the crew back at the paper. He knew everything there was fine. He got daily reports from Franco via email that ran from assignment choices to family news among the staff. Naturally he received the paper online, but he also received alerts of kids' graduations, deaths, births, and marriages of not just staff, but people back in Latrobe that Franco knew he'd want to send a personal note to. It helped having a staff to keep a supply of note cards on hand, but each note was handwritten, often with a favorite and appropriate quote from literature or scripture. To one kid about to embark on his college experience, he wrote, "Remember: Good judgment comes from experience, and a lot of that comes from bad judgment. Make your Dad proud, and don't embarrass your Mom."

A toast offered by Phil awoke Monroe from his reverie. "To Monroe Taylor, our generous host and friend, and the next President of the United States!" There was a chorus of "Hear! Hear!" and an inebriated attempt to sing "For He's a Jolly Good Fellow," which fell apart after the second measure because no one was in the same key, and the laughter that ensued prevented any serious effort to restart.

"Jesus! How drunk do you have to be to fuck up 'For He's a Jolly Good Fellow'? It's a song made for drunks!"

The next day started in earnest, the sensitivity to bright lights and loud noises was not as bad as some may have expected. The inability to harmonize was chalked up to high spirits rather than intoxication, and it promised to be a productive third day on the beach. Gary had a full schedule of interviews, speeches, and events queuing up over the next two weeks, and there were still plenty of issues to explain.

"We've been talking about how candidates ought to release the names of their cabinets and advisors," said Kate Frachette, a tablet balanced on her crossed legs to take notes. "Besides the vice president, there are fifteen cabinet members. We should be thinking about who to talk to about these positions."

"You're right," affirmed Monroe. "And we've already been tossing names back and forth with Dino and Dex and the Undersecretary, but you guys already know about those. With the campaigning, I haven't had any time to personally research or reach out to prospective candidates. And honestly, I really don't know what the proper protocol would be to contact these people."

"But," added Ted, "we do think we need to keep it quiet until we have some serious talks with whoever we decide on." He passed out packets of info. "This is condensed. We had some of the reporters back at the paper working on pulling info."

"Well, gee whiz, guys," Sam cried, "What do you think you're paying us for?"

"I wonder that almost every day!"

"Gotta say . . . we've also been a little light on representing the military," observed Ted.

"WE haven't," boasted Sam. "TPC has been talking to dozens of retired generals and admirals about you. We have several that would love to be included in the campaign. And incidentally, we already have dossiers on prospective VEEPs and Cabinet positions. I actually expect there to be a significant amount of overlap between our list and the one your associates have prepared."

"Duly noted. Any of them prospects for VP?" asked Monroe. "I'd love to find a Centrist with a war record. Someone like John McCain. Only about my age. And speaking of Centrists, we need to grab from Republicans AND Democrats. We are gonna slice through this party unity BS once and for all."

"Who you got?" asked Phil, rubbing his hands together with glee. "Why don't we start with Secretary of State?"

"State. David Greene. Republican."

"Well, for crying out loud, we know who David Greene is."

Monroe ignored Phil and plunged ahead with his own self-indulgent commentary. "Former Governor of Arizona, former Ambassador to Russia and China. Speaks Spanish, Russian, and a bit of Mandarin. Scratch golfer. Five kids. Don't know how he had time to crank out five kids . . ."

"Treasury?"

"Treasury. Stefan Wolstan. Republican. PhD, Columbia economics. Jensen Prize . . . look, I'm only gonna give you the first-tier names here, we have selected alternates down to five deep in some cases, but I wanna hit the beach this afternoon, okay?"

"Okay. Wolstan is a little bit wonky. Your second string might have someone with a little experience in business or finance?"

"Yeah, I'm not sure," explained Monroe. "This is the first time I've seen the whole list. I mean I recognize some of the names, but this is scaring me. Maybe I should've been on top of this already. I feel unprepared."

"Are you kidding me?" Sam and Phil asked in unison.

Sam explained. "No candidate would be drilling this deep at this stage in the campaign. In fact, some people might claim it's premature. But if we can get some agreement on these prospects, we can actually sell a team, and even have them assist in the campaign. AG?"

"Attorney General. Francesca Hernandez. Democrat. US Attorney for the Southern District of Florida. Oh! We should pay her a visit while we're in the neighborhood!"

"What about Defense?"

"Defense. Spencer Andersen. Former NATO commander. General. Valedictorian at West Point. Rhodes Scholar. Obvious overachiever . . ."

"Interior?"

"Interior. Brenda Storey. Another Democrat. This looks fishy. PhD in meteorology from Penn State. Hmm! Local girl! Stints with NOAA and Woods Hole Oceanographic Institute. Now I get why it's a good fit."

"EPA?"

"EPA. Paul Reynolds. PhD from USC. Climate scientist. Greenland Ice Sheet Project. Wow, I'll bet he froze his ass off up there! Interested in climate change. Tree-hugger."

The TPC crew was starting to roll their eyes. Monroe kept the editorial comments coming.

"Energy. Bruce Hayes. Republican. Nuclear Engineering. PhD from MIT. Now we're talking!" he looked up to see if anyone was still paying attention. Sandra had her head back on the lounger, mouth agape in mock deep sleep.

"Education! Stephanie Richards. No party affiliation! PhD in elementary education from CUNY."

Kate was still processing. "Wait a minute. You said you had *The Independent* running research on the campaign? Is that legal?"

"Well . . ." drawled Monroe. "Sure it's legal! First of all, they were paid for the service. And second, when we began the campaign, right after we announced, we established an internal organization, separate from the paper. So we have a firewall between activities, accounts, and timekeeping. Just in case it becomes an issue."

"Plus we have Ron Le Quang's guys auditing the campaign on a regular basis," interjected Sam.

The conversation went on for another hour as they passed around the dossiers that Ted had shared. Monroe enjoyed the deep dive into the individual characteristics of the team he sought. They spoke about the vetting that would take place and what approaches they might take for each of the prospects. Some might favor a more nuanced approach while others would appreciate the direct style.

"What about Chief of Staff?" asked Kate.

"Ted Polanski, if he accepts. No reason to change there." Ted reached a fleshy hand to his best friend after wiping the condensation from an ice-cold Budweiser on his trunks.

"You do realize," began Ted, "that I know nothing about protocol or the mechanics of that particular position."

"Yeah, I know. But you're a clever lad and Sam and Phil will hook you up with the right coach."

The sun was inching higher in the sky and Monroe excused himself to take another stroll along the beach. Fredo tagged along. They headed north toward the pier. More people in that direction and Monroe enjoyed people watching. It would be especially fun since he was again incognito. He started to ask Fredo about his family. Fredo was Puerto Rican, born and raised in the Miradero barrio in Mayaguez, a municipality on the west coast of the island. At nineteen, he enlisted in the US Army and because his aptitude tests were stellar, when he requested paratrooper training the only question the recruiter had was 82nd or 101st? He opted for the 82nd because he coveted the prestige of going through jump school. He rose to the rank of first sergeant and did a tour in Mosul. Once home he sought a job in law enforcement in DC.

Chapter 24

"Yeah, I went from one US territory to another," he explained to Monroe, chuckling. "At least in Mayaguez I didn't have to pay income tax."

"Well, you still had to pay the state income tax . . . but I guess it's not a state tax 'cause it's . . . well, not a state."

"That's right, we still pay a territorial tax. But even the Puerto Ricans below the poverty line have to pay the territorial income tax. The lower limit is much lower than on the mainland, and many people are way below the poverty line. We sure were."

"Mmmm." Monroe's mind wandered in silence as he thought about the crummy hand that Puerto Rico had been dealt. It wasn't as bad as say, Haiti, but then again, Haiti wasn't a US territory. And then there was the Hurricane Maria debacle. Recent polling suggested that two-thirds of Puerto Ricans favored statehood. *Where would we put the fifty-first star?* thought Monroe absently. *Well, fifty-one is divisible by three, but, well, Christ! Figuring out how to get another star on the canton is a bad reason to deny statehood. Some clever designer would think of something cool.*

I wonder if he is even paying any attention to what I am saying, wondered Fredo. *Maybe all of his 'engagement' with the public is just an act. A façade.* Fredo pondered, looked around scanning the environs for latent threats. That part of his brain always on a low boil. Regardless of what he thought of this guy as a person, he still had a job to do, and he was a professional.

"Do you think the polling is accurate about wanting to become a state?"

Fredo was so surprised by the renewed interest that he chuckled. The guy might really be tracking. "Yeah, I think it is. Especially after Maria."

"Yeah, but you wouldn't want to let that be the reason, now would you? It would make it look like a welfare grab. Guam is in a similar situation . . . a territory with no votes in Congress, territorial income tax. It's just so damn far away. But I mean Puerto Rico is what? A thousand miles? We ought to look into DC while we're at it. They're paying full freight."

"You'll get no argument from me," Fredo's voice trailed off as he observed a couple about thirty yards away on a collision course with them. He relaxed his arms and tapped the pocket of his swim trunks to reassure himself that the retractable baton was at the ready. He did not have a good way of holstering the SIG Sauer P229 that all of the bodyguards were issued. Some opted for other sidearms, but TPC had standardized on the same .357 SIG carried by the US Secret Service. At the beach house, the guards had discussed transparent protection for the candidate, since he wanted to remain as incognito as possible. After the scolding they had received for posting obtrusive-looking guards outside the "compound," they decided to not arm themselves when in beachwear. And they couldn't very well wear body armor or suits on the beach. Sam and Phil were cautious, but Ted and Monroe weighed in and were comfortable with the concept.

Monroe recognized the couple as the ones he'd met in front of the house the previous day. "Hey, how are you guys?" he extended his hand and introduced them to Fredo, who remained professionally aloof, but greeted them nonetheless. "How about a drink at the tiki bar tomorrow night?"

"Oh, sorry," said the woman. "We're leaving in the morning. This is our last night in paradise!"

. . .

224

"WHAT THE HELL IS KEEPING THEM?" said Phil to no one in particular. Then turning to Bill Williams, the head of the security detail, he asked, "Do you think we should go looking for them?"

Bill hesitated, and then held up a finger. A call was coming through his earpiece. "It's Fredo. They're down the beach. At the tiki bar." He grinned from amusement as much as from relief. He did not relish the idea of mounting a search party at twilight on the beach. He'd been trying to reach Fredo but the reception was uncharacteristically poor. He'd be taking that issue up with his Comms Chief directly.

"How's that grouper, Suze?" asked Monroe between bites of an enormous Cobb salad.

"Oh, it's great, Monroe! Have some! Hey! Is that Lindsay?" She stood up and waved across the courtyard.

Fredo sat down next to Monroe. "Hey, Boss. I just called in for reinforcements. They were getting edgy."

"Well, that's their job I guess. Try some of these fries, man. They're great."

Fredo scooped a forkful onto a plate, thinking that he would feel better once the rest of the security detail arrived. Here he was in an uncontrolled setting, lots of booze around, and all he had to protect the asset was the baton and a slippery hand covered with deep fryer grease. He surveyed the crowd.

Monroe sensed the anxiety and draped an arm over Fredo's shoulder. From across the table it looked to Suze and Don Baylon like two friends having a good time. Fredo understood that it was Monroe's way of securing a bit of privacy over the guy covering Jimmy Buffet's catalog. Usually where live music was involved, Monroe found the volume was way too loud for casual conversation. This entertainer however was more laid back, and the music was styled for background ambience. Monroe spoke softly into Fredo's left ear, "Relax. We're safe here. I don't think the cavalry needs to bring its firepower."

Fredo was impressed that Monroe read his anxiety so well.

"But call them back. And ask them to bring Ted along with the credit card. I'm not gonna be able to cover the tab with what I got on me."

Don Baylon was from Toledo, the son in Baylon & Son Contracting, a firm that provided industrial and commercial electrical services in western Ohio and eastern Indiana. Don had come up through the trades bending conduit and pulling wire after school. He was about to buy the business from his father, and this was the first vacation he and Suze had taken in nearly three years. The problem was that when they had the time, they didn't have the money, and vice versa. This year he decided to treat Suze to a week at Fort Myers Beach.

Suze reminded Monroe of Denise. She was a gregarious girl, and had accumulated a variety of friends wherever she went. One of them was Lindsay, an attractive blonde who loved to wear high-cut one piece bathing suits. She breezed in with a flourish and took a seat at the ample table next to Suze. Fredo and Monroe shared a glance, also sharing the understanding that the role of the bodyguard was as much about protecting him from himself as protecting him from physical violence. Bill Clinton should have been so lucky.

It was a target-rich environment, and everyone was having a good time. The natural beauty of the beach and the setting orange sun, the warm air kissing your face and arms, the alcohol-induced buzz, the vibe of the bar. . . .

Suze was explaining something to Lindsay in low tones. As she spoke Lindsay looked up at Monroe periodically. Monroe stood to introduce himself and began to introduce Fredo as well.

"Oh, I know all about you. I'm from the heartland, and let me tell you something Mr. 'Elitist Liberal Playboy': you don't have a CHANCE of beating President Trump! We LOVE our president in the heartland!"

"Really!" Monroe paused. He was simultaneously amused and annoyed. "Well, that's just fine. Why don't you relax and join us anyway. We're gonna order some more appetizers and drinks. Can I get you anything?"

"Not on your life! You'd probably slip me a roofie and date rape me! No thanks!"

"Lindsay!" scolded Suze. "Settle down! Here, have a sip of my Chardonnay!" Then addressing Monroe, "I don't know what's got into her, I swear!"

"Well, I'll tell you Missy!" replied Lindsay. "I don't need a lecture from another East Coast liberal who has no respect for the president! We love Mr. Trump in the heartland!"

"That's fine! That's fine!" protested Monroe. He'd had a couple beers, and he realized that maybe he was a little less inhibited than he ought to be. He also realized that there was no one to rein him in. Fredo was there, but Fredo was not going to drag him away from a potentially embarrassing situation. As he was considering this, Fredo, who NEVER drank on duty, was lucidly observing the conversation, his eyes darting from Lindsay, to Monroe, to Suze, to Lindsay. He felt like a deer on a highway. With a collapsible baton. Woefully unprepared for what may happen.

Where the fuck are the TPC guys? Fredo thought. *Should I lead Monroe out of here? Or would that create a scene?*

"Tell me," said Monroe patiently. "Exactly what is it about Mr. Trump that you admire?" He adopted his earnest expression. It was sincere and he knew from his reporting experience that he could rely on it to get people to open up during interviews.

"He tells it like it is! He's one of us! He's not just another bullshit politician!"

"Mmmm. I see. So he appeals to you because he is similar to you. He understands your concerns. He's like all the good people out in the heartland . . . pays his taxes, changes the oil in his car, mows his lawn, picks his kid up from daycare. . . . Don, do you think Donald Trump has ever changed the oil in his car? I mean, does he even know how to DRIVE a car?"

There was no reply as everyone sat looking at each other. Then Fredo looked up to see another woman, a friend of Lindsay's recording this exchange on her iPhone. Fredo stood, and Monroe reached up and grabbed his arm. "It's okay," he said. "It's fine. Let her be."

Ted, Phil, and the rest showed up at that moment. Ted regarded the situation, and said in a voice that was too loud, "Hi! What's going on?"

Monroe explained that Fredo and he were just enjoying some food and drink with their new friends. He introduced everybody, and then said, ". . . and this is Lindsay from the heartland, and her friend . . . I'm sorry, I didn't get your name."

The friend said "I'm Mia." Then she did an about face, grabbed Lindsay by the wrist, and led her into the crowd.

"Nice girls," nodded Monroe. "Sam, Phil, have a seat. Kate, what would you like?"

Phil looked at Don and Suze, offered a deferential "Would you excuse us please for a moment?" draped his arms around Monroe and Fredo, and asked them quietly to stand and accompany him.

The rest of the TPC contingent (minus Bill and the security team, who took up posts on the perimeter), sat down and engaged in persiflage in an effort to assess the appropriate level of damage control that may be required.

Phil asked Monroe, "What the hell just happened?" Then he looked at Fredo accusingly and said, "What the hell just happened?"

"Look, Phil, don't bust on Fredo. He did nothing wrong. Nothing happened. I'm lucid. There's nothing to worry about. Just an honest exchange of opinions. With any luck it's on YouTube by now."

Phil wasted no time, he turned away and searching the internet with his phone, immediately got a hit on Twitter with "@ Monroe Taylor Myers." He walked off the property toward the beach, where he could study the content objectively, in a quieter environment. His eyes were glued to his screen as he nearly bumped into the guy blowing the conch shell to herald the setting sun. A few people in the vicinity admonished him. He did not look up, but mumbled a vague apology as he navigated to the screen shot of Monroe sitting at the table, a blue circle with a white triangle covering the center of the screen. He tapped the triangle and watched the scene play out. The audio quality was surprisingly good considering the ambient noise. He replayed it. And replayed it again. He stood mute, shaking his head slowly as a grin spread over his face. He had to hand it to Monroe. The guy was a natural-born politician. He DID appear lucid. He was polite, measured, and most importantly, he did not come off as a smartass, even though he had every right to be. Instead he came off as witty and genuine. Phil slowly lowered the phone to his side and looked at the pink band of horizon that glued the rippling gray gulf to the laminous gray clouds. A contented wave of tranquility washed over him, and he now thought he might be able to relax and enjoy the evening. He exhaled, turned and strolled back to the table with his team.

They had ordered more appetizers and a fresh round of drinks. Monroe was standing with about a dozen curious tourists who had come over after the commotion with Lindsay. He was talking to them in a casual tone and introducing himself to others who were gravitating to their area. This had the potential to get out of hand, so Phil caught Ted's attention. Ted immediately grasped Phil's intent and got up. "We should wrap this up and migrate back to the *hacienda*, huh?"

"You're a real buzzkill," Monroe replied discreetly. "I'm earning votes here."

"Free beer does that. And it probably violates a couple FEC laws. Come on. We can come back to the beach again tomorrow, Timmy."

"Hey, we gotta get going," announced Monroe. "It was so nice to be able to spend some time with you! Enjoy the rest of your stay!" He shook hands with Suze and Don Baylon, and hooking up with his entourage, walked back to the beach house, feeling invigorated. They repaired to the pool deck.

. . .

"GOOD EVENING, AND WELCOME to this edition of 'Eyes On 2020', as we dive deeper into the presidential campaigns. Tonight we begin with Dexter Manfred, a Harvard professor of Political Science, and a consultant to the Monroe Taylor campaign! I'm Monica Vickery and this is 'YOUR AMERICA!'"

The show broke for commercial and Phil explained, "I think we can rely on this lady for one of the town halls. She's heavy conservative, but that's what we want, right? She's respected at her network, she has a very favorable rating among Conservatives and Libertarians, and her people say she's interested in the spot."

Monroe sat silently, reconsidering his earlier stance. He had been pushing hard to get into the deep red districts so that he could persuade Conservatives to vote for him. But right now it seemed a Herculean task. He vacillated again between caution and confidence. The program was back on, with the camera on Dexter Manfred.

"Dr. Manfred, you have been coaching Monroe Taylor for some time now. What are your topics and why does he need your services?"

"What a bullshit question!" spat Ted. "Like 'Have you stopped beating your wife?'"

"Shh!"

Dexter proceeded thoughtfully. "I have been consulting on the Taylor campaign for about three months now, reviewing a range of domestic policy. Every candidate is wise to take some counsel of experts. I find Mr. Taylor to be especially adept at grasping complex concepts."

"So you explain domestic policy to him and he memorizes talking points?"

Dexter laughed. "Not at all. Monroe Taylor was already well-versed in domestic and foreign policy. He's been writing about it extensively for thirty-five years."

"Oh, come on!" challenged the hostess. "He's the editor of a rinky-dink, ten-page rag in Podunk, Pennsylvania. He's written editorials about garbage collection and potholes! I hardly think he's taken on peace in the Middle East!"

"If you thought that, you'd be wrong. Monroe certainly has an active interest in the local civic concerns of Latrobe, but he also possesses an astonishing intellect. He's the kind of guy who can synthesize concepts and analyze events. He has a BA in history, and he uses those skills to take a long-term view of a wide range of complex problems. He has an intellectual curiosity regarding many topics of global interest."

"Whatever we are paying Dex, I want it doubled," joked Monroe.

"Can you tell us who else is on the payroll at Taylor For President? For consulting?"

"We have frequent sessions with Judge Dino Andropoulis who is a constitutional law scholar. Monroe Taylor is not ideologically bound to one party. Judge Andropoulis is a life-long Republican.

Monroe Taylor seeks the best advice regardless of party. And that's the way he will govern."

"She sounds like the queen of the harpies," Ted commented.

"Well, it has to be done I suppose. Make the call, Phil," instructed Monroe. "Dex knocked it out of the park, huh?"

.   .   .

27

"NO, NO, NO! NO NO NO NO NO!"

Franco DeMario looked up from an ad layout of a local merchant. He had been summoned to the layout table of Joe Fiore, one of the old-timers. Joe preferred to block content out on paper rather than rely exclusively on a computer screen. Joe peered over his designer half frames as a refrain of groans and "what the fuck?"s echoed through the newsroom. The two looked at each other as Franco's gastric glands dosed his gut with hydrochloric acid and enzymes. He headed out into the newsroom to see his employees clutching at their scalps, looking at the ceiling, or frantically dashing and clicking their mice.

"We're infected!" gushed Sheila Burns. "Everyone is fucking infected!"

"Computer virus?" asked Franco innocently.

"No! Syphilis!" barked Smitty.

"Hey! Settle down!" hollered Franco, insulted. "What is it?" He turned his attention to Sheila's laptop as she tried to open her files in Windows Explorer. The first file in each folder was an instruction on how to recover their files. It involved a $3 million ransom to be paid in cryptocurrency. "Jesus. Somebody did this to Monroe," said Franco absently. "No one gets hit with this much ransom. Sheila, call the IT guy and Albert Messing. He needs to know about this. I'll get ahold of Ted." He shouted to the newsroom, "Everyone! Power down your computers! NOW!"

As he walked back to his office he considered that it probably didn't make a bit of difference if everyone's computers were left on or powered down. The genie was out of the bottle at the speed of light, or however fast data traveled across their network, which come to think of it, was not that fast. So maybe that really was a valuable moment of inspiration. He closed the door and called Ted.

"Bad news, Ted. The office is shut down 'cause of a computer virus. It's ransomware and it's on everyone's machines. The bastards are looking for a $3 million payout."

"Three million dollars? The whole paper isn't worth three million. Whoever is behind this doesn't know shit about newspapers."

Franco explained the measures he'd taken, and Ted asked him to sit tight for a while until he could discuss this development with Monroe. They were in Dayton, Ohio, today pushing west through Lindsay's heartland. The Twitter feed attacking the "one-of-us" theme had provided some momentum. This tour had already been scheduled for the campaign, but the video of Monroe deriding Trump's populism was fortuitous.

"You gotta be kidding me!" groaned Monroe. "What happened to the security software we have?"

"This got through it. Must have come in on an email and then got on the server. Every file is encrypted. Franco has called in the IT consultant. He wants to know if you want him to bring in the hacker who went after Denise Dexter's computer."

"Hell no! Let's leave this to the pros. This has to be a political attack. No one in their right mind would expect $3 million from a paper." He fished his iPhone from his coat pocket and called Phil, who called Fuller Thompson. Fuller was skeptical about the ability to track down the culprits with any kind of forensic analysis. Fuller also raised the specter of the incident being triggered through a political adversary rather than a random cybercriminal. The ransom was just too high to be anything other than a specific attack against Monroe, so he was obliged to look into it.

Ted fumed and Monroe stewed. "I guess there isn't a damn thing we can do about it," began Ted philosophically. Then, exposing his visceral emotions, "But Jesus Christ! I'd like to flay these sonsabitches!"

"Yeah, you and me both. What idiot thought that cryptocurrency is a good idea to begin with? The whole concept fosters crime. We're gonna outlaw it in a Taylor administration. What are they doing back in Latrobe?"

"Complaining mostly. But they are actually getting out the next edition. I mean the computers are hamstrung, but they aren't out of commission. The files are all backed up online. Except for Smitty's porno."

"Don't even joke about that, Ted. Fuck."

"I thought a little levity might cheer you up. Nevertheless, *The Independent* soldiers on. Expect a scathing editorial by DeMario."

"I want him to pass it through . . . wait." He dialed Franco himself. "Franco, Monroe. I want you to have Albert look at the editorial before you publish it."

"I'm not going to libel us!" protested Franco.

"Be that as it may."

"Whatever," he responded dismissively. "Who do you think is behind it?"

"I don't know. How bad is it back there?"

"I've only had to restrain a dozen or so people. When you remodeled the place, you should have included the padded cells like I requested. How are YOU holding up?"

"Me? What's the matter? Don't you read the papers? I'm great. We're sitting in Dayton, about ready to hit an interview. Gonna shake some babies and kiss some hands."

"Yeah. You kissing babies. I can imagine. They better be at least eighteen."

"Hey! Watch that!. . . . Well, take it easy, Buddy. I know *The Independent* is in capable hands."

"Yeah. Sheila has it covered, boss. Take it easy."

The team headed to a conference room downstairs at the hotel to tape an interview. They passed by an architecturally interesting bar and as they entered the institutional-looking conference room, Monroe considered how regrettable it was that these places always put their efforts into the bars and restaurants instead of the halls where people are going to spend most of their time. The walls were drab, the tables were covered with a plain white fabric. He summoned Kate Frachette over as the TV crew was setting up.

"Pat Metiore and Gary Davidson were okay with this?"

"Yes, Monroe, I guess they were."

"And you're okay with this?"

"It's going to photograph a lot different. We'll bring in some background."

"It would photograph well if we were producing the segment. But we're not. We're at the mercy of whatever intern or local drone they have to set this up. It's gonna look low-rent. And if we complain now, we're gonna look like ungrateful malcontents. Bringing in some plastic ficus trees isn't going to dress this up."

Kate looked around and sighed. "You're right. Would you feel comfortable in the lobby? There might be some traffic there, but it looks out over a busy sidewalk. We can post Bill Williams and the boys out there to scare away college kids who want to make

237

faces behind you. Let me catch the front desk and the interviewer. I think we have time."

Monroe thanked her and turned to Ted. "That's what I'm talking about. Why don't we schedule an interview in front of Trump Tower?"

"Better yet, why don't we do it in front of Trump Plaza in Atlantic City? I thought that presser with Clinton standing in front of a defunct Trump casino was brilliant!"

"Yeah, but that would make us unoriginal, and I'm not sure, but that casino may actually have been demolished by now. Plus, it didn't work."

"We can check. If you had listened to me and established the Latrobe Renovation Trust, we could be having interviews back there in LEED-sustainable luxury." Ted was needling him. That was Monroe's idea back when he claimed the lottery ticket. It seemed like a decade ago, and yet it was less than a year ago.

Kate came back with the good news that they would move to pleasanter environs. It was a cloudy day outside and the lighting tech thought he could position the floods without getting any reflection off of the picture windows that looked out onto the cloudy street in front of the hotel. Monroe was introduced to Harold Gibbons, the interviewer, a middle-aged man with a friendly face that belied political acumen. He'd seen that look before, and recognized it. Mainly from his mirror.

Monroe smiled and made small talk with Harold Gibbons about his background, and learned he had skipped up and down the Midwest with stints at TV stations in St. Paul, Des Moines, and St. Louis, before returning to his hometown of Dayton. And even though he had worked for some larger markets, it was Des Moines that Monroe was interested in as he quizzed Harold.

"Of course Des Moines was one of our first stops. Those stations there must really love the elections!"

"Oh, yeah!" admitted Gibbons, "That's a lucrative gig. And being on the political beat there is a dream job for a journalist."

"So why did you leave it?"

"There was a lady involved," he replied with a wink and a broad smile.

Monroe recognized that this, like practically every one of his previous interviews, was not going to be a puff piece devoted to his virtues. He was frankly beginning to tire of having to prove himself to every journalist and their respective audiences. Yet he knew this was the only way to gain a foothold in the area. In spite of the sophisticated social media presence that had been established by Gary Davidson's team, Taylor for President and TPC had always known that traditional media was also going to play a strong role in persuading voters.

But it wasn't just the votes Monroe was now after. Sure, those were important. At this stage in the campaign, at this stage in his life, he was every bit as interested in molding opinions, in framing his policies, in explaining to the American public that the current system of party politics—and more importantly, the current administration—was corroding the future of America.

His unvarnished critiques had by now caught the attention of the foreign press as well, who had been sending correspondents to campaign events. Those reports had initially been more of a human interest nature, assigned by curious editors in England, Germany, France, and Canada. Now there were more serious interviews (many taken by high-level staff) from organizations like Al Jazeera, RT, JNN, and Korea Newswire. Monroe welcomed them all.

As he settled into the lobby chair and adjusted his posture and mike, a few patrons of the hotel recognized Monroe and he waved to them. Gibbons took note of his popularity and as the tape rolled he captured an impromptu and candid exchange of the candidate and the public, even before the introductory comments. This was to be a segment for a local station that was going to be aired as part of a series of reports on the importance of the Midwest "fly-over states" and their impact on American political discourse. Local stations did not typically produce such lofty documentaries, but Gibbons had won two regional Emmys for his insightful reports in St. Paul and St. Louis, and his current GM had given him free rein to bring some of the prestigious hardware to Dayton. Gibbons needed no other incentive, but the networks were calling now too, and that didn't hurt.

"I see you have some fans here," observed Gibbons. "It must be rewarding to be getting recognition."

"We have a wonderful team with the campaign. We're very fortunate that our message is being spread throughout the country, and yes, it's always great to see those efforts succeeding."

"Well, welcome to Kasich-Country! Today we are speaking with Independent Presidential Candidate Monroe Taylor, who is passing through western Ohio on his way to spread his message through the Midwest, America's Heartland. Tell me, Mr. Taylor, how do you think your message will resonate in a state as red as Ohio?"

"I believe that our message is universal, and will resonate among thoughtful voters of any political party."

"And because we are in Ohio, I have to ask your thoughts about former Governor Kasich."

"I've got to say, I'm a fan of the Governor's. The only time I have ever registered in a party is to cast a vote in a primary against a particular candidate. I'm happy to tell you that John Kasich got my vote in the Pennsylvania primary."

"So you did not vote FOR him as much as you voted AGAINST Donald Trump or Ted Cruz?"

"That's accurate. Although I have to say that voting against Trump AND Cruz was a twofer. A magnificent way to cast a vote, and it was for a decent guy like Governor Kasich. So yes. It was all good, except for the fact that Kasich came in third in that primary."

"You have commented extensively on why you are running as an Independent, but you recognize the many handicaps associated with having no party affiliation."

It wasn't a question, and unlike some interviews in which Monroe's lawyerly instincts were on alert, Monroe appreciated the open framework of Gibbons' style. "Right. We don't get any funding from a national committee. We receive no protection from the Secret Service. On the other hand, we don't get beaten up in a primary campaign. We don't adhere to a party line. We march to the beat of our own drum. And ultimately, that is the path, the ONLY path in my view, that can lead the country out of the miasma of gridlock inherent in a two-party system.

"Can you imagine," he added as an afterthought, "how it must feel to run for office after your opponents . . . FROM YOUR OWN PARTY! . . . have dissed you? It takes a lot of ego to put yourself out there to run for office. I don't know how guys like Ted Cruz can swallow that much pride."

"Does that mean your ego is easily bruised?"

"I'm human. I've taken some pretty hard hits during this campaign. But I like to think I am resilient."

"Let's talk about some of those hits."

241

Monroe looked at Gibbons with a mixture of caution and disquietude.

"You've been associated with a licentious lifestyle. You have been accused of being a womanizer, gay, a Papist, a tax-and-spend Liberal, weak on defense, poor character, irreligious, and having a violent temper."

"Gee, I wish they would make up their mind and arrive at some sort of consensus.

"Where do you want to begin? *Argumentum ad hominem.* These are personal attacks on my character . . . for the most part . . . rather than critiques of issues or policies. As I stated during my announcement, I am a healthy adult male, and for the record, I am heterosexual. Not that it's anyone's business. But yes, I understand that by virtue of placing myself in the public eye many areas of my private life are now subject to scrutiny. What I don't get is the public's fascination with sexual orientation, or sex for that matter. It's a message that is incessantly used in the media to sell stuff. At my newspaper, I exercised strict control over advertising and 'news' that was gratuitous in its representation of human sexuality. I'm not in favor of censorship, mind you. But I can remember a time when children did not know the slang words for sexual acts. Toilets were forbidden by the FCC to be shown on TV programs. Married couples slept in twin beds. Bill Bennett once said that there was a time when personal failure and perverse tastes were accompanied by a sense of guilt or embarrassment, and now it's an invitation to go on national TV to talk about it. He said this back in . . . I don't know . . . the nineties. I mean . . . he wasn't wrong! And I have spoken about Dan Quayle's comments about the relaxation of morals. Here we are twenty years later and the culture certainly has not improved. And so-called conservative networks have not raised the bar of morality with their programming, so I find their criticisms to be hypocritical.

"And yes, it's true I have never had a wife. You know what else I never had? An extramarital affair. Am I immoral because I never got married? Whose business is it how I live my personal life?" He stopped just short of saying, "*I want to know. Bring these cocksuckers before me so I can face my accusers.*" He shifted in his chair.

"Let's talk about the religious aspects. You have said that I have been accused of being both irreligious and a Papist. I was raised in the Roman Catholic tradition. This is not a defense. It is a statement of fact. My feeling is that one's religion is a personal choice. In fact, isn't that EVERYONE'S feeling? Isn't that why we have a separation of church and state? 'Congress shall make no law respecting an establishment of religion, or prohibiting the free exercise thereof.' Yet we have these cascades of political candidates every election cycle who aim to prove that they are holier than thou. It matters not one whit," he said, shaking his head. "It's a personal choice, and has nothing to do with being an effective leader. If it did, we would elect religious leaders. We'd have imams or mullahs or bishops running the country."

"What about national defense?" asked Gibbons.

"The US needs a strong defense. The issue is what do you spend the money on? Aircraft carriers? Rapid deployment forces? Drones? Cyber warfare? Next-generation Abrams tanks? Imagine that you are a homeowner out in the country and you buy a rifle to defend your property against bears and wolves. And then your house is attacked by termites. That's how I compare the choices in selecting what defense programs to sponsor.

"The US spends more on defense—in real dollars—than China, Russia, and Saudi Arabia combined. There's no question that defense spending is an important aspect of our national economy. It's something like three-and-a-half percent of GDP. We need to be careful about how that money is spent, and make sure that we avoid getting trapped by the military-industrial complex that Eisenhower warned about sixty years ago."

Gibbons was shaking his head impatiently. "But what about national defense policy? You're talking about budgets. I want to know about execution of national defense. The US has been fighting in Afghanistan for seventeen years. In Iraq for fifteen years."

"Again, let's start with the War Powers Clause of the Constitution. Only Congress has the right to declare war. Let's either declare war and win, or not declare war and remove troops. I want to talk to military leaders to get a better understanding of how effective our military actions are. Nobody wants war. It's a terrible solution to political problems. Yet if you look back through our history the US has been at war . . . or some variation of it . . . for over 90 percent of the time since 1775.

"But once the US declares a war, the military should be in a position to quickly and decisively terminate that war. Something is wrong with a military solution that takes fifteen years to resolve.

"You know more civilians than combatants died during World War Two. That's a terrible situation. I am not in favor of harming civilians, but you have to acknowledge and recognize that if a country is going to go to war, then damage is going to be inflicted on the country we are at war with. And it is my belief that you have to give the citizens of an oppressed country the tools they need to self-govern if that is what they want."

"I'm confused. Can you elaborate?"

"I mean that armies inflict casualties and that if a people want to avoid mayhem and destruction, then they need to be willing to step up and overthrow an oppressive government. Bush 41 gave the impression that he would do that in Iraq, and then it didn't happen."

"Now you sound like a hawk."

"I am not a hawk. I just believe in having a clear vision for defending the Constitution and citizens of the United States. And that vision is guided by the Just War Doctrine: namely, the threat of aggression is grave, all other means of avoiding war must be exhausted, the prospect of success is certain, and the use of force must not cause greater harm than the threat of the aggressor."

"That comes from your faith, does it not?"

"It does. But just war traditions go back to ancient Egypt and the Hindus. It's a human concept; not a religious concept."

"You never served in the armed forces."

"That's true. I never did. I thought about enlisting in the army when I left high school, but my father was dead-set against it. He saw heavy action in Italy in World War Two. He had these absolutely gut-wrenching stories about war, and he naturally wanted to protect me from those horrors. So he talked me out of it, and now I regret never having served. Selective service ended in 1975, right before I turned eighteen, and so I never even had to register for the draft.

"It's one of the many third rails in politics, but I think a draft would be a good opportunity for young people to serve their country. I know I will be pilloried for this, but I believe any organization derives greater strength through a heterogeneous sample. The military has done a good job of recruiting qualified personnel in the four decades since it's been a volunteer force, but there are a disproportionate number of poor and minority recruits. Comfortable white kids like me need to step up."

"That's incredible! What would you say to a soccer mom, or a father like James Madison Taylor, whose son or daughter you want to draft?"

"I'd say two things: First, if your child does not want to join the military, there are plenty of other programs available for them to serve the country. And second, I think the discipline of getting up every day and being part of something greater than yourself is a noble cause. A lot of the kids I see today are pretty soft. America did not become a world power by wearing pajamas, drinking hot chocolate, and talking about getting health insurance."

Gibbons paused, letting the moment that Taylor lost the election wash over him. He recollected himself after considering that he now had a third Emmy in the bag, and a smile spread across his face, as he was barely able to contain his glee.

"Have you selected a running mate?"

"We have been speaking with some candidates. Unlike the current president, I am not willing to discuss who we are talking to."

"Why not?"

"It risks embarrassing those that are not selected. This is not a beauty pageant or a reality TV show. I'm not interested in pitting people against each other or parading them in front of the nation to see how it polls. Our campaign will select the best qualified people, and the voters can judge the ticket on the strength of the decisions and policies we put forward."

· · ·

28

"BREAKING NEWS THIS MORNING, Brian. Yet ANOTHER disastrous set-back for the Taylor campaign as they try to walk back not ONE, but TWO catastrophic missteps that occurred yesterday!"

"Samantha, I don't think you can characterize these comments as missteps. These are full-blown examples of a COMPLETELY unqualified candidate trying to play in the big leagues!"

"Tracy, I am absolutely BESIDE myself! Mortified that a so-called candidate for the highest office in the land is MAKING FUN of shaken baby syndrome! What an insensitive, I'll just say it . . . EVIL! jerk this guy is!"

"Well, Samantha, what do you expect from someone who supports abortion? I mean, he obviously has zero respect for human life, but that is to be expected from a progressive, ultraliberal, elitist, pseudo-intellectual!"

Monroe sat with Ted over their morning coffees, absorbing this display of arrogance. Both men were processing this, realizing that a private cell phone conversation had been hacked. Ted was silently formulating a plan to drive to New York City to throttle these bastards. Monroe noticed the apparent lack of reaction to the pointy stimulus, and took it to mean Ted was preoccupied. He sat quietly, waiting for Part Two of the televised dissection of his campaign and qualifications. He knew the next words would be about his comments about reinstituting the draft. This part was expected, but he was anxious to see how they would spin it. He screwed his mouth to the side, resisting the urge to speak, as the stunning conservative correspondent met his expectations.

"Now he wants to reinstitute the draft, because he obviously feels that the military is incompetent. A guy who never wore the uniform! Such disrespect for our heroes!"

Monroe's iPhone buzzed, then paused, then buzzed again while Ted's started to buzz. Rather than dump one more obligation on Ted, Monroe simply texted TPC1 that he would be with them in thirty minutes. TPC1 was the inner circle, INDY was *Independent* staff, and so on. He got up and refilled his mug with the horrible brew that Ted had made in his room. They hadn't yet emerged from their rooms this morning. Back in Latrobe they would sometimes share an unplanned fifteen minutes of relative peace and quiet over coffees before all hell broke loose. Those occasions were not as frequent as either would have liked, owing to the late nights and late starts that Monroe had. Since the campaign had mobilized they had tried to spend some time alone to compare notes, discuss strategy, and for Ted to outline the day ahead. It was akin to the duties Monroe expected his Chief of Staff to perform. That is, on the mornings when Ted was not otherwise occupied with Sandra. Lately, Monroe noticed that Ted was becoming more and more available.

"Everything okay between you and Sandy?" It was a complete *non sequitur*.

"The fuck?" exclaimed Ted, taken aback. "Don't you have headier issues to worry about than my love life?"

"Yeah, but . . . you know. If your head's not in the game, maybe you need to recalibrate."

"Hey!" Ted barked. "My head's fine! You're the one who better start tracking! And maybe if you were a little bit more 'socially active,' you'd take less interest in MY love life!"

"Settle down, Tiger! Jesus! It's not like I live vicariously through your peccadilloes! However perverse or entertaining they may be."

There followed an awkward pause. All the more awkward since these two friends rarely shared awkward pauses.

"I was just asking. As a friend. You seem distracted."

"I am not distracted. I am only distracted by these fucks on TV."

"You said you weren't distracted. Make up your mind already."

Ted rolled his eyes, drained his mug of disgusting coffee, and left Monroe's room to retreat to his own where a hot shower and pressed clothes awaited him. He passed Fredo in the hallway, and jerking his thumb in the direction of the room he just exited, said, "Do something with that guy, will ya?"

Fredo gave a smile and a knowing nod, but had no idea what the hell Ted was referring to.

They had flown last night to Green Bay, Wisconsin, after the interview with Harold Gibbons. The team convened in a conference room where Sam, Phil, and Sandra were already animated, discussing how to counter the attacks. Monroe pre-empted them.

"I want to go on with Samantha, Tracy, and Brian."

"Are you crazy?" blurted Sandra. Monroe glanced at Ted to capture any expression that registered. He caught Ted examining the floor. "No good would come of that!"

"Call Gary. Get me on the show. Preferably in their studio so I can read their body language. I don't want them to have me on a remote. Then they hold all the cards. And it has to be live. No taping so that they can cherry-pick and edit. Do it. Do it now."

"Monroe," assuaged Sam, "We understand how you feel. But please trust us. Trust our professional judgment. We think it's a bad idea."

Monroe walked over to Sam, and placing a hand on his shoulder said, "Sam, I know what I'm doing here. They have an audience, and that audience needs to hear me. And if they don't accept the offer, then we put out a press release calling them a bunch of pussies. Sorry for the language, Sandra."

"Hey," she looked aside and held up a hand, "no offense taken. They are a bunch of pussies."

"Can we get off of the slang please?" protested Phil. "All we need is for someone to pick up this conversation, and no, this room has not been swept. Monroe. Please. Don't do this. Not now."

"What is your problem? I am not gonna lay down and let these cretins march all over us. If we wait then the moment will be lost. They will spin it like I had to consult with a bunch of speechwriters and lawyers. Fuck that noise. I'm going in."

"See, it's that kind of language that scares us."

"Sam. Relax. I'll be fine. I've done this before."

"What about the events in Cedar Rapids, St. Louis, and Denver?"

"If you get me in tomorrow morning, I'll be in Cedar Rapids by what? 1 PM? 2 PM? We have a jet. Oh. Nevermind. You guys need the jet. OK, I'll charter one. Problem solved." He turned and left to pack an overnight bag.

Phil looked at Ted with suspicion. "Why is he hell-bent on going alone to New York?"

Ted gave a how-the-hell-should-I-know shrug and left to see if Monroe needed anything, or if he had any instructions to be followed in his absence.

Phil turned to Sam and Sandra, and asked in a low voice, "You think he has some action on the side up there?"

"You never know," admitted Sam with a sigh. "Put Fuller on it. I don't want to risk anything at this point."

Back in the suite, Ted called ABC to get her working on a charter jet reservation from Green Bay to LaGuardia. Alice looked up the time from LaGuardia to midtown Manhattan and reckoned it could be done. Monroe intended to travel alone, which was unusual. "He travels the fastest who travels alone," he reasoned, quoting Kipling.

The day proceeded as scheduled with a meeting with a dairy association and the local chamber of commerce. He had to cancel a scheduled tour of the Oneida Nation of Wisconsin. Sandra and Ted would go to speak to the leaders. Monroe felt comfortable with the substitution.

The meetings were at least cordial, and the chamber presented Monroe with a Packers jersey with his name glued above the number 2, and the usual lame jokes about earning votes if he could switch his allegiance from the Steelers. He took it in stride, but allowed that he would have been more apt if they had issued him Number 1. "If I find out you gave Trump a Number 1 jersey, there's gonna be a tax on cheese in a Taylor administration." There were good-natured guffaws all around, and then Monroe was ushered to a limo to take him to a waiting Learjet 31A, which had been flown in from Chicago. Ted rode with him to the airport.

"Lot of speculation about why you insist on going alone."

"Why? You wanna come along? We can buy you a toothbrush inside the terminal."

"I'm not your bodyguard. I'm not gonna take a bullet for you!"

Monroe laughed. "You've taken plenty of bullets for me!" He looked out the window and thought of his security team. "You know, it's not like we have Secret Service protection. I'd never expect any of the guys to do anything heroic."

"I know. Just do us all a giant favor and keep a low profile up there. Dinner in your room, get to bed early . . . and NO HOOKERS!"

Monroe laughed. "Shut up!"

"And tomorrow. On the air. Please don't resurrect the bit about mast . . ."

"Shut up already!"

". . . tication."

Monroe was in the hotel lobby across from the studio by 8:30 PM.

He loved New York City. The amazing variety of ethnicities all in one concentrated place. The food, the architecture, the salad bowl of humanity. He had no time to take in the sights tonight, to stroll without purpose down a sidewalk crammed with attractive women of every nationality. But he did happen to notice a stunning black lady in the lobby, dressed casually in jeans and boots, and wearing a sweatshirt that was way too big for her. When she caught him noticing her, she demurely went back to checking her phone. Well, that would have to be the extent of his people-watching this evening. He had a Skype session scheduled with Kurt's team for nine fifteen. Enough time to order room service and grab a shower.

Gary Davidson had confirmed that Monroe was scheduled to go on at seven, an hour after the show began. Monroe was up at four, grabbed a plate full of what passed for a continental breakfast in the lobby, showered, and dressed. He was out the door and at the studio for prep at six thirty. After checking in through a large security portal he was directed down a corridor to meet with a production assistant.

The PA was a young man who was disarmingly polite. Monroe regarded him with suspicion, thinking maybe this was the enemy's way to play good cop/bad cop. Then he considered that this kid was probably just being a professional. He had a job to do and was being pleasant and professional. Period. Monroe scolded himself for being so skeptical. He was moved to the green room where he checked messages before he texted a status to Ted, who was now in Cedar Rapids.

A harried middle-aged woman entered the green room and introduced herself as the executive producer. "We'll set you up on the couch during a taped segment about ICE and the wall, and then there will be a commercial break. From there you'll be introduced by Tracy, who will ask you a few questions, and you can do whatever it is you do. We're on a three-second delay."

Well, that was rude and informative, thought Monroe, shaking his head imperceptibly. He sighed loudly, prompting the producer to ask, "Are you annoyed or nervous?"

"Probably just nervous," Monroe lied.

And the next thing he knew he was being led to the couch, seated next to Samantha and Brian, while Tracy wiggled into her seat. The two women were stunningly beautiful, even in person with all of the makeup and hair product. Monroe wondered if the extreme cuts of their dresses were for the benefit of the viewers or intended to intimidate the guests. He reckoned that male or female, the guests had reason to be intimidated. Samantha and Brian greeted him warmly. Which struck him as hyper-hypo-critical. *If it's hyper-hypo, then it's just "critical." Heh! At least that part of my brain still works!*

Because he was on a couch, there was no way to adopt his defiant posture of slinging his arm over the back of a chair. Kurt would be gratified by that. He realized that the cushion he had been directed to was of the same fabric as the others, but his was much softer. He sank into the seat while Brian and Samantha sat atop theirs like royalty. He saw there was time to spare so he snatched a stack of magazines that lay on the table in front of him, and sat on those. The three hosts looked at him as if he had kicked a dog. He smiled back at them warmly as the assistant floor manager counted down the time to air.

"We are back this morning with Independent candidate for president Vaughn Monroe Taylor, whose campaign made a special request to join us amid recent controversial comments he has made." The broadcast showed a close-up of Monroe's reaction to Tracy's intro. "Welcome Mr. Taylor."

"Thank you. I appreciate the opportunity."

In Cedar Rapids, Kurt watched the TV with the others, providing quiet and fast-running commentary. "Calm. Erect posture. Confident. Well-modulated voice." In Falls Church a sample focus group of eighty likely voters sat with neuro-testing dials to indicate their emotions as the interview progressed.

"Mr. Taylor, we played some audio yesterday that has gone viral online," began Samantha. "It's so disturbing that we are not even going to play it again today. Can you tell America how you can make jokes about shaken baby syndrome?"

"No, I cannot, because your analysis of the audio referenced is completely out of context. It was not a joke about shaken baby syndrome."

"Out of context?" fulminated Brian, his eyes bulging. The two women sat shaking their heads dismissively.

"Exactly so," explained Monroe calmly. "The conversation you eavesdropped on was between me and my editor at *The Latrobe Independent*. We had just suffered a directed computer hacking attack, and at the close of the conversation I used a spoonerism to break the tension."

"A spooner . . . ? Tracy asked, the camera picking up her eyebrows raised in incredulity. "Is this another one of your . . ."

she paused and looked at her colleagues in exasperation. "I don't know . . . innuendoes?"

"A spoonerism is a literary device often employed for humorous effect. I'm surprised they didn't teach you that in journalism school, Tracy." He smiled only enough to appear sincere and a bit sorry. "What I actually said, in, what again, was a very private telephone conversation, was that I was going back out on the campaign trail to shake babies and kiss hands. See, ordinarily politicians KISS babies and SHAKE hands, and by mixing up the phrases, well. There's your spoonerism and your humor."

"Don't patronize me!" scolded Tracy.

Monroe was having fun, but he realized he was here to make a point and win hearts and minds, not come off as the smartass they made him out to be. Back in Falls Church the dials move hard to port.

"You know," continued Monroe, "from my perspective the more newsworthy aspect of your story is the fact that a private cell phone conversation of a candidate for president was tapped. How is that not a serious offense?"

"It is a serious offense, no question. And the FBI is looking into it," nodded Samantha.

"So what you are saying," drawled Brian, "is that this comment about shaking babies is a joke. A gag. You were playing it for laughs." The smirky, dismissive attitude was really pissing Monroe off.

"No, Brian, what I am saying is that it has nothing at all to do with shaking babies."

"Aren't you one of these Progressives who likes to chant 'WORDS MATTER'?"

"I've built an entire career around words as an editor, as a journalist, and now as a politician. My message to you is that you should exercise some journalistic integrity and listen to all words, and stop tilting the balance by taking words out of context. It's like the distortions about Nancy Pelosi's remarks about passing the ACA to find out what's in it. Without context it sounds ridiculous."

Brian was agitated and rolling his eyes. Monroe tamped him down and pressed on.

"Look! I am not a big fan of Pelosi, but I detest bad reporting for political effect. Well, I detest bad reporting in any case."

A cacophony arose as the three hosts began talking at once, but Monroe overtook them. "Listen, you just have to be fair in your reporting. You can't cherry-pick your sound bites. It's like claiming that Lincoln said "we cannot dedicate, we cannot consecrate this ground." Out of context, it's meaningless. Root out the facts. You're all smart people. Make a case built on truth. You have a responsibility to your viewers."

The dials in Falls Church twisted to the right of center. The producer's voice came through Tracy's and Samantha's and Brian's earpieces. "Get control of this fucking interview, please!"

"What about your comments about the failed military recruiting?" challenged Samantha.

"Once again, that is a false premise."

"False how?"

Monroe reached out with his right hand and laid it gently on Samantha's forearm. "Eww! Don't touch me!"

He quickly retracted his arm. "What I said in the Gibbons interview is that a draft would ensure that the military is more representative of America. Affluent white kids are underrepresented and they need to step up. People should go to Taylor2020.us to get access to the full interview."

"Why do you hate President Trump so much?" asked Tracy, her brows knit in an expression of disdain and skepticism for whatever answer might be proffered.

"Hate is such a strong word. An ugly word." Monroe looked up thoughtfully. He was considering whether now was the time to go nuclear. It was exactly the feeling he had back in Greensburg at the first news conference when that jackass from Harlon's Super PAC asked him about pornography. He felt his ears warming and he knew that it was not just from the studio lights. "He may have some good qualities. I've said before that no one is wrong all the time, and there have been times when I have agreed with some of what he has said and done."

"Like what?" she challenged. This interruption was robbing Monroe's mojo.

"He's right about term limits for Congress. I agree with placing America's needs first, in a fiscally responsible manner. And I think if I was president I might be tempted to call out certain politicians for stances that I think hurt the country. Take obstructionists like Mitch McConnell and Ted Cruz for example." Brian started to interrupt him but Monroe raised his hand. Monroe went for the full monty anyway. He glanced at Samantha who was subconsciously petting her forearm where he touched her, as though wiping away the cooties. "But to answer your question about my regard for President Trump, yeah . . . I guess you'd have to say that I do hate him. I mean, I have a Shakespearean vocabulary, but I find it insufficient to describe the loathing and execration I often feel for him and his administration."

Samantha looked like she had just swallowed a fly. Tracy was dumbfounded as though stuck mute by the Archangel Gabriel. Brian exercised his role as defender of the womenfolk, and sputtered, "PAH! At least now it's out in the open. You admit it!"

"Read my editorials! I've never hidden my disdain for this presidency! And let me ask you something: why is it that you give him a pass? Tell me that! He's recorded talking about grabbing a woman in the most inappropriate manner, in language that is unsuitable for public consumption. Yet I make a joke about 'shaking babies and kissing hands'—in a private phone conversation—and you call me an 'evil jerk.' What hypocrisy! How dare you?"

"Yeah, okay, so it's a big joke," answered Samantha, now recovered.

Monroe reached into his back pocket and retrieved his wallet. Fishing out a twenty, he handed it to Samantha. "Buy yourself a sense of humor. Honestly. The whole country needs to take a pill and lie down. Why is everyone so easily offended? This is one thing that Trump actually gets right occasionally. Americans are CONSUMED with political correctness. Bill O'Reilly makes a joke about the singers in *Jesus Christ Superstar* having tattoos, and he gets annihilated on social media. Men and women can't joke in the workplace."

Tracy thanked God for this gift. It was a perfect segue into her next question which was about Monroe's defense against the sexual harassment lawsuit filed by Denise Dexter.

"So you approve of men joking about women in the workplace?" Tracy, Monroe thought, is a real pain in the ass.

"I never approve of violence or harassment of anybody. But sometimes you have to give common sense a chance. Men and women really are supposed to like each other, and the current climate of the Me Too movement is, in some ways, an overreaction. I've read reports of women who feel uncomfortable because of the way a guy looked at them . . ."

"So you think it's okay for a guy to ogle a woman," asserted Tracy.

"Have you ever been uncomfortable when a man looked at you, Tracy?"

"Yes. Yes I have. Many times!" Samantha nodded a "Me Too" nod.

"Well, here you are on national TV wearing a low-cut dress with a hemline that's what? Twelve inches above your knee? You're on this conservative network selling your sex appeal, Tracy. If you don't want guys leering at you, I suggest you wear a burka. Because you are an attractive woman and you're gonna garner a lot of attention if you dress like you're in a hip-hop video."

"Get this shit under control, people!" commanded the producer, screaming into their earpieces. A couple of the dials in Falls Church actually broke at this point.

"It's certainly interesting that you have such sensitive views about women, Mr. Taylor," mocked Tracy.

"Yes," said Brian. "We are joined now by someone with a different perspective, Denise Dexter!"

The lights went up on stage left to reveal Denise Dexter, wearing a smart business suit and sporting a short pixie cut.

"Denise!" gasped Monroe, "I don't know what to say!" There was a dramatic pause. Everyone on set knew they had taken Monroe completely by surprise, and the producer relished the moment. "Didn't your lawyer advise you against appearing here? On national TV? With me? What's wrong with him? He should be protecting your case!"

"Oh, Monroe," she whined pathetically. "That lawsuit was my brother's idea. Someone approached him and made a case to bilk you out of your lottery winnings. I never wanted to hurt you!"

"Oh for God's sake." He got up, unclipped his mike, and went to her. The producer cut abruptly to a commercial about car insurance. Monroe put his hand on the back of her left arm and tenderly rubbed it up and down, the way a kind father soothes his kid after striking out in the big game. The segment was over and a couple PAs came to usher Monroe and Denise off set. Monroe turned and walked briskly back to Samantha, realizing there was not much time before the end of the commercial break.

"I'm sorry if I offended you by touching your forearm."

"It's alright. I may have overreacted. It startled me, that's all." While not exactly contrite, she did appear a bit more human.

"Well then, I apologize for startling you." He stood and shook hands with the other two. Brian returned an aggressively firm handshake. Monroe thought about breaking the tension with a joke about kissing babies, but discretion prevailed. He thanked the hosts for their air time and excused himself quickly, which the production staff took as a sign of his professionalism.

· · ·

HE LANDED AT THE EASTERN IOWA AIRPORT at Cedar Rapids at 1:15 PM and the Learjet 31A taxied to the hanger where Taylor One was parked. Ted was standing outside a limo, his phone pressed to his ear. There were six security guards; two flanking Ted and two each in black SUVs parked in front of the limo. Ted looked at Monroe with an inscrutable expression as they got in the car.

"What's up?"

"We're interviewing for a new position. Sandra just turned in her resignation. She's gonna go to work for a health care lobbyist."

"Really! Did you see that coming?"

"No, but I should have. It explains her recent attitude."

"Mmmm. Maybe it does. But it doesn't explain why she's been so distant from you. I mean, in theory, in a normal relationship this should be a good thing for the two of you. You're no longer colleagues. No dipping the pen . . ."

"Shut up please. I can't believe you're not concerned about what this does to your campaign."

"What does it do? She's an overpaid cog in the machine. Just like you," he joked. "Who's gonna replace her? What about Alice?"

"No!" Ted exclaimed brusquely. "Alice is good, but she doesn't have that kind of juice. She'll be a good assistant to provide continuity during the transition."

"Geez. First Blake and now Sandra. They're falling like members of Trump's cabinet. Ah, I shouldn't be so glib. Sandra will be missed . . . she's a valuable member of the team. . . . What's up with all the fresh security?"

"There have been some threats incoming from your interview. Apparently your performance was not universally appreciated."

They stopped for a burger at a diner before going to the first event, a speech outside the National Czech & Slovak Museum & Library. Monroe was supposed to speak to an audience of about a thousand people who had signed up online to hear him discuss the importance of the NATO alliance to America's defense. Two of the guards remained outside. Two sat at the counter across the table from Ted and Monroe, and the other two took tables on either side.

"Who is being considered for the job?" asked Monroe while they waited to be served.

"Kate for one. Sam is talking to a guy from the outside too. They might already have made a decision. I dunno. It's not a position we want to have open very long."

"You think Kate has the juice?"

"She's reserved, but she does have a ton of experience. She's worked on a Senate subcommittee and for a few lobbyists."

"Senate subcommittee?" Monroe asked skeptically. A waitress came to take their order.

". . . and we're in a bit of a rush ma'am," Ted said apologetically. The waitress gave him a look that said she understood he was a self-important asshole. She turned without replying.

"Senate subcommittee," repeated Monroe. "That could be anything. Was it Fisheries or Defense?"

"How should I know? I haven't read her goddamned CV. Why are you being such a hardass about this?"

"I don't know. Sorry. I've been uptight ever since I gave that interview. How did it play?"

"Fifty-fifty. Kurt thought you did pretty well under the circumstances, but Phil and Sam aren't grading on a curve. They are dealing in absolutes."

"Well how do YOU think I did?"

"I thought you invoked a little too much smart-assidry."

"You're making up words you know. It's the only reason your vocabulary is allegedly larger than mine. Seriously. You think I was too hard on them or on Trump?"

"A little of both."

Monroe paused. "I was thinking of sending a fruit basket to them. And maybe some flowers to Samantha."

"Apologies for tapping her arm? Might not be a bad idea . . . mess with them by showing how kind, sensitive, and contrite you are. Or, it might set a bad precedent. You never sent anything to other interviewers."

Monroe remained silent. Ted stared at him. The food arrived with a clatter of plates and Ted asked, "Did you?"

"I did. I sent flowers to Lori Spalding."

"I guess I'm not totally surprised," remarked Ted as he adorned his burger with mustard. "You're the last of the gentlemen. Plus, she was a total babe."

They finished the meal in relative silence, with Monroe sending burgers outside to the two security guards. After Ted paid up they rode to the Library and Museum with plenty of time to spare. Monroe debriefed TPC about the missed meeting with the Oneidas (they were a little miffed), and then awaited the verdict on the interview. Kurt explained that the focus group thought he hit some rough patches with an inadequate explanation of his views on a draft. His comments directed at Trump were exactly what you would expect: People who hated Trump loved his explanation, and the die-hard Trump supporters thought Monroe was an unpatriotic sonofabitch.

"I could have told you that," Monroe said with no sarcasm. "How much time and money did you waste on this focus group?" It was a rhetorical question.

Monroe was introduced for the umpteenth time by David Evans, who was back on the trail. The crowd gave a roaring welcome and Monroe leapt up to the dais. A lectern had been provided but he abandoned it, preferring instead to roam the stage as he spoke. He had convinced Kurt that at certain lower-profile events that he performed better without a prepared speech. Instead he relied on outlined notes that projected on the teleprompter screens. They had rehearsed this strategy many times in auditoriums, and found it to be effective. After thanking the crowd and briefly acknowledging the recent controversy over his remarks (with no apology necessary), he continued.

"I have been irritating my campaign team. I'd like to acknowledge Kurt Bastille, who was been a great communications coach. When we kicked off the campaign, we used speeches written by me. Because I'm a journalist, I've rejected speechwriters on the campaign, opting to write my own stuff. As an editor, I have passed my work on to other members of the team for their input. Politics, like a newspaper, is very much a collaborative effort.

"By not using prepared speeches, we've been able to avoid delayed reactions to the daily, and sometimes hourly, shifts in the news cycle. The politics surrounding the Trump administration is so fluid and dynamic, that it actually is much easier to just be extemporaneous, and so we are able to react to current events quickly. Today's topic is about NATO though, which is certainly timely, but so far today we haven't seen any tweets from the president in which he insulted our allies. Yet.

"Donald Trump is often described as a 'populist.' He's fixated on his popularity, but populism as a political term really has nothing to do with being popular. The word means 'one who supports the concerns of ordinary people.' That sounds like a legitimate cause, and who could argue against being for your country? America First. There's not much for an American to disagree with there.

"But 'populism' as an ideology is associated with nationalism, anti-immigration, anti-Muslim, anti-free press, authoritarianism, and a disregard for expert opinions. The term has been applied to movements in countries like Hungary, Turkey, Italy, France, the United Kingdom, and the Philippines. Nigel Farage is the former Member of Parliament who advocated for Brexit. Marine LePen ran for president of France under the National Front party banner. Prime Minister Viktor Orbán of Hungary, Tayyip Erdogan of Turkey, and Rodrigo Duterte of the Philippines have all been described as populists. Nationalists. Anti-immigration. Authoritarian. Anti-free Press. For a country that cherishes the Constitution, it's hard to reconcile these traits as desirable for someone running for office. And yet, here we are.

"It's peculiar that this nationalist sentiment is rising all across the world. Much of it has to do with Islamophobia, as with Marine LePen. Much of it has to do with preservation of sovereignty, as with Nigel Farage and Brexit. Much of it has to do with national-ism, as with the Alternative for Germany party, which is another Euro-skeptic organization. Here's a question for you: Does the world really need a right-wing anti-Europe party in Germany?

"Nationalism is dangerous. America First is a nice slogan as long as everyone understands that America, like all countries, functions within a global economy. A global community. The problems that face the US are problems that face other countries. We rely on maintaining strong relationships with European allies like NATO, as well as global partners like Japan and Australia. But the Trump administration is amenable to criticizing and irritating our allies, while at the same time cozying up to leaders who threaten our political system, as in the case of Russia, if not our actual existence, as in the case of North Korea.

"I am in favor of engagement; not isolation. I think it's a good idea to have meaningful discussions with North Korea. My hope is that someday North Korea will become a member of the international community. My thinking is that if you establish trade with a country, there is less of a chance of hostilities. More butter, fewer guns. On the other hand, I have argued that a strong defense is necessary for the US, and a key component in our defense is a strong NATO. Russia needs to be put on notice that the west will not stand for either military or political aggression. Regions in the Middle East that have been destabilized by Al Qaeda and ISIS require the resources of a strong united defense, and that includes our NATO allies."

Monroe continued lecturing about the roles of civilians at the head of the military. He acknowledged that, if elected, he would be the fifth president since Bush 41 not to have served in active duty. But he also pointed out that there were ten presidents before Clinton that never had military experience. And he further explained that while he was never required to serve, neither had he chosen to serve. He felt compelled to elaborate on the reasons he never volunteered, but he thought it would sound like an excuse. An alibi. No one would want to hear how he left law school to come home and take over the family business for his elderly mother. He opted to omit that portion. It was already in his official bio, but it had not received a lot of attention. Maybe he would ask TPC to clarify that portion of his CV. Or something. His mind drifted dangerously as he concluded his remarks, and he was afraid of sounding like a disorganized thinker. Unorganized and undisciplined.

At least he spoke in complete sentences.

· · ·

30

TED LONGED FOR A BREAK FROM CAMPAIGNING. It was easy for Monroe to be enthusiastic. He was the flavor of the day, every day. Ted was just along for the ride. He missed harassing the gang back in Latrobe, he missed being able to set his own schedule, and he missed Sandra, who had flown back to DC. He called her every day, but lately he was leaving more messages. "Ah well," he thought. "That was fun while it lasted."

He tried to shake himself out of the funk that he felt descending on him. He felt uneasy, unsure of himself. He was worried about his health. The results of his recent EKG had revealed an arrhythmia, and the lipids showed high LDLs, which was no surprise given his diet. Since he had been campaigning, his diet had certainly not improved. It had always been pretty poor, the result of having too little time to prepare real food. The self-inflicted demands of his job at the paper also led to inadequate physical activity, though he did manage to take extended walks at lunchtime when he was back in Latrobe. A hyperextension of his knee during his senior year as a running back for the Latrobe Wildcats prevented him from taking up jogging, to the mutual chagrin of him and Monroe. He had been on medication for hypertension since he turned fifty. He lay in the hotel bed struggling to get his socks on.

"Fuck. One day leads to another and the next thing you know you're sixty years old, inflexible, overweight, and have a bad ticker. Fuck."

He got dressed and joined Monroe in his room for their morning coffee ritual.

"Hey Dude," Ted greeted Monroe without enthusiasm.

"What's wrong? You look like hell."

"I'm just tired I guess. Tired and worried."

"Worried about what?" asked Monroe dismissively. "We're doing great!" Monroe considered for a moment, and then realized that he once again risked turning into a self-centered jerk. It really WAS about him, but he needed to exercise some of the empathy that he was famous for back at *The Independent.* "Hey. Sorry. For being a jerk. What's troubling you?"

Ted explained his symptoms then elaborated his concerns about his effectiveness as Monroe's right-hand man. "How am I going to be a Chief of Staff if you get elected?"

"Ted, look, we have known each other since seventh grade. To a large extent, I am the person I am because of our friendship. You and I have been influencing each other's worldviews since we rated Miss Blakely's dresses in algebra class. You're a part of the team whether or not you wanna be. Quit your bellyaching. And take a vacation. Go back to DC and spend time with Sandra."

"No, that ain't happening. She's too busy to return calls anymore. That ship has sailed."

"Okay, sorry to hear that. But take a vacation anyway. Get healthy, have some fun, and get back here as soon as possible. I need you. Oh. And stay out of trouble!"

Ted was worried about going anywhere remote by himself. What if something happened to him or what if he missed some important challenge on the campaign? What if he had a heart attack and no one was around? On the other hand, he was getting dull from the travel and the daily grinding away of his senses on the campaign trail. The trip to Fort Myers was a short respite for the team, but Ted had arrived late, so it was even shorter for him. A change in latitude would be good for him, but a visit back home would be better. A week away might be the ticket. Give him a chance to recharge in Latrobe without having to look after Monroe's business interests and worry about a battery of medical tests. Plus it would allow him to lick his wounded ego after Sandra's abrupt departure. While he was back in town he would be able to spend a little time at the paper to see how they were getting along without him and Monroe. Assess the prospects for the future just in case Monroe lost the election. Heck, a week might not be enough time to address the dozens of items that he had just added to his "To-Do" list.

Ted took a long draft on his coffee and sighed contentedly. "Okay. How about I head to Latrobe for a week or so? Clean up a few details, get my affairs in order for the eventual move to Washington, and check in on Franco."

"Sounds like a plan," assented Monroe.

Ted landed at Arnold Palmer Regional Airport the next day on a charter arranged by a staffer working for Alice. Franco was going to send Ronni the Mole to get him, because he was up to his neck in work and worries. On reflection, he thought it would be better if he met Ted himself. That would give him a chance to take him to lunch to pick his brain about the campaign and get any fresh leads for what now amounted to a serial feature in the paper about the national campaign.

They ordered salads at the restaurant upstairs, and Ted filled Franco in on the recent successes.

"Are you really that jazzed about his chances, or are you just drinking the Kool-Aid?"

CHAPTER 30

"No. He's really doing well, especially since the incident in Fort Myers."

"Oh my god! Everyone in the office just went completely nuts when he asked if Trump even knew how to drive a car! They were high-fiving each other! We sent Smitty out to Toledo to interview the Baylons."

"Really! We're scheduled to be in St. Charles and St. Louis in a couple days. He should hook up with Monroe out there."

"Well, naturally he would like to drop in and see Monroe and the campaign first hand, but we have him doing more background stuff. He's working with Ronni on a story about Lindsay O'Connor."

"And you know who Lindsay O'Connor is from the Baylons . . ."

"Right. She ID'd her. Lives in St. Charles, which went heavy for Trump in 2016. Typical nut-job. Ronni assembled a dossier on her from her social media posts. Sanctimonious, holier-than-thou hockey mom."

"How's she working out? Ronni?"

"Great," answered Franco matter-of-factly. "She pretends she doesn't know that we know she's a mole, and we pretend that she doesn't know we know she's a mole. She's actually a damn good reporter. Clean writing, good research. I kinda hope she stays after the election. I mean, provided we still have a paper then. Hey! Wait'll you see the office. We have the campaign schedule posted everywhere, and a map of the US with colored pins that show where he's been, and where he is on any given day. It looks like the invasion of Normandy!"

Franco dropped Ted off at his house after lunch. It had only been a couple weeks since he'd been home, but the place looked abandoned. He started sorting mail, stacking papers, and doing laundry. The drain on his laundry tub was leaking, so he laid a towel on the floor, gathered some tools, and went to work to tighten the slip nut on the P-trap tail piece. When he laid down he got a little light-headed and wondered who would find him—and when—if he should pass out under there. "Screw it," he thought. "I'm not gonna be controlled by health worries." But he did pull out his iPhone to make sure it was within easy reach. Once the leak was repaired, he cleaned up and went out to stock up on provisions.

At the grocery store he was stopped several times by well-wishers inquiring about Monroe and the campaign. He observed an elderly couple both wearing TAYLOR'S VISION 2020 caps. He surreptitiously took a picture of them and texted it to Monroe.

He thought about Sandra while he was waiting in the checkout line, and he thought he might call her later tonight, just to say hello and perhaps to say goodbye. Some closure might be appropriate. Sandra was logging long hours to catch up with the pharma lobby she was now managing. She would make a big splash there, but Ted recognized that now they were on different sides of an issue. One of the planks in Monroe's platform was to impair the influence of lobbies. The means to affect that would be to promote term limits for all elected offices. Ted and Monroe had talked about this at length and Monroe had expounded this view often, even before he won the lottery. Monroe understood that the likelihood of amending the Constitution to limit terms for Congress was nil, but the discussion had to be initiated.

This was one of the few issues where he found himself in the unnatural position of actually AGREEING with Donald Trump. The day after they are first elected, politicians are most concerned with getting reelected. And that takes money. The money comes from individuals, of course, but much of it comes from lobbies with axes to grind, and influence to peddle. If the politicians didn't worry about getting reelected, they could govern more effectively without corruptive influences.

He called her that evening around nine thirty, and she answered politely, if somewhat stiffly. After inquiries and reports as to each other's well-being, Ted affirmed that there was little likelihood of maintaining a long-distance relationship, given their workloads, travel schedules, and competing interests. It would have been trite to say, "Well, it was fun while it lasted," or "We'll always have Paris," so he offered her his best wishes and a vague intent to stay in touch.

At least that was over with.

As he set down the phone and picked up a glass of Merlot, he felt a burden lift from his chest. He exhaled sharply and looked around his living room, wishing somewhat bizarrely that his hectic schedule could permit him to own a cat. Well, maybe after the election.

Tomorrow he would go to the office to see what was shaking, thank everyone for their hard work and their support for the boss, and assuage their fears over what the future might hold. For now, he absorbed a few minutes of peace and quiet until his obsessive nature overtook his intellect and he compulsively tuned the TV to the cable news spectrum, jumping between the ultraliberal attacks on Trump and Taylor and the ultraconservative attacks on Clinton, Obama, and Taylor. *Christ, it's 2019 and they're still bitching about Clinton and Obama.*

"Whatsa matter? No herald trumpets?" He asked Franco on entering the office. "No virgins scattering rose petals in my path?" Franco smirked and led him into the meeting room to cheers. A TAYLOR banner was tacked to the wall above the whiteboard and a mockup front page for November 4, 2020, lay on the table, with the headline proclaiming "TAYLOR WINS IN LANDSLIDE." The staff's enthusiasm for their boss was to be expected but it was still a heartwarming sight. Ted placed several cardboard boxes on the table and opening them he started to divvy up a new batch of promotional apparel. Taking a rolled-up T-shirt and stepping back to throw a pass to Sheila, who was standing back against the wall, he quipped, "Look! I'm Trump in Puerto Rico passing out paper towels like a boss!"

After the revelry subsided he explained how energetic the campaign was, and how proud both he and Monroe were that the paper was doing so well. Everyone knew that part of the rejuvenated financial health of the paper was due not only to Monroe reinvesting, but also the fame accorded his campaign. For the first time in its history, *The Independent* had a national reporter. Paper circulation and online subscriptions were up due to sales in major cities across the country.

"It's been a helluva publicity stunt!" remarked Barlow.

"I hasten to point out that the increased sales and advertising revenue remains less than 1 percent of the outlay in cash that Monroe made to run for president."

"It's a good thing he's a serious candidate!" opined someone.

"He's got my vote," offered another.

"I'll pass that along to him," said Ted. "Just make sure you're registered. Which raises a good point. In Pennsylvania, you can't vote in a primary unless you have a party affiliation. So if you want to help Monroe, the way to do it is to register in a party you want to defeat and cast a vote against the frontrunner, often known as the candidate you detest the most. Although as we all know, the Pennsylvania primary happens too late to have any effect on national politics. But the word can be spread in the early vote states."

"Except for New Hampshire and South Carolina which are open," added Sheila.

"One in every crowd," said Ted, rolling his eyes. The meeting adjourned, he met with Franco and Sheila to catch up on details. "How badly were we affected by the ransomware?"

"It hobbled us for a couple days. We were able to get most of the files back from the online backup service. We had our IT guy bring in a couple of hired guns too. Made sure we updated all of our antivirus software. We even brought in the kid who hacked Ronni's laptop that time to run some security checks."

"Alright. I guess that's just going to be a thing from now on. Another cost of doing business. Sucks." Ted paused, thinking, then continued. "Too bad we couldn't have used this episode as a diversion when we had our problem with Ronni. Did she ever get wise to your safecracking?"

"Not as far as we can tell. Either that or she's a damn good actor."

"Being tied into TPC I can guaran-damn-tee you she is a good actor. They are the real deal."

"And I guess the hacker is the real deal too," added Franco.

. . .

31

GARY DAVIDSON WALKED PURPOSEFULLY across the stage at the Vespucci Arena in St. Louis. Taking long strides, he approached David Evans, who was in conference with the stage manager on stage left. Gary was uncharacteristically frazzled, shouting complaints about the lighting. Kate Frachette was in tow, pausing while on her phone and then rushing to catch up. She had the ninety-three item checklist of details to review prior to every appearance. And that was just the production-related details. There were similar checklists for security and admissions, and those were always reviewed in advance with the events centers.

There were always compromises and specifics that were peculiar to the locale, whether they were requirements of the local fire code, the authority having jurisdiction, or limitations of the site itself. Today it was a lighting *faux pas* that was exercising Davidson. The word "SLEAZEBALLZ" was projected against the back curtain, the result of a gobo having not been removed by the rock concert's lighting crew from two nights before. "This is why we do dress rehearsals," assured the stage manager, retaining his calm demeanor.

Monroe was still at his hotel suite going over some policy bits being tossed at him randomly by Kurt, Dexter, and Dino. Phil and Sam were observers who peppered Monroe with suggestions too numerous to be of much value. They knew it too, but hoped that maybe some of it would sink in through osmosis.

"Guys, look . . ." Monroe attempted to deflect some of their good intentions. He leaned forward setting his GO FOR MONROE mug, his fourth cup of coffee today, on a low table. "If I don't project the image by now, it ain't happening." He wished that Ted was here. Ted would have understood that at this point their suggestions were really just unintentional attacks on his self-confidence.

"Sorry. Sorry, Monroe," Sam apologized. "We're just trying to polish it a bit, it's no reflection on you."

"Absolutely! Absolutely!" cajoled Phil. "Listen. You're the best candidate we have ever managed. We all agree." He looked around to the others for their nodding confirmation.

Monroe threw him a skeptical look and murmured, "No need for a smoke machine at the Vespucci Arena . . ." They shared a chuckle.

In fairness to TPC, they had invested emotionally in Monroe's campaign. It was not just about business to Sam and Phil (although Monroe was paying them handsomely), it was not just about their professional reputations (although accepting Monroe at the outset seemed like a bit of a risk). Now it was about getting this guy elected because he had good ideas, a rock-solid work ethic, and a commitment to his country that matched that of any other politician they had ever represented. That he was likable, photogenic, and spoke in complete sentences was the icing on the cake. And tonight was another high-stakes event. The format would be similar to the town hall meeting in Lubbock, except that tonight there would be no panel of journalists. Instead there was a single moderator who would supervise the audience and ask appropriate follow-up questions. In yet another self-inflicted effort to remain impartial, TPC had secured Monica Vickery to be the moderator. Vickery's presence would guarantee high ratings.

Kurt and his team had been roughening Monroe's hide with too-personal questions and snarky comments. They practiced every evening for the past three weeks, covering the gamut of domestic and foreign issues, even during his overnighter in New York, with some of the sessions stretching to two hours.

Monroe took a call from Ted while riding in the SUV to the arena. He wished him good luck and reported on what he learned today back at the paper. Phil leaned forward as if to say something, reconsidered, and leaned back, with Monroe's raised eyebrows inquiring what was on his mind. Phil silently shook his head. He had just heard some news from Fuller Thompson about the phone tap, but did not want to risk upsetting Monroe before the town hall meeting.

Monroe marveled at David Evans' enthusiasm as he worked the crowd prior to this evening's town hall. "Wow, if I had half of his charisma, I'd have this thing locked." He drained the remaining swallow from a bottle of water and handed the empty to Sam, who offered to take it from him. Monroe understood the importance of remaining hydrated during these sessions. He balanced that against a fear of having to excuse himself during the meeting to hit the restroom. But there was to be a brief intermission.

Sam smiled and laid a hand on Monroe's shoulder, saying, "I have news for you. David Evans admires YOUR charisma."

Evans provided a short but unnecessary biography of Monica Vickery, then introduced her to moderate applause commensurate with the balance between conservatives and liberals in the audience. He then laid out the ground rules, explaining that a dozen questions from the audience had been preselected but not submitted to Taylor for President or the candidate himself.

Additional opportunities to ask questions would be provided live, at the arena, with people selected by lottery to ask questions at one of three microphones set up on the floor. Evans then welcomed Monroe, who bounded enthusiastically onto the stage, greeted the audience, thanked David for the introduction, thanked Monica Vickery for moderating, and thanked the national television audience for viewing.

Once the applause died down Vickery charged. "Mr. Monroe, you have recently been quoted as saying that you HATE President Trump." A very loud chorus of boos echoed through the arena. "You said you wanted to elevate the political discourse, yet you spew hateful language to describe your opponents. Isn't that hypocritical?"

Well, here we go. His ears heated up and he considered whether he should just answer with a simple "yes," and move on, but that would be disingenuous and only invite additional scorn. *All that preparation . . . all that practicing . . . Why the hell did I ever decide to put myself up here? What a pain in the ass.*

"Monica, yes, I understand why it appears to be hypocritical. And I think I have raised the level of discourse in my campaign already by talking plainly about the many serious issues we, as Americans, face. And the reason I am standing on this stage tonight, facing difficult questions, criticism, and scrutiny, is that I cannot tolerate seeing our country fall apart under the watch of a guy whose claim to fame is telling people they are fired. I cannot abide an administration that lies about so many things that there appears not to be any consideration given to the truth. An administration that offers 'alternative facts.' An administration that has provided no answers to questions of impropriety, conflicts of interest, and possible corruption, because the president refuses to show us his tax returns.

"So yes, I hate the way he has conducted himself and his administration. Tell me, what is there to like about him?"

A small chorus echoed now, but these were cheers. Monroe tamped them down.

"Now having said that, I will say that there are certain issues I agree with the president about: Term limits, diplomatic engagement with our enemies, and a healthy disregard for political correctness . . . not to say 'disrespect.'

"Honestly, I wish he was better than he is. I wish I didn't feel like I have an obligation to get up here and explain to people why I feel the way I do. And to try to educate the people who voted for him about civics and decency. But TV and social media educate people now, and education and experts are frowned upon in a populist regime. I'd rather be on a beach somewhere."

"Perhaps St. Lucia?" she asked rhetorically. The reference to his rendezvous with Mona Dupuis stung Monroe. An inauspicious beginning.

"Our first preselected question this evening comes from Mr. Gavin Black. Mr. Black."

"President Trump has proven his toughness by standing up to our enemies. He withdrew from the Iran deal and he put North Korea on notice that their nuclear program is unacceptable. Why do you criticize his foreign policy?"

"Thanks for that question. The Iranian nuclear program is obviously a threat to Israel and the rest of the Middle East. The problem is complex, but withdrawal from the Joint Comprehensive Plan of Action has several negative consequences. The first is that it takes us further down the path of isolating Iran rather than engaging them and negotiating with them. It puts the Joint Comprehensive Plan of Action in a state of limbo and does not ensure compliance with the terms of the agreement, which is really a step backward in terms of monitoring their nuclear capabilities. I'd hate to think that Trump withdrew just to make Obama look bad, but my professional skepticism makes me wonder. A more serious consequence is that withdrawal from this deal damages the credibility of the US in any future negotiations with any other country. Just like withdrawal from the Paris Agreement on Climate Change did.

"Regarding North Korea, I don't equate name-calling with putting anyone on notice. The one positive thing has been the engagement of Kim Jong-un with the US and also with South Korea, but to date we don't know if this is just theater to cover a nefarious purpose, or if Kim is really serious about dismantling his nuclear weapons. There have been indications that he still has nuclear weapons. So Trump has not mitigated that threat either.

"But I want to go back to the Iran question because it raises some additional points. The first is that Iran is a proud sovereign nation, and like us, they don't want to be TOLD what to do. They feel that they have a right to build nuclear reactors for electric power generation and also to build weapons. Imagine you are an Iranian, and the US has nuclear weapons, but says that you are not allowed to possess such weapons. How are we to convince them? I'm not suggesting that we unilaterally disarm. I'm just trying to frame the problem empathetically so that a diplomatic outcome is more likely than a military outcome.

"The second point is that the Iranian people do not hate America. Years after the hostage crisis there were reports that showed Iranians' affection for America. The politicians hate us, but the people do not.

"That was a missed opportunity. It's just another example of a lack of follow-through. It would have been much more effective to engage a receptive country than it would be to threaten them and isolate them.

"Back in the Cold War there was a massive propaganda campaign directed at communist countries. With all of the sophisticated, targeted advertising that comes out of American commerce . . . think Madison Avenue . . . you'd think we would be able to change hearts and minds more easily, wouldn't you? Wouldn't it be a good idea to expose hostile countries to our ideals? Look at the ads during election cycles. If propaganda . . . ads . . . didn't work, why would we spend so much money on them? Why don't we apply the psychology that sells you things you don't need to foreign countries to sell them on American ideals. Why don't we put America's best foot forward in the countries that threaten us the most?"

The next question came directly from Vickery. "Since you hate the president so vehemently, why don't you support impeachment? Are you afraid of running against a Pence administration?"

"I'll answer your second question first. No, I don't feel that a Pence administration would be difficult to run against, since he has the same problem that Al Gore had in 2000: guilt by association. I have to figure that Mike Pence is complicit.

"The answer to your first question is simpler. There are no grounds for impeachment without hard evidence. If a president could be impeached for incompetence, then sure, I would support impeachment. But to date there has been no evidence of high crimes or misdemeanors. If such evidence comes to light, that is when impeachment should be discussed. Not before then. These Democrats that talk about impeachment should understand that the founders never intended it to be wielded as a political weapon. That is completely insupportable."

"Let's take a question from the audience." Monica was getting production feed from her producer who was screening potential questions from assistants on the floor. "Sir, state your name please."

A tall, well-dressed man was standing at one of the mikes. "Uh, hi. Good evening. My name is Calvin Davies, and I own a small business in Glendale. President Trump made a fortune as a businessman before he ran for office, and the stock market seems to have benefited from his policies. You have no business experience, and you made your fortune from a lottery. Why should anyone vote for you?"

Monroe was frustrated. Here he stood before a mostly hostile audience, and it was now nearly a year since he had begun his crusade. And these idiots just were not getting it. He took a breath and told himself to not lose his temper. This required a rational explanation.

"If I understand, your contention is that Donald Trump is a good president because the economy is great, and the reason it is so robust is that he is a fantastic businessman. My initial reaction is that it's hard to even know where to begin. But patience, facts, and reason are a good place to start. Let me acquaint you with the facts.

"Donald Trump has bankrupted not one, not two. Not three or even four. Donald Trump has filed Chapter 11 bankruptcy SIX times, the most recent in 2009. SIX! And friends, let me tell you, it's a good thing that the USA cannot declare bankruptcy because with his record deficit spending he would do the same to our country.

"You asserted that I have no business experience. I've maintained a newspaper for thirty-five years before I won that lottery. To be sure we had some lean years, and we managed the risk by investing successfully in other ventures, but we never declared bankruptcy. We've created jobs, we pay our taxes, we never stiffed anybody by not paying them, we never defaulted on a loan.

"Further, the stock market continued a rise that began under Obama, up until about twenty-three months into the Trump presidency. But forget about that. You don't want to hear that the stock market began its rise under Obama. And furthermore, it doesn't matter, because study after study has demonstrated that the market simply does not care if a Democrat or a Republican is in the White House. There is no correlation.

"So this narrative that Donald Trump is a great businessman and therefore a great leader is to me incomprehensible. A good businessman knows how to build teams. He has had, I don't know . . . I've lost count . . . something like eight cabinet-level positions resign under pressure? When he ran for office he bragged about how he loves his generals. Remember that? Michael Flynn? John Kelly? James Mattis? H. R. McMaster? All gone. Different reasons for their departures, to be sure, but all gone."

"Following up on that, are you suggesting that the economy is not robust?" Monica Vickery was back on the attack.

"I'm suggesting that I don't know anyone who is tired of winning." The crowd cackled ambiguously.

"That's really a very evasive nonanswer," Vickery challenged.

"I'll be more specific," Monroe corrected. "The Dow Jones was on a pretty steady climb since 2009. But the stock market is not the best indicator of economic health. The government is fond of reporting unemployment numbers. But these statistics are historically misleading because the numbers don't represent people who fell off the unemployment rolls or those who are underemployed. Engineers who deliver pizzas now. Managers who drive for Uber. Manufacturing and construction workers stocking shelves at Home Depot. The economy is always cyclic. There are always people who are doing well, and many more who are not. The problem is a lot more complex because we truly work in a global economy, and US manufacturers are competing against those in China, India, and lots of developing nations."

"And a Taylor administration can naturally solve all of those complex problems," she drawled sarcastically.

"A Taylor administration would understand that a better way to boost US manufacturing is to spend money improving our infrastructure, while maintaining a healthy environment. Who loses when we remove restrictions on particulate emissions from a steel mill? The neighbors, the workers, and the guys who build and install the baghouses. Which by the way use a lot of steel. That's just one example."

"I want to keep it focused here," Vickery said, reminding Monroe of a schoolmarm. "Maybe we'll get a question about the environment that merits your answer."

Exasperated, Monroe turned his back and walked briefly upstage to take a break and get some water. His hand shook as he reached for the bottle. He was surprised he was so rattled. Taking a sip, he wondered why these questions were jacking him up so much. Glancing back at the bottle he saw that it was caffeinated. *Christ! That makes for maybe six cups of coffee I've had today!* He turned back to the audience and noticed that Monica Vickery was eying him suspiciously.

"It's caffeine in the water," he explained ingenuously. Then to someone offstage he asked, "Could I just get some unadulterated H-Two-Oh?" A soft rumble of chuckles passed through the front rows of the arena.

"Time for our second preselected question from the audience. This from Jane Withers. Ms. Withers?"

"Mr. Taylor, you have stated that you are pro-choice. We here in the heartland consider that a vote for abortion, for terminating a life. Some might call it 'murder.'" There was another chorus of cheers and clapping and Jane Withers smiled and nodded her head in approbation. "Why do you think it's right to end a human life?"

"Thank you for that question, Ms. Withers. It's a very broad question that I want to answer, but I will get back to your specific question about abortion in a minute. Aside from conducting wars, the government ought to have no responsibility for taking human life. This is why I am opposed to capital punishment. I am strong on crime prevention, but I am vehemently opposed to capital punishment. The US is not in really good company when you consider what other countries have capital punishment: China, Iran, Saudi Arabia, Iraq, Pakistan. . . . And when you consider the number of people on death row who have been exonerated, it's a good reason to impose life sentences rather than perform executions."

People were wondering why Monica Vickery wasn't admonishing Monroe for straying from a direct answer about the topic. But Vickery relished the evasive wandering into liberal territory. *I'll give him enough rope to hang himself on national TV*, she thought coolly, and then she nearly snorted from the irony.

Monroe continued, "Some countries retain the death penalty for treason during times of war. That may be justifiable. And it's hard to feel compassion for someone like Timothy McVeigh. But imposing the death penalty is a slippery slope, and I am in favor of abolishing it across the board. I think a life sentence in maximum security is a very harsh punishment. As harsh as the death penalty.

"But you asked me about taking human life in the context of abortion. I have to tell you honestly that my opinion is evolving on this, and may never be fully formed. And there are several reasons for this. The first is, I am not convinced that an embryo is a human life any more than a heart or appendix are." There were some gasps.

"Second, I am influenced by my Catholic faith, which is admittedly not strong. My religious beliefs have been scrutinized, but they are personal, and I have said repeatedly that one's religion should not be a test for political office. As you know, the Church is strongly opposed to abortion.

"Third, and perhaps most importantly, I think everyone can agree that abortion is not, nor should it ever be, the primary means of birth control. If we use that as a starting point to find common ground and solutions, then at least that's a beginning.

"And finally, abortion is a very dangerous issue for voters and the country. It's why the religious right voted for Donald Trump. They overlooked the many, many questions about his character . . . because they are single-issue voters. And the issue that convinced them to vote for him was his current stated position against abortion. I say it is his current stated position because his position has changed. And look, he is entitled to change his mind. Changing one's mind when new evidence is presented is a smart thing to do. Politicians accuse each other of flip-flopping, but only an idiot would adhere to an untenable position.

"But Donald Trump is not going to do anything about abortion. Neither are the Republicans. A lot of Republican women don't want it overturned. If it is overturned, they may stop voting Republican. . . . Lyndon Johnson is said to have told an aide, 'We have lost the South for a generation.' He was talking about the Democrats and the Civil Rights Act. The Democrats didn't lose the south for a generation. They lost it for several generations. And still haven't gotten it back. Johnson understood the ramifications, but he did the right thing anyway and signed the Civil Rights Act into law in 1964. Similarly, Republicans are afraid of losing the votes of millions of conservative women if Roe v Wade is overturned.

"Don't believe me? If they are serious about overturning it, why have they not put it up for a vote? It would never pass in the

Senate since they need sixty votes for cloture. But that is no excuse when you consider that they have repeatedly tried to pass laws to wipe out Obamacare, despite knowing the bill would never make it through the Senate. They don't try to pass legislation against abortion because they aren't really serious about taking direct action to end abortion! They don't want to risk losing the votes of conservative women who are pro-choice.

"But, Ms. Withers, let's say that Roe v Wade IS overturned. Then it's up to the states to decide whether to outlaw abortion. That just kicks the can down the road by forcing the state governors and legislators to face the issue. And they face the same problem: namely losing the votes of conservative women who don't want the government interfering with a very intimate, very personal decision.

"Let's examine which states are most likely to outlaw abortion. They're the ones that require mandatory abortion counseling, parental consent, mandatory ultrasound images to be shown to the mother-to-be. Texas, Alabama, Georgia, Florida. . . . If it becomes illegal in those states, there will be a cottage industry of transportation of poor minority women to states like New York and California where abortion is likely to remain legal.

"You know, when you see a pro-life billboard it often depicts a forlorn white teenager. Maybe she exercised some poor judgment. Maybe some rotten kid coerced her. The reality is, 60 percent of the women who seek abortions are already mothers. Most are in their thirties. Most are poor. Most of them are people of color. Will we see the white Republican establishment line up to protect the pregnancies of unwanted children that are born to poor brown and black women? They haven't sent a bill to be voted on. Maybe they are afraid that those poor children will grow up in poor homes and become a burden to society. Ask them.

CHAPTER 31

"The number of abortions has actually decreased since the nineties. And that's a good thing. I'd like that number to be zero, but I don't want to eliminate that option."

A pall fell across the arena. After a moment, Monica Vickery called for an intermission. Monroe exited the stage to find a restroom. Sam handed him his cell phone to speak to Ted. "Brother, you are KILLING it tonight! I wish I was there!"

"Well, you are in spirit. Thanks for the feedback. I was afraid I was getting too anxious. Listen, here's Sam, I'm on a mission!"

"He needs a restroom, huh?"

"Ummm, could be," confirmed Sam uneasily.

"What do you guys think?"

"Overall it's a solid performance. No gaffes. Phil is happy, I'm happy. Kate is watching the results of a focus group in real time with Kurt. Of course they are taking copious notes, for download to the team."

"Just like a football team watching game tape on Monday, huh?"

Monroe was back onstage. There was a genial buzz of conversation as he waded into the crowd with three unobtrusive members of the security team close at hand. Unbelievably, Monroe was working the crowd during intermission, shaking hands and chatting with people. A camera caught him speaking to a smiling elderly couple wearing MAGA hats.

"The caffeine must have worn off," remarked Phil as they watched the monitor from backstage. "The guy is fearless."

A gong announced that the end of the intermission was imminent and once settled, Monica Vickery introduced the next participant.

"The next question is from Mrs. Alva Watkins," said Vickery, gesturing to an elegant elderly lady. She looked frail but spoke with a clear voice that had a hint of a southern accent.

"Thank you. Mr. Taylor, I am concerned about crime and drugs, and I want to know how you propose to deal with the immigrant caravans along the southern border?"

"That's a good question, Mrs. Watkins. I don't believe that anyone is for open borders, but I want to point out that unlike Donald Trump, I do not believe that everyone who crosses from Mexico is a rapist or drug dealer. There are problems in South American countries that are forcing people to look for a better way of life in America. And let's be honest with ourselves, we need the help in unskilled labor. I am not in favor of taking jobs away from US citizens, but many of the jobs these people want are those that Americans do NOT want. So I am in favor of work visas, I am in favor of American companies employing migrant workers and PAYING TAXES ON THEM! I am not in favor of illegal immigration, but I know we can streamline the process in the short-term.

"Now in the long-term, I think the US needs to help solve the problems facing these people in their home countries. That means foreign aid and perhaps assistance in dealing with crime, cartels, and corruption. I am NOT in favor of spending one single dime in building a wall, a fence, or a barrier. That's only a symbol used to promote a slogan. Walls can be climbed over, or tunneled under. Steel slats! That's brilliant! Ever seen a car jack?

"It's absurd, really! 'Build the wall' they chanted. And Trump said Mexico would pay for it. Why would they? Instead he shut down the government because Congress had the temerity to say 'NO'!"

"Now if you want to worry about a migration crisis, wait twenty or fifty years when sea levels rise. This migrant caravan is just a small dress rehearsal of what the future holds for people displaced by climate change."

"I don't believe I will need to worry about that," joked Alva Watkins.

"I may not be around then either, Mrs. Watkins, but I do worry about it. Climate change is already responsible for severe weather events, and sea level rise is already affecting places like Miami Beach. And don't forget that when sea levels rise, so do river levels. That will affect people inland. And that's another reason to take a look at my plan for homeless and displaced persons."

The second half of the town hall meeting wore on, with questions about the military, energy independence, and a follow-up about privatization of government services. Then Monica Vickery introduced the final question for the evening.

"My name is Lindsay O'Connor, and I'd just like to say that there are PLENTY of conservative women in the heartland that appreciate the great job that President Trump is doing. AND we are pro-life. And we most certainly DO NOT appreciate the criticisms of liberal elites like you!" About a third of the audience cheered, with a significant portion giving Lindsay a standing ovation.

"Hi Lindsay. Nice to see you again. Did you have a question?"

"Yes. Why don't you go back to whatever rock you climbed out from under?"

"Well, it was great talking to you too, Lindsay. You take care. God bless you. And God bless America. Thank you for coming out, and our thanks to St. Louis and the wonderful people of Missouri for the—mostly—warm welcome. Good night!" Monroe waved and turned to Monica to give her time to conclude the event. He then calmly descended the stage and into the audience.

As he greeted well-wishers and those who did not wish him well but were nevertheless curious and polite, Lindsay worked her way through the crowd, drawing the attention of Fredo

Martinez. When she was within arm's reach of Monroe, Fredo intercepted her.

"Get your hands off me! You filthy Mex . . ."

"Fredo's actually Puerto Rican," Monroe interrupted. "He's a decorated combat veteran and a valuable member of our team. It's okay, Fredo. She's harmless."

"Harmless?" she challenged. "Conservative women like me are your worst nightmare!"

"I'm sure you're right!" Monroe smiled. Network cameramen were jockeying for position around the perimeter of the small crowd.

"You're never gonna defeat Donald Trump! Decent people are never gonna vote for you!"

This was hopeless. He shook a few more hands and excused himself.

• • •

"WOW, WHAT A CLUSTERFUCK that turned into!" complained Monroe to Ted.

"Yeah, it was a goat rodeo. But it made for some great TV. You looked very together. Very professional. Gotta admit though: I was a little bit worried you were gonna smack the bitch."

"Mmmm. I won't say I wasn't tempted. Well, she got her fifteen minutes of fame."

"A few more than fifteen. She's all over cable news this morning. The darling of the conservative stations."

"Well, the people get the government they deserve."

"I know," sighed Ted, empathetically. "I don't blame Donald Trump. I blame the assholes who voted for him. It's not like he didn't give them every reason in the world to NOT vote for him."

"Amen. How you feeling? When are you joining us? I don't wanna rush you but I coulda used you there last night."

"Be back on Monday. I need to close up the house better this time. Check on your pad . . ."

"Did you plant the seed?"

"Yes, I gingerly let Franco know that a contingency plan exists. In case . . ."

"AH!" Monroe exclaimed. "Don't say it! Don't jinx us!"

"Dude, there is no jinx. I can't believe that a just Supreme Being would provide you a fortune only for it to be wasted. This campaign has legs."

"Mmm. See you in Falls Church then. Bye Dude."

Monroe was headed to Denver this morning, completing the swath cut through the plain states. After this there was a brief strategy session scheduled back at TPC and some meetings scheduled with still-skeptical-but-needing-to-face-reality party politicians in DC. The Denver trip was going to be a cakewalk after the hostility he faced in St. Louis. He wanted to admonish Phil and Sam about not having stacked the deck a little more in his favor, but he also knew that the ultimate path to success was to change hearts and minds; not to needlessly energize the base.

On the flight he would be briefed by Kurt and Kate who had analyzed the data from the focus group. It would not be a long flight so there would be no opportunity to chat with Dino or Dexter for some last-minute coaching. After takeoff Phil preempted Kurt.

"Hey what was that thing you didn't want to tell me on the ride over to Vespucci Arena?" asked Monroe, preempting Phil.

"The thing I'm going to tell you now?"

"Yeah," Monroe stroked his chin. "That thing."

"We found out who tapped your call with Franco DeMario the other day." Monroe waited. "It was Harlon's people."

"How did you find out?"

"Two words. Blake. Mrzowski."

"Get the hell outta here! How is Blake tied into Harlon's conservative wingnuts? He was with Progressive Socialist whateverthehelltheyare."

"Strictly speaking, he's not with Harlon."

"Goddamn, Phil. Enough with the Pythian riddles. What the fuck does Blake have to do with Harlon?"

"Sorry. Fuller did turn Blake. You didn't want the publicity of prosecuting him, and in hindsight that was a very good decision. So rather than just letting him off, Blake returned to Progressive Democratic Socialists on the pretext of being burnt out from being undercover. So they kept him on as an analyst."

"I wouldn't have thought they were funded well enough to maintain staff," observed Monroe.

"That's the point. We learned that Harlon Michaels funds them."

"Seriously? He's an ultraconservative!"

"That's right, but he plays both sides, funding conservatives, liberals, and excavating dirt on his political enemies."

"Christ! We're all just dancing to Harlon's tune. Marionettes on his strings!" Monroe sat back, stunned. "What the fuck! Is this just a hobby for him? If he's that loaded, and wants to exert his influence, why doesn't HE just run for office?"

"Well, Boss. . . . It takes a special personality to put yourself out there in the public eye." Phil smiled, gave Monroe a wink, and relinquished his seat to Kurt, who opened a thick binder and began to describe to an inattentive Monroe which of his many topics alienated various voting demographics.

· · ·

33

TED DROVE A RENTAL CAR TO FALLS CHURCH. He'd had a productive working vacation back in Latrobe. The troops at the paper had been assured that regardless of the outcome of the election, the paper would remain in business for the foreseeable future. Whether Monroe would take an active role in that endeavor remained to be seen, but everyone understood that he felt an obligation to preserve his father's legacy.

Further, he'd spent some time with his PCP to review his health concerns. "Stop worrying," his doctor admonished. "This is completely manageable. All you need to do is take your meds, change your diet, lay off alcohol, and get some moderate exercise."

"Just shoot me," was Ted's unironic response.

He briefed Monroe over dinner on Monday night. They went out to their favorite steakhouse in Tysons Corner where Ted ordered a salad, no cocktail, and no wine or beer with dinner. "So no adult beverage, huh? Is it that serious?"

"Well, let's just say I'm trying to follow their advice."

"How you feeling?" asked Monroe. He was truly concerned.

"Like I want to punch somebody in the fucking throat." They both laughed heartily.

Meetings were scheduled throughout Tuesday and the rest of the week at the TPC offices. There were double the number of people there since the last time Monroe had visited. He could practically see the dollars floating away, but he had braced himself for this aspect of the campaign. His concerns were assuaged when Alice Conway assured him during the meeting of the Finance Committee that donations had exceeded outlay in the last month. He made a note on his iPhone to call Khalil and Blaise anyway. He wanted to verify how the private portion of his portfolio was doing. The stock market had not been kind to most investors in the latest mash-up of Trumponomics.

Checking on his finances was not something he regularly did. He had made a decision after giving the money to the financial planners to not obsess over it. Sure he would have oversight. And he still relied on his accountant Nancy Maguire and his personal attorney Fred During to oversee the quotidian aspects of his portfolio. But he wanted to enjoy life now, and in balance the campaign actually allowed him to do that. The schedule was grueling but he reveled in the engagement with people and policy.

"One measure of the success of our campaign is the number of invitations we are receiving from foreign governments." Sam was beaming. He knew he had no right to cast himself in the role of kingmaker, but he was nevertheless gratified that the Taylor campaign was gaining international recognition. This was going to be great for the next phase of the campaign.

"Well, I'm happy about all of this, to be sure," agreed Monroe, "but why are we taking time away from campaigning to take a victory lap for a victory we cannot yet claim? It's a little premature to break out the brandy snifters and see-gars, no?"

Phil and Sam looked at each other, surprised. Then Phil quickly recovered. "Monroe, sure it is, and now it's time for the full-court press. Remember, we wanted to get you back to DC so you can meet with some of the congressional leadership. We need to build those relationships but we also need to put you on the world stage."

"I get that. I just want to keep this fire stoked. And I am also looking forward to meeting with some of the candidates for vice president and Cabinet while we are here."

"And let's make sure those meetings are on the QT, huh?" warned Ted. "How are we making sure that happens?"

"We have a series of rotating sites . . . hotel suites booked for the week . . . scheduled across the metro area; interspersed with public appearances so that the media won't get suspicious. You'll be seen in public, and that will be a bit of a diversion while you meet with the candidates. Kate has a team organizing that."

Monroe was at the coffee station with Ted, Phil, and Alice during one of the breaks between the morning sessions. Through the glass walls Monroe saw Denise Dexter talking to one of the TPC staffers. She was wearing a name tag on a lanyard hung around her neck. Monroe gasped audibly and looked at Ted, alarmed. Ted gave a silent shrug that said "How the hell should I know?"

Monroe set his mug down and walked over to her. Denise gave him a little hug, and was discreet enough not to display the full extent of her affection and appreciation in such a professional setting. He carefully lifted her name tag to inspect it.

"Denise Dexter. Taylor Campaign Staff. Advance Team. Mmmm."

"Oh Monroe, thanks so much. When I asked Jenn if there was anything I could do to make up for the trouble my idiot brother caused, she suggested I send a resume to TPC. And they hired me, and I know they didn't have to. But it was because of your kindness, and I swear I won't be a problem for you!"

He stroked the back of her arm like he did the last time he saw her not sure what to say. He looked away from her to avoid prolonged uncomfortable eye contact. His glance landed on a stunning black woman rounding a corner, talking quietly to Fuller Thompson. She looked vaguely familiar. He knitted his brows and recollected that she was the lady in the hotel lobby in New York. Denise followed his gaze, which was now a full-on stare. She noticed an attractive black woman, and her immediate thought, an unkind one, was *Wow! This guy is SUCH a cockhound!* Denise knitted her brows and gazed at the woman. She looked vaguely familiar. She recollected that this was the lady that sold her the bogus ISP contract in Ligonier.

Tonya sensed she was being watched and glanced up from the page that Fuller was holding in front of her. She saw Monroe and Denise, and realized that not only was her cover blown, but that it also did not matter now. "Shit," she muttered. Fuller looked up and said, "Shit," chuckling. Tonya walked over to the two of them and introduced herself as Tonya Jackson, a member of the TPC research staff.

"How nice it is to meet you both," she said, then excused herself.

"She sold me bogus internet service in Ligonier!" exclaimed Denise. "How do you know her?"

"I think she was tailing me in New York," explained Monroe uncertainly. He stroked his chin. "Oh well! Glad you are on board, Denise." He excused himself and clutching Ted's elbow moved back into one of the conference rooms.

"Why didn't you tell me about this! About hiring Denise!"

"I didn't know!" Ted said surreptitiously, even though no one was around.

Phil poked his head around the door. He entered with Fuller behind him. "Ummm. We thought it might be a good idea to keep a closer eye on Denise. After your New York interview we asked Jenn Hensel to reach out to her to see how she was doing. We knew she needed money and we figured if we offered her some financial security it would solve two problems."

Fuller added, "And by putting her on the advance team, your paths are not likely to cross. Keep your friends close. You know?"

"Mmm. I would have appreciated not being blind-sided like that."

"Sorry. We thought you knew."

Fuller and Phil turned and exited with their collective tail between their legs. "Hey," said Ted, "I'm having dinner with Sandra tonight. Wanna double date?"

Monroe passed a hand over his mouth and went to find his next meeting.

· · ·

OCTOBER 29, 2020—five days before the election

"Samantha, it's just INCREDIBLE! It's hard to even characterize this . . . what we hope will FINALLY be the FINAL misstep of the Taylor campaign. People, hang on for this unbelievable new development in Campaign 2020!"

"Absolutely right, Brian! This latest catastrophe for the Taylor campaign is simply unfathomable! His OWN EDITOR . . . Yes, the editor of *The Latrobe Independent*, Mr. Franco DeMario has written a scathing editorial . . . IN THE PAPER THAT IS OWNED BY VAUGHN MONROE TAYLOR! In which he tells his readers to NOT VOTE FOR TAYLOR! Tracy, have you ever?"

"Oh my gosh. It's hard to know even where to begin. How to process this information. Take a look at this editorial."

Successive screens switched to a graphic with black-on-white text:

"DON'T VOTE FOR MONROE TAYLOR By Franco R. DeMario, Editor-In-Chief"

"Don't vote for Monroe Taylor because he seems smart. Taylor is not smart."

"Don't vote for Monroe Taylor because he seems to be a good speaker. Taylor is not a good speaker."

"Don't vote for Monroe Taylor because he seems to know what he is talking about. Taylor does not know what he is talking about."

"Don't vote for Taylor because he seems to be a good leader. He is not a good leader."

"Don't vote for Taylor because he seems to have good moral character."

"Don't vote for Taylor because he seems to be too wealthy now to appreciate what it's like to be middle-class."

"Don't vote for Taylor because he is just plain lucky."

"Don't vote for Taylor because he criticizes President Trump."

"Samantha, it's just what we have been saying all along. Taylor has been ineffective, outmatched, unqualified. And even his own newspaper says so!

"I don't expect that Franco DeMario will have a job at *The Independent* by the end of the day!"

Monroe's phone rang. He saw Franco's name displayed, so he put it on speakerphone so Ted could participate. "What's up, Buddy?"

Franco was despondent. In tears, he cried, "Did you see what they did? Jesus! Monroe!"

"Take it easy, Franco. I saw it. It's gonna be fine."

"This was my *magnum opus*! This is the best piece I ever wrote!"

Ted was already on his phone trying to reach Sheila. If they were in close proximity, Sheila might need to keep an eye on Franco. If they were not in close proximity, Sheila would need to get someone to keep an eye on Franco. In the meantime Monroe looked into Ted's eye as if to appeal for some help as he tried to console Franco.

• • •

Editorial

DON'T VOTE FOR MONROE TAYLOR
By Franco R. DeMario, Editor-In-Chief

Don't vote for Monroe Taylor because he seems smart. Taylor is not smart. He is brilliant. The depth and breadth of his knowledge are exceeded only by his respect for knowledge. Nor is his intelligence merely based on an encyclopedic grasp of facts. He reasons. He is able to take seemingly complex issues and boil them down to their essence. And then he is able to explain those relationships to those who lack his analytical skills. Vote for him because he is brilliant.

Don't vote for Monroe Taylor because he seems to be a good speaker. Taylor is not a good speaker. He is the closest thing to a natural orator since Daniel Webster. Taylor can explain those complex thoughts we mentioned above in terms that the average citizen can understand. The passion he exhibits when he talks about causes that he believes in is no act. He is genuine. Vote for him because he is an orator.

Don't vote for Monroe Taylor because he seems to know what he is talking about. Taylor does not just know what he is talking about. He has made himself a subject matter expert on a variety of issues that are important not just to Latrobeans or Americans, but to citizens of the world. His views are not informed by prejudice. They are informed by fact and investigation. Vote for Taylor because he is informed.

Don't vote for Taylor because he seems to be a good leader. He is not a good leader. He is a great leader. He could have dismantled this newspaper at any time in the past twenty years, but he had a vision to improve it and make it stronger. It's true that he has reinvested some of his winnings into it, but he did not have to do that. He could have taken his winnings and retired to a tropical island. But he has always been interested in his employees' welfare, and he has always been able to build consensus and strong teams. That's what strong leaders do. Vote for Taylor because he is a strong leader.

Don't vote for Taylor because he seems to have good moral character. He has great moral character. His associates call him "The Saint" with no irony attached. Monroe Taylor is the finest human being we have ever known. We are proud to have been associated with him professionally, and we are proud to call him our friend. He is empathetic. He was generous even before he won the largest lottery in the history of the United States. He gave time and money to many local civic causes, as well as to international ones like water projects for Haiti and shelters for tsunami victims in Indonesia. When *Independent* reporter James Plinther lay in a coma, Taylor sent groceries and Christmas presents to his family. That was twenty-five years ago, but we at *The Latrobe Independent* remember it, and so does the Widow Plinther, who sends Taylor a mass card every year. He is a mensch, and deserves your support. Vote for him because he has your own values.

Don't vote for Taylor because he seems to be too wealthy now to appreciate what it's like to be middle-class. He is wealthy. But he retains his middle-class work ethic. Taylor has been known to put in sixteen-hour days. Should he end up in the White House, you can rely on him to work as hard for you as he does for all of us here at *The Latrobe Independent*. Vote for Taylor because he is a hard worker.

Don't vote for Taylor because he is just plain lucky. He is lucky, but when most people would retire and relax, Taylor's sense of devotion to the country and its citizens has compelled him to set aside the luxuries afforded him and run for an office where he can affect the best outcome. For you. For us. Not for him. Vote for Taylor because he is unselfish.

Don't vote for Taylor because he criticizes President Trump. He does criticize him, without apology and without mercy. He criticizes him because he loves this country and its citizens. He does not want to see the country his father fought for turn into a cesspool of corruption. He believes in the rule of law, and in the US Constitution. Vote for him because he is a *true* patriot.

* * *